Red Wine

Red Wine

Amina Zaydan

Translated by
Sally Gomaa

The American University in Cairo Press
Cairo   New York

First published in 2010 by
The American University in Cairo Press
113 Sharia Kasr el Aini, Cairo, Egypt
420 Fifth Avenue, New York, NY 10018
www.aucpress.com

Dar el Kutub No. 2265/10
ISBN 978 977 416 389 0

Dar el Kutub Cataloging-in-Publication Data

Zaydan, Amina
        Red Wine / Amina Zaydan; translated by Sally Gomaa.—Cairo:
   The American University in Cairo Press, 2010
            p.   cm.
        ISBN 978 977 416 389 0
        1. Arabic fiction   I. Sally Gomaa (trans.) II. Title
        892.73

1 2 3 4 5 6 7 8   14 13 12 11 10

Designed by Andrea El-Akshar
Printed in Egypt

Great deeds do not take a long time.

To my daughters, Hamees and Farah Abd el-Azeem,
and Suha, who I did not give birth to. I love you.

Overture:
Forty Years of Slowness

This time was different from all the others. I did not run away or hide behind my mother's mirror or submit to my uncle's will as I did every other time, going along with what my father would always advise, "Be like the palm trees, above grudges, yielding their best fruits when stones are thrown at them."

No, not again. If palm trees were handled gently, they would yield their best fruits: dark, sweet dates would fall off ripened by the pure air of great heights.

This time I did something so different and so right that it helped me overcome the aftermath of my relationship with Essam, except for the nightmares I pull myself out of with terrifying slowness, choking and gasping and fearing death for long moments, until I wake up and realize that I'm now quite far from those ages haunted by my uncle's ghost or Essam's ghost or Andrea's ghost.

This time my resolve to make a new beginning is unshaken. It comes after suffering punishments for a total of almost twenty years, years that divided my brief childhood from my current age, a few months over forty, and being disturbed by nightmares every time I fall asleep: my blind grandmother comes for a visit. She is beating my body in circular motions

1

with her walking stick. She keeps dipping it in bright red mud and I keep trying to stay clean, which is like trying to swim without getting wet.

My father is running with an amputated leg dangling in his trousers, looking for a new country on which to dump his patriotism. I'm trying to catch up with him to reattach his leg to his thigh. He keeps rushing forward and I keep stumbling like I'm carrying a heavy load. In the meantime Asaad is watching, arms crossed, sneering at my inability to catch up with my father. . . . Or with anything else. I look back surprised by his regular appearance in nightmares about my father. All my life, like a fool, I keep looking back.

My brother Selim is a toddler crawling. He stops to play in the excrement he has uncontrollably dumped. He puts it in his mouth to taste it. This gives him chronic intestinal diseases with regular outbreaks that keep him skinny and delirious. Older now, and dreading another fit of diarrhea, he decides to stay at home. If he ever leaves, he rushes back, going straight into his room where he always shuts himself up. We only see him on his way to the bathroom. I shudder, pretending to be disgusted and bored, which is my way to avoid seeing him or helping him.

My mother, whose attention I'm trying to draw by pulling on her dress, is nothing but an image reflected in every mirror—an image with no tangible presence.

Then there is my uncle who is 'playing God'—inflicting suffering and expecting people to love him and fear him. I actually love him, not like a strong support, but like a contradictory idea that speaks only when he is lost in the narrow alley of himself under the influence of drugs. Then he seems real and I don't want to be afraid of him. He says, "All I hoped for was liberty, equality, fraternity like the French or the Bolshevik Revolution or just for the sake of humanity."

Finally, there is Andrea, watching with a neutral smile. He used to love cinematic improvisation and ruled over every detail of every scene with his eyes and his smile. I would closely watch his face trying to figure out how good I was at playing the part he had given me, which I don't think I ever got to play.

Until I reached this point: slightly over the Big Four Zero and still hearing drums playing in my head, lifting me up, then plunging me down, becoming louder and louder until they match the sound effects of a parody in which I play all the parts. I try to escape its snares to forge a new, peaceful beginning inspired by the part I know I have to play regardless of what others want. So I write on the mirror with red ink:

"Remember to say no, no, no." With no equivocation. And in yellow ink:

"Be careful."

"Fear nothing."

And on the last line: "Justice and mercy. 'The male is not as the female.' Those are your verses."

To all respectable people: do not misjudge if you happen to see a woman taking off her clothes and stretching out her body under the moonlight; she is most probably over forty, forlorn, and calling on the moon to help her figure out who she is.

The difference between what is true and what is made public is so vast that it verges on alienation. God, what would stop the agony of being lost in the desert of my soul where tyranny roves like a horse on fire, tipping the balance of the universe, setting off the destruction upon whose ruins I quietly dance until I fall asleep?

I rush back to the middle of everything. I choke on the smell of coffee and gas leaking from the stove and the way being forty feels as I stand in front of the mirror not knowing who I am; I stare harder and turn my face toward the right then toward the left. I smooth over the wrinkles around my eyes and my lips until boredom and a fly buzzing near my face force me to move. I want to weep and to feel that the whole world is conspiring against me in the name of love or friendship or marriage or solidarity or even coincidence. Since they keep intruding upon my daily exercise in saying "no," I finally decide to take my mother's advice: "Do not lean on a wall for support; a sudden raid may knock it down."

This is how I was when Essam set me free, or perhaps right at the moment when he announced our divorce three times in the presence of my uncle and other witnesses. He did so not only without reluctance, but with such resolve and relief that my uncle did not have to pressure him to sign the divorce papers. Naturally, I got what I thought was fair. Our history together left no room for hesitation and our rejection of each other was certain. Strangely, I still felt crucified, floating over a gulf of grievance without knowing the extent of my punishments, which were ripping my soul apart. I wrapped my head in a black veil and I grew a hundred years older every day. I was never tired of digging a grave I filled with inertia and lethargy laced with bitterness and filled with memories.

After a hot shower, I make another resolution to leave. Running away is not reactive: it is erasing a chapter from decades of nonexistence in my pseudo-lives that are now passing by as if projected on a black glutinous screen. There was nothing I could do except wait for a lucid moment to reveal a gap in this siege. For some time, all I had was light sleep interrupted by gasping and soundless screams.

Now, I must go out, face everybody, and search for myself in the old haunts, starting with Khairiya's shed, which her landlord demolished to build a huge apartment building with long balconies so that his sons could occupy the upper floors while he presided over the first one. I should also stop by the university, home of the political party, and all my friends, including Asaad and Rebecca and others, in a constant search for a family tree to which I could belong.

If water can bear ships, life can bear with me.

Like a strong woman, I go back to my father's house so that he can hold my hand and cry over my mother's death. She threw herself off the balcony that faced the narrow alley and fell to her death on the concrete that government workers had previously poured over small French tiles. How I missed the way they glistened and the sound of the raindrops rolling over them. What my dad and I believed was different from what my brother, my uncle, and the rest of the mourners thought. They believed she fell while hanging out heavy wet clothes over clotheslines worn out by the sun and the humidity of the summer. This tragic scenario was not totally removed from the truth because my mother was actually hanging out clothes and she might have decided at some point that nothing worked and nothing removed dirt. She used to scrub clothes in large amounts of detergent with her bare hands time after time without reaching the level of cleanliness she sought. Even after the clothes dried, she insisted that dust from outside made them even dirtier than they were before, so she would wash them again, which is what Dr. Shawki called being obsessive-compulsive. But his pills did not work because she would secretly spit them out after my brother forced them under her tongue.

I was easily able to visualize my mother pushing herself over the high fence of the balcony and see her body smashed in the blood that trickled from her ears all the way to the main doorway. I could smell the odors and hear the noises that surrounded her right at the moment before she died. I saw all that despite being deplorably late and missing the funerary rituals and the burial ceremony because my decision to leave Essam came exactly at the moment when her emaciated body hit the ground and nothing could protect her skull. I did not answer the phone, which rang with ruthless insistence, because I was trying to muster all my energy to pick up my luggage and leave permanently so that I could have my new beginning there with my mother, my father, and my brother. The pounding on my door would start off furiously loud and wind up in silence; but I had no reason to get out of bed. However, as soon as my uncle was done receiving condolences at the graveside, he got into his car and drove nonstop for four hours until he reached my door and started pounding on it and angrily yelling, "Open the door, bitch. . . . Your mother is dead."

"Really?"

When I say that, he slaps me and drags me by the hair to shove me into his new car while I'm in a state of utter shock and disbelief. This is my first time ever to be in his car. It hurls me to the point of dissolution where I cannot see or comprehend anything. I try to remember how my mother looked, but I can't make out her features, which used to confront me with suspicious persistence every time I looked into the mirror. I look at his hands, one tightly gripping the steering wheel while the other twirls cigarettes in nervous circles, a motion that is making me restless.

The car flies into space and lands upside down after spinning three times on the edge of the narrow strip which separates the paved road from the abyss of the waterway. Right at that moment, I see my mother standing tall and smiling through the car windows, which I later learned were made of shatterproof fiberglass that did not distort any of the details of her face, which materialized as a free shield against death. I step out of the car completely off balance to take her in my arms but she keeps fading further and further away with the sun, which is now falling behind the mountain. I weep and heave desert sand over my face and scream like a wounded animal, "Mother, mother, mother. . . ."

I must have needed that death to unleash an animal not too self-conscious to wail in agony. I go over our lives together, over how many times

I rejected her embrace, how many opportunities I missed to kiss her hands or her cheeks; years of negligence and resentment toward her insanity; how I showed no mercy when I harshly shrugged off her obsessions.

Now my uncle is facing me with his legs apart trying to hold on to the earth after he lost his balance, earnestly saying, "What the hell do you think you're doing? You never loved her. You wished that she would die so that you wouldn't have to deal with her madness. So what's new, Muhammad Galal's daughter? You and your father finished her off a long time ago."

Everyone here is in mourning mode: black clothes and Quranic verses recited by Sheikh Abdel Aal crouched in my father's chair rocking back and forth. My father is entering brief states of unconsciousness, haunted by his memories of the woman he loved as much as she rejected his world, which she occupied like a color missing from a rainbow until she escaped through death: either she spent all her life waiting for it or it cut through time to carry her off directly from her mother's womb and into its cave so that her name and her features would fall off the face of the earth. An old woman was lost forever; she walked out on life dragging all her faces, which none of the mourners, enveloped in sorrow and help-lessness, have ever seen. Did my mother really exist?

"Take good care of yourself; your father and your brother need you."

"Our hearts go out to you."

"We're here for you."

"You know, God has taken her into His mercy. She's at peace."

"May God forgive her sins."

"May God rest her soul; she never did anyone any harm."

"Cry, my daughter; may tears bring comfort to your heart."

Do waves find comfort when they hit a stone wall? Did I need my mother's death to switch from slow to hurried steps trying to make up for what she missed in me? Or have all open endings combined to push me simultaneously toward and away from everything? I could never grasp one end so that I could use it as a start. Nights of receiving condo-lences became shorter and limited to people who found out about her death later—until there was only me, my father, and my brother and a final visit from my uncle, who seemed as if he was severing his bonds with us when he finally said, "I owe Nadia two and a quarter acres of land. I took care of the funeral expenses. This envelope has money for

6

the land and for her share in the family house. I bought them. What the family has already lost is more than enough. Goodbye."

Asaad stops by at midnight to see if there is anything he can do for us, which he does not really mean. So, once we thank him and my father gives him his blessings, he leaves.

Which train am I on now? Coming or going? I leave in order to dispel the sadness that haunts my memories. Where to? Where from? I take leave of this agony, which over forty years of sadness and emptiness has become ubiquitous. It turned arid and brittle under the scorching sun of those years. There is no friend encouraging me to hurry up. The train is completely still, frozen, unmoved by the whirring noises, heedless of my hesitating footsteps, which shuffle slowly on the platform. The platforms care nothing for the passengers regardless of how many times they walk back and forth. I look for my face in the shadows reflected on the window-pane, but I see nothing. I stare into the night pierced with faint lights from the distant city on the way south while the train slows down for a quick stop to deposit my feet on the platform. Dewdrops fall on my unsteady form. Where do these tiny drops come from? The sky is overcast and shows no signs of life. The buildings and the temporary commotion at the gate of the railway station have no life either: an uncanny stillness I walk through like a distant ghost.

This time is not like any other time. Despite my small suitcase, I decide to buy my father something special.

"A bottle of Bordeaux wine and a carton of Marlboro Reds, please."

Other than the long look he gave me, the sales clerk did not say a word. He wrapped the bottle with two full pages from an old newspaper and then put it in a black plastic bag. He shoved it into my hands after I paid him. I carried my luggage and left thinking about my father. It's no longer possible to buy a bottle of wine in our city, but my father needs to run away from everything for days I cannot count, or maybe I can but choose not to, as usual. As the bus speeds, leaving Cairo's lights and wet streets behind, the darkness of the desert outside absorbs me. I see only darkness and complete void. Mixed recitations from the Quran envelop the air with a rare radiance. My father is going to enjoy my special gift for a few days. As I'm about to enter the city of Suez, I decide to ignore the actual city.

Instead, I conjure up the old city buried deep in my consciousness, a city where everyone, as my mother used to say, was "switching from linen to khakis." Despite the new construction that stretches ahead for over twenty kilometers, my old city appears. Here are the international observers who usually arrived too late watching food and water come in. Small vans carry canned meats, sardines, sugar, tea, and a few newspapers to be checked before they are allowed in. The general is making excuses for the Zionists: "Let them eat. We should improve our image. They are civilians after all. Show the world that you have mercy. Let Dr. Kissinger manage your affairs in his way; he understands."

Hunger makes me anxious. I can almost taste the cumin crackers which the soldiers and officers of the Third Army used to generously distribute as if we were having a dinner party under the missiles.

Here is the area called the Triangle and the railway repair stations. How would history have turned out if my father and his companions had not bravely broken the siege while their blood ran between the tracks and trenches? Tanks and bulldozers were immobile, smothered in their own fumes. Was I a traitor to feel sorry for the fallen enemy soldiers, crying for their mothers, screaming and weeping over the abrupt end of their stroll through the city that seemed inhabited only by ghosts? They had no way of hearing the hearts that would not submit to tyranny or seeing the dreams of six years in Tel Aviv when Asaad, Andrea, and all our noble friends were cheering our armed vehicles heading toward the east bank. Everyone erupted from the debris like fires that only death could quench. Everyone played his or her part in this well-written drama of the Resistance.

Those days are now gone, leaving me in a deep slumber, waiting for a visitor to ring my bell although my expectations are usually disappointed. My hunger is deep and undefined. I'm quite hungry but not for food. In the end, I look like a small 0 quivering beside a patient 4. I polish the photo of my parents' wedding where they look perfectly yet proudly different, like day and night. I have no choice but to emulate the life I share with my father and my brother in their voluntary confinement. Each one of us is closed up in a solitary universe uninterrupted except to silently point out, "This is your fault."

Perhaps the sorrow that peeks at me from my mother's mirror, hung like a cross, is not enough. I doze off and wake up with a start while sitting on the bamboo chair in front of the mirror, as if guarding my bad dreams, which absorb me into their core. I cannot fall asleep in my bed. Figuratively, I'm molded into nonexistence. I come to reality only as quickly as it takes to prepare an instant meal. If I try to hold my pen, I find one billion Christians and 1.6 billion Muslims crammed on the white page. I gallop through them on my imaginary decrepit horse. My fate will have to differ from theirs by taking fanciful flights. I try to set my imagination free but I look like an ancient woman sitting on a rock under the moonlight that descends on my black clothes and my black headpiece. I try to carve a meaning for my existence inside the social sphere. My mother's ghost haunts me as regularly as she used to serve me pies and tea with milk. Andrea leaves under a false promise. He has missed our date at the bay. Every day before sunset for more than twenty years I wait without even a trace of him. My mother's ghost does not stop watching over me despite my having estranged myself from her by choosing my father over her. Hostility becomes formal attire for everyone, including me. I decide that arriving late is better than not arriving at all. My life is like a broken bottle of perfume gushing out over a cold floor with no scent.

The smoke that I'm ravenously inhaling makes my heart palpitate faster—as if I'm trapped in an elevator hurtling down past many floors or suspended in a boat without oars. No heartbeat is like another. Rumors are spreading about me. A farce created by frustrated men devouring the corpse of a dead woman on their table in a scene from the daily drama of poverty, oppression, and hunger.

But the man who knows that my uncle is Atef Bey lets me go. I run away from the shed unable to shake off the sight of the shiny floor where Khairiya laid down furtively clutching two coins. The damp dirt road takes me to my uncle's house, which is as pitch black as the city that forced me out twice. My voice keeps calling Khairiya's name while she is soaked in blood the way I'm soaked in dreams. The same thing that happened to you happened to me, to a certain extent. The doors and windows of a rundown shed where ghosts and rats run amok are locked to me. The same rotten wooden foundations are used to construct a luxury building.

I keep trying to ward off nightmares. I place a sharp knife under my pillow like my mother used to do to fight evil spirits; or she would stab a slice of the watermelon she saved for my father with a sharp knife until it rotted and was riven with yellow worms before she threw it in the trash-can. These worms would upset me and drive me to scratch my head hard until my short hair was disheveled.

For twenty years I have been looking for imaginary models, watching justice turn into a nonexistent value in a life where I don't belong despite being fully enmeshed in it. I fake living until death suddenly invades me like an unwarranted thought, as it did with those who are now gone and will never return. Andrea proposes make-up appointments that only I keep while he travels abroad and leaves me behind. Asaad provides me with smothering care that erupts as suddenly as the anger my father feels toward the photo of my mother standing next to him in her short wedding dress. She has one arm around his shoulder and another holding a bouquet of roses whose colors faded to something between the whiteness of her dress and the blackness of my father's jacket that falls down to his thighs as he sits with legs crossed. He no longer remembers when exactly he lost her or hides not having forgiven her for leaving him, without saying goodbye, saddled with an emotionally handicapped boy and a daughter who packs and unpacks her bags so many times, muttering to herself, "You only have to say no once and you won't need reading glasses regardless of how your eyes hurt; you won't need your sleeping pills and anti-depressants regardless of how you seethe with anger or hatred at the life you're about to begin. You will immediately begin this new life with learning everything you missed, including dancing. There is no more time to waste. It is okay to miss sleep trying to make up for what you missed for forty years and for twenty before them, which belonged to my mother. I will add them to my list of reparations."

I will start with language; Greek should be first. I will wipe the past's mark off my face and assume the 'look' that suits me no matter what others think. I will become me, owner of the name that makes me ashamed every time I hear it. I will look for Andrea. I will settle every unresolved issue in my life. I will make a fresh start. I will study the curricula so that when I go back to teaching, my students will be able to say and do whatever they want because life is stupid and foolish and offers nothing but misery.

I'm lulled to sleep peacefully as if in an infinite soft space. This optimism surprises me with a sweetness that showers my smiling face with a dazzling beauty; my cheeks flush with the loveliness of contentment. All of this happens in the course of a few hours after midnight. A different woman is going to wake up tomorrow singing. . . . I am alive.

I still believe, while I have not completely lost my sense of wonder, that names have their own significance. When Sartre claimed that hell is other people, he was not wrong, but he forgot another hell, more burning, which I have never managed to avoid when I stand on the other side of *me*, watching *her*.

Suzy . . . how many times have I tried to resemble her to no avail even when I tried different hair colors and contact lenses, or even when I quickly switched the personas others gave me, which I embellished for each person individually. Of course, I had to add my own touches, which I was never able to get rid of and which my memory cannot specifically recall; for what is reflected in my mother's mirror becomes quite confusing given its preoccupation—my memory, that is—with knowing the future—obscure—at least as far as I'm concerned. Despite the stifling obesity with which I'm suddenly afflicted, I'm still obsessed with repeatedly returning to point zero, although not exactly like Siham with her frequent transformations and dramatic haircuts.

The more my age advances slowly and incompletely from one stage to another, the more I fall for the temptation of the beginnings that lick their lips, hungry for a horrific ending. A sort of death takes over my body in my sleep, so I wake up in a different one, stupefied by the lifelessness that banishes a moment as fast as a meteor falls.

In this case I may have to wait for the Big Five Zero in my life to see my own features reflected on others' faces again. Mathematically, it is very simple. I was born in the year 1960, which grew like a malignant cancer over nineteen centuries. I can no longer count the random white hairs on my head. I forget about trying to color them because I cannot deny my admiration for their resilience; they would spring from mysterious spots in my skin, which is the color of "henna soaked in vinegar," as my dear Asaad used to tell me on our way to school.

Are these introductions enough? At any rate, an introduction is important even if repetitive and predictable—like an actor's face bruised by rotten tomatoes thrown at him by the audience while he insists on reciting his lines to the end even after the curtains fall on his withered soul and the crying members of his troupe.

11

One may think that his or her life is a series of predestined events. This type of thinking may make one feel special even if no one else is aware of such hidden design given the usual ignorance and misunderstanding that are so common.

I should stop acting like a woman over forty who has not showered or changed her clothes for over two weeks and who is being as playful as if she has suddenly received an invitation for a romantic date on a dinner cruise. A gentle rain showers my face as I stand at the window in front of the mirror. Its shiny drops quickly dissolve after they stroke my skin. They distract me from the memories of the years chronicled on my face. Exactly the way I must have looked in my mother's arms when she gave birth to me. She said that in the small white baby clothes prepared beforehand I looked like someone found half dead among the waves. Then I began to come to life, arching my body toward the dim light of the yellow lamp hanging from the ceiling by a thick cord coated with white cement. White was the color of the walls in our home, which were retouched during the city's renovation campaign once bullets and gunshots stopped scraping layers off them and leaving deep holes in them. White was the color of my father's coffin buried deep in a drawer under my bed.

What a pain-triggering memory. But I must resist it and for one last time go over the words I will learn to say in the new language. They sound as definite as the train that used to travel so fast and whistle so loudly through the night that it made the floors shake in our house. I would lie down on the floor and stretch out on my belly when I was no more than six months old to feel the earth shaking underneath me, which was so powerful given my tiny size. When the train moved away, an 'optimistic smile' would briefly appear on my face, but it would vanish for a long time as another train passed by and still another and so on and so forth. That was what my father told me. But this time is not like any other time. I have prepared everything with as much determination as the tip of the bay that protects the city against the waves while submitting to the full force of their sharp blow. How can I translate this metaphor into Greek? I should have a chapter for language in my master's thesis arguing that Arabic is a broad canvas, maybe rough at times, but capable of absorbing the colors of any other language without much reluctance, perhaps even with some romance.

Now is the time to fight silence, to develop a language that can confront the other, and to stop being angry at historical omissions.

Come as you are but stop coughing as you sneak by my windows and spitting your germs through the dim shutters. What is the use of words against a gentle morning automatically breaking through the clouds or against a sudden gust of blustery waves on a wall surrounding a calm bay?

Sleeping Beauty was not awakened by words or by the noisy play of dwarfs. A kiss goodbye accidentally woke her up at the end of the tale my mother used to tell me every time I demanded a bedtime story at the age of three.

Act 1

Cosmopolitan:
A Woman at Age Ten

The image is received on two levels: one is an integer and cannot be divided; the other is floating and temporal and may later turn into the vicious memory of something like mass murder. Cartloads of bodies are drawn by a donkey that shudders but can't shake off the flies sticking to its open sores or to the blood-smeared corpses with obsequious flags. The bombing of historic buildings, the sudden fumes of bursting missiles, the massive violence and cruelty together with the oppressive heat breed hostility among the living and discourage their communication.

"God is great; God is great. . . . There is no God but God."

The sound of the call to prayer comes from a nearby mosque or perhaps from my own head branded by a backdrop of devastation, the First One Zero in my life from which tales would burst past this brief, intermittent sermon heard after each raid: "Those who came out alive should thank the Lord and pray for His mercy on the souls of our martyrs; those who were injured should wait patiently until God's will is done and the Jews' scheme is overturned. God is great; God is great."

A church bell somewhere starts tolling, infusing the silence after the raid with the echoes of a skeptical resignation and forgiveness.

There is no place in our home for a crippled being called Love.

"I have had enough of fumes and debris and bombing. The chaos has clotted our souls. We're leaving; we're definitely leaving. I want to see the Nile and the green land and the soil teeming with life and with people living in peace. I'm sick of rushing to dimly lit and stifling shelters not knowing if we should step over the dead bodies in our way or stop to pick up their pieces. We're leaving."

That was what she said as she marched up and down the two floors that were long and narrow to make up for the small size of the plot of land that was my father's unfair share in my grandfather's estate. My father continued to play the same inferior role until the very end. It was reinforced by his wife, the elementary school teacher of Arabic, who ranked her suitors according to some irrational rules of a language only she could speak as a former writer of prose so lyrical that it could have competed with Nazek al-Malaika's poetry. Or at least that was what she told me about her life before me as she tilted her head to stare at the white ceiling. Its whiteness did not make the room seem any larger because the walls were cracked and covered by the dust from the repeated bombings that had collapsed some of the neighboring homes.

In the meantime, my father would protest using nothing but silence and petulant gloominess much like the house itself. He would stare at the chaos echoing through the window. Sometimes he would furiously crush objects in his hands and shake the bed rails or slam the doors of the closet for no reason; his flushed face and bulging eyes made it seem as if some uncanny force was grabbing him by the throat and torturing him.

At the moment their eyes met, she was holding the big mirror while he was holding his head. They stared back at each other shocked to find an unfamiliar face in the room; but the faces were theirs. They embraced after he fastened her mirror to the opposite wall. They looked odd as I watched them through the bedcovers. They were not my mother and my father; they were like the heroes in the American movies the civil defense used to project on the wall in the fire station, trying to hold back their tears, my mother in my father's arms trembling all over. Then words were banned in our house and everything turned to silence.

The conversation was resumed where it ended: Asaad was next to Andrea; I was sneaking behind to take them by surprise. We were heading toward the checkpoints along Sinai's coastline to look for the defeated soldiers who were trying to return in small boats and floating vehicles;

the faces of the soldiers and the officers had the same expression of terror and shock. We were looking for a way to join the training camps run by the local Resistance groups. I sadly pointed out that after the first blow, the city was swimming in khaki and blue, and overalls became the national uniform. In two days my father had to make overwhelming quantities of them. He made them at his sewing machine after he figured out the measurements. When I asked why overalls were not made according to size, Asaad laughed saying that all sizes were equal but people were not. Only his head could be seen as he pushed the thread through the needle of the black sewing machine and pressed its pedals with his bare feet buried in the piles of blue and khaki. The turning of the sewing machine was our way to resist giving up as our minds traveled past the hundred and eighty meters that separated the city from the Israeli flag, whose mast proudly pierced the morning sun, while two American boats sailed through the water to place another flag in the middle of the canal under the very eyes of the international observers.

A whole year passed by in bewilderment before national security started a war of attrition that shook the earth like a volcano. The bombing of petroleum tanks covered the skyline and people's chests with the fumes of burned oil for days; visibility and breathing became difficult. Fires burned firefighters and swallowed them up completely, spitting out only their melted helmets.

Glistening crows and gray rats infested the city and outnumbered the tables laid out with meals after each bombing. Rats were seen nibbling on a human finger torn from the body of its owner as he lay moaning in agony. A pack of crows bit off pieces of raw flesh from the corpse of a man whose life did not count, a man who was killed on the job while guarding the gate of the prep school. That was Amm Gibril whose smile used to light up his dark-skinned face and the lonesome schoolyard, and who used to stop students on their way in to make them read him some of the newspaper headlines. During recess, he would chase after Asaad, Andrea, and Ijith to discuss news stories and recent events, carefully trying to discern their significance. He always referred to my school friends as "kids":

"Should we believe this, kids?"

"These kids will build a great nation."

"Playing football exhausted the kids."

"These are not kids; those are the leaders who will make our country great."

"The kids drove me nuts today!"

"You know what, kids? I want your horizons to be as broad as this. . . ," opening up the palms of his hands like a big ball before he sadly let them fall down. "Ignorance is like darkness; you keep stumbling into it until you lose your eyesight and fall down dead."

The "kids" would laugh like grown men at his jokes as they walked away with a playful obedience. Amm Gibril would then go back to his bench that was big enough for him to sit with his knees bent up, holding his gallabiya between his legs and keeping a smile on his face until the school day was almost over when he had to chase the kids who were trying to skip the last period.

"That lot is going to ruin our country. Each kid should go back to his classroom. I swear that I will lock up in my room whoever I catch, and you don't want to know what's in my room."

Although none of us would dare go near his room even out of curiosity, not a single kid stopped trying to skip class and not a single instance passed without Amm Gibril using this strange threat while I watched from a distance.

"Why did they bomb the school and kill the security guard?" I ask, not expecting an answer from my father as he drinks half a glass of water to take an aspirin. There are no painkillers to obliterate his pain or the pain in my heart as I mournfully wait for him to come home after each one of his ventures.

He changes into one of the shirts he usually wears to appease my mother instead of the white gallabiyas that keep him comfortable during the extra hours he has to put in the sewing shop. The shop was a gift from my grandfather to make up for long years of neglect; he also bought him the first machine in Egypt to automatically make buttonholes. My father thus became the king of buttonholes in our city and all across the canal coastline. Asaad would carry over piles of clothes, gallabiyas in local and modern styles and shirts, and dump them all in a room on the first floor. My mother and I would spend the night splitting open the buttonholes ever so gently so as not to rip the fabric.

There was nothing like the deadly fumes that clung to our chests and made us stay up coughing all night.

"Prayer is better than sleep. . . ."

Which sleep was the muezzin referring to? There was no difference between sleep and death in the moonlit nights favored by sudden bombing and the consequent scramble for refuge in the shelters topped with sand and big chunks of debris. Poppy plants and bushes quickly grew around them, their branches entangled to create a hidden doorway to a cave whose inhabitants were steeped in fear and palpable terror. We could hardly find the entrance to the shelter, whose gate separated me and my mother from the season of moonlit retaliations heralded by the abominable sirens. They kept ringing in my ears as my feet involuntarily carried me through the newly formed wasteland and the mire of body parts soaked in bright red. My eyes were staring at the kind of death that took by surprise noble people now proudly melting in the great fires. My soul, scorched by my hot tears, humbly wished them goodbye without waving or holding a white handkerchief or even apologizing.

Terror strikes me in the creepy shelter with its dim lights and half-sleeping figures. I try to ask who I am but silence envelops me. I close my eyes and try to imagine streets aglow with abundance and safety, supporting the feet of the wealthy, who curse the war only for keeping them from vacationing in spacious resorts.

A cut I received from a castor plant burning on the wall of the shelter suddenly opens in my hand. My attempts to hide it fill me with self-disgust and guilt because I did not burn completely like those with melting eyelids who screamed as they gulped down fire. What was their pain like? What was their anguish like? With the discomfort I'm feeling from the hot walls, I try to imagine the terror of their pain. I say without words, "Please forgive me because I did not join you in crossing the accursed gate, because I'm still here enjoying a temporary sense of security on the ruins of your torment."

My mother holds a cup of red tea and she tries to soothe me by talking over the silence of the city, "Cheers to you, our city; cheers to your burned trees like the trees in a Hitchcock movie; cheers to the inescapable dimness of your lights; cheers to your mosque whose broken minaret is down on its knees hanging by the last rusted iron post and dancing to the bells of the church. The church's pews are lined up in the middle of the street and its altar is swaying back and forth in front of the dilapidated wall—yet another performance by Miss Suzy and her courageous father, heroes of the City of the Dead."

My mother usually uses words I cannot understand, especially when it comes to matters of life and war, and proper nouns to which she gives titles and adjectives that seem like the ravings of a crushing feeling of inner rage that make her pain unbearable. She drinks some tea and calms down a bit while my father chooses to keep quiet.

"Is this the paradise you promised me, harbinger of happiness?" my mother asks.

In the early days of the war my father would go to show support for the troops on their way to a calculated defeat. He would run after the armored vehicles journeying to the east bank, pushing their wheels with his own hands, hands that seemed to defy gravity. A great spirit was sweeping over Sinai; unique was the scene of boys climbing up tanks in a Sufi-like journey toward victory aiming for Tel Aviv—a wild dream unabashedly courted with visions of greatness.

But after days of murmuring trying to describe the debacle, the army returned; what was left of it was punctured with the sand of the lost desert. Parched, frustrated lips offered no explanations. Over there the desert was immense and no one knew what happened or who planned it or why the uniforms once rigidly held up were now old and worn out. For no compelling reason we buckled down and turned to silence. My father did not lose the war, but the warlords lost it and left us mourning among the debris and the ruins. That was until July 1969 when Sinai's Liberation Organization attacked a Jewish post at Port Tawfiq and a just war began to take place.

War was slowly approaching, reaching the sky in retribution, while my mother was demanding an instantaneous paradise to be rendered by my father.

The sky shivers in shades of white and red. I pull the top of my blouse together to protect my neck from the foam splashed by the waves breaking against the rocky wall of the canal. The wall extends in a network of lines abandoned by the birds drawn to the sun's cry for help before it drowns in the gulf. I, Suzy Muhammad Galal, pray silently to this which my

20

presence desecrates. My dry lips smart under the biting of my teeth. I call up my conscience stained with my actions. I enter this jungle willingly, an insect under a canopy of vines, embracing its snakes and befriending its creatures. I scrutinize with a secret dread the reasons for connecting eating meat with having sex in a culture that brings two different species together while simultaneously believing that he who gives loses and that one learns survival of the fittest from the school of nature; nonetheless, I believe that there is some goodness in others. . . . Sometimes.

Wouldn't it have been fine and reasonable for me to be able to say no? At least in the way Ijith did when he defended his reasons for staying although he did not have to. That was in a harmless debate run objectively by Asaad with Andrea, who could not leave his family. I was there watching Andrea; how beautiful and full of light he seemed amid the exquisite ruins by the deserted shore. . . .

"Besides it won't be that long. I listen to the Voice of America and I know there won't be a war; just a few raids to reassure the Egyptians and to indicate that Nasser's courage has been seamlessly transferred to Muhammad Anwar al-Sadat. I will be gone with my family to Alexandria for maybe a month and we'll be back; it's just a vacation."

His Greek family usually spent the summer in Alexandria with some relatives who lived there. There was no sky here. It was more like a huge white tent lifted up by the heat into the space that witnessed my eleventh year. But age followed different rules in wartime.

Based on this conversation, I wondered where I would be next summer. I had none of Andrea's self-confidence. Ijith was saying, "As for me, I'm an insignificant Indian. Because we were poor and from the countryside, my father could not wait until I started school in my divided country. We came to Egypt; we came here to Suez and I don't know any other place, so why do I have to relocate or emigrate? I'm staying here with you even if I die. I only ask that my ashes be thrown over the spots where we used to play and walk. Right, Suzy?"

I smile at Ijith while my eyes light up for Andrea; I turn to Asaad to help me hide my feelings as he helps my father with his sewing. My father has adamantly refused to leave and given up on dissuading my mother who has made up her mind. She tells me with finality, "You and I are leaving. I will show you how to make a lovely life, at least a life free of raids."

21

When I tightly close my eyes on that new world, I see nothing but black pages from a notebook in the bombed schoolyard where smoke reeking of chalk mixed with devastation and ghastly screaming. I see life here as a bright idea, perhaps often dimmed by death, but under the explosions of random bombing, people smile trying to coax death into seeing how much life needs them. My mother keeps talking angrily to herself, "Shut up, Nadia; talking is a useless torture. For someone who is playing the hero, shouldn't he use his superpower in helping me out or at least asking me not to leave?"

During the day, I ruthlessly rebel against my mother; at night, I apologize and feel guilty. That day, it was not yet nighttime when I invaded her space, trying to find the most painful words.

"He's worried about us, Mama. If something happens to us, he'll never forgive himself; I know him."

"You know him and he knows you, and both of you know nothing! You want to live like guerrillas."

She ignores my presence and continues talking into the mirror.

"He is trying to make himself feel better like any other man, but he is being ridiculous acting like he is going to defeat the Jews."

I try to deeply hurt her by repeating what I heard from Asaad, "Zionists, Mama. There is a huge difference between Judaism and Zionism."

"Is that right?!"

"Yes, dear, it is."

Now it was nighttime, time for bed. I appease my conscience by kissing her. I climb up on the sofa in the bedroom where we have been sleeping since the number of raids increased and became almost nonstop. I watch them: my father never rests. He keeps tossing and turning, expecting the first sign or the first siren. I never fall asleep before at least one of them does; their tight embrace eases away my shivers and my fear of sleeping through the sign, which remains secret until it erupts suddenly. But they do not fall asleep either—their heavy sighs are entangled and twisted in the hot air. They try to cool off their angry faces by fanning old newspapers. Then they start a long argument with words they pick to scorch each other with like fire. The night will be almost over and my father is still lying down trying to fall asleep, my mother is crouching at the edge of the bed against the wall, toying with the short strands of her hair. She tries to wipe the stings of fear off her beautiful shoulders. They end up with nothing: two bodies next to each other shrouded by the fog of a graveyard while I'm up high judging both of them. Eleven years could not have prepared me to comprehend the quick and intricate turns dispensed by the sound of sirens, which rules out the chance of the arrival of a morning safe for sleep. We run along the deserted and devastated Hamdi Alley to Army Street, an even more devastated area. The three of us flee in the early winter of a year that joins our running with that of other human shadows. We try to escape the bombing in despair because the road from our home to the shelter of Ambulance Square is so infinitely long. Although we are not asleep as we were supposed to be, we are still caught up in the rhythms of amputated dreams until my mother's reproaches, echoing down the nightmarish road, wake us. The wrecked homes now appear in the road's enchanted center as if it were an infinite, invisible ball of fire. Like flames, we burst into the shelter across from the hotel where foreigners and movie stars used to stay.

If I were asked about what I saw in the darkness of the vault, I would have said nothing about the spots of light that continued to explode like a carnival of fireworks, incessantly echoing the multicolored ghosts that flashed through the dark hotel. They peeped through the windows that were broken in different, abstract shapes on each floor, casting calm, kind smiles on the shivering bodies inside the shelter.

But no one cared to ask me about what I saw, so I did not have to lie. My father would mumble a few words in an anger that was not unusual in this type of situation, my mother would stamp the floor with her little feet as if to greet everybody, some people would be laughing, and some would be crying while others did not care whether it took a long or a short period of time. Things would end up the same and we would walk out wet with sweat or urine or tears or blood, all the same. More debris and dead bodies and another search for any house that was still standing. "That was one tough raid!"

"Fifteen rockets in less than half an hour!"

"In addition to the diarrhea of bullets the sons of bitches dumped on us."

"Eww, that's disgusting!"

"Hey, has anyone seen Said Khater?"

"I saw him taking the gas tanks inside."

23

"I called after him and thought I heard him saying he was right behind me."

"It would be such a catastrophe to bomb the gas station!"

"But what difference would it make?"

"You're right; nothing but fire eating fire."

"And bodies being grilled."

"God will punish them."

"*We* should punish them. Tomorrow we'll show them and humiliate them."

For me, "tomorrow" was the day I completed my eleventh year by packing my belongings. After long negotiations, it was concluded that my mother was entitled to take me away. They could not have understood the feelings of a fish taken from a saltwater sea to my mother's stagnant freshwater pond. "Tomorrow," the life of the child who used to play in rocket-hit homes, feeling their hot walls with her bare hands and betting with her friends on which house would be hit next, would be over. Most of the prizes that consisted of candy and whistles went to Asaad, whose predictions usually came true as he led us through the hard-hit homes and reminded us of how they were as of yesterday, an arrogant boy who cared nothing for Abdel Halim's love songs, grinning stupidly when I poured them into his ears to carry over to Andrea.

"Pack what is important; indispensable items only. The rest we'll find there."

"Mama, please let us stay; let us stay with Dad."

"You're insane and he's even more insane. Do you think this is a game? This is a real war: death, devastation, hunger and thirst, and no guarantee of tomorrow or even five o'clock; you'd spend the rest of your days running from death, trying to compress your entire life into one moment before a bullet or even a piece of shrapnel ends it. There is safety there, which means life, which means order: hay in springtime, grapevines planted in March, planning on doing such and such in the future, there is only one month left before eid. . . ." I remain quiet as if I do not understand, as if her argument is convincing; maybe that would stop the drama for a day or so. I should fill my bundles with heavy stones so that she may feel for me and reconsider her decision.

My father says, "This is the way women are, my dear."

"Well, then I don't want to be a woman, Dad."

"Who said you would be like that?"

He nods his head, adding that I'm not like anyone else, that I'm his backbone that will never break, that my youth will last for a hundred years, that pain will make something great out of me, and so on.

My father and Asaad are peacefully sitting in the silence of the mosque. Their faces light up in kind smiles. I'm outside, hiding behind a stone column to conceal my overwhelming desire to accept their invitation to join them in this benevolent space. I resist for no reason. Is it shyness or the usual running away from good opportunities?

"Now, we should turn your constant running away into a memory; come with us, Suzy. I will show you something you won't forget every time you enter a space somewhat damp and dim during the daylight; it will rise in front of you declaring the death of everything, the death that will obliterate all your beliefs. I will inoculate you with this vaccine because I want you to quietly sit down and thank the divine fulfillment that will infuse your otherwise ordinary face with a huge smile shining through all your damp and dim memories."

Vast distances separated my father from my mother, a world of fairytales between the mountain and the valley, mud, and sand. While for my father I had great prospects ahead of me, I was digging a hole to bury the pain within my soul. I was looking for something everywhere, perhaps for a future whose image I should grant my father, a valediction for mourning broken promises as we walked among the graves of the victims of the previous night's raid in the poor, dusty graveyard. Into empty drug containers and wine bottles we stuffed the names of the dead—but those bottles, filled with identifications, were bound to roll over, causing the dead to lose their names. What I feared most was losing my father among the bottles and the graves, which would subject me to my mother's will so that she could live her second life through me.

"I have dreams for you that are more than what I had even for myself. I want you to have what I could not have. I want you to be more beautiful and better off. That's why we have to run away. Lives are snuffed out here day and night and I don't want to die before I make sure you're safe. Do you understand?"

My mother's departure date was postponed because her full-size mirror, the most important possession she had to take with her, was impossible to move in wartime, especially because it had a delicate frame made in Istanbul and plated with pure French gold. It was an heirloom that belonged to the aristocratic family whose standing was not tarnished by the scandals of Selim Bey the Turk, lover of boys. No scandal fazed him as he proudly strutted in his wool jacket through the gate of the small palace, guarded by two stone eagles, to the garden where his gentle daughter gave him a white flower. Had it not been for his mysterious disappearance, my grandmother would not have accepted a local tailor as a husband for the apple of her eye.

Black attire dotted the roads. Houses were cast down in silence for the secret rites of a sorrow that could not be lifted. Memories stubbornly haunted even the arteries and fine ligaments of deeply wounded hearts. A martyr in every household. Hands were touched in the dark by the spirits of the loved ones who died smiling at a future cut short by death, leaving behind the promising beauty and wisdom of youth obliterated by a war they never regretted fighting. No one could disentangle rubble from human remains; blood and fire mixed to make an open grave for civilization and people. On Sidqi Street—the street that vomited the debris of its residents and buildings on the black stones of the road—what was this atmosphere that reeked of death and its secretions, and why did these successive images suggest different meanings to shadows? I lived over sand bags where RPGs were propped up, hidden under heavy turbans to split the helmet from the sweating, throbbing head.

"Hearts do not pound when you are fighting; they are already dead. The mind has only its energy reserves to use," my father says as he and Asaad walk me through the dim city to share with me everything he sees every day from daybreak until sundown. He breaks his silence only to describe the sites we pass by, his strong words adding to my heartbreak at seeing them. He says that when evening comes, death becomes an eastern hero in a life waiting for reception like a TV. Meanwhile, radios play victory songs, prayers for safe return, and statements of gratitude and praise for the devout leader.

Loud weeping is heard at some grave; handkerchiefs are dripping with tears and despair over a son, a brother, an uncle, or a woman, who never bore arms. Wailing quickly moves us to tears over the lost ones whose good company and kindness are lost. The odor of death permeates the whole city and gathers within us; every minute, since by the law of war, new graves are continually dug, death itself presides over both gravediggers and gas lamps. One coffin fits all corpses, whether gutted or split open, cut into random pieces or left for days under stabbing debris or growing mold. No way to identify the dead except by guessing according to their clothes or small pieces of paper crumpled like scorched butterflies inside fractures and holes. Sometimes a casket contains random limbs and parts. The gravedigger works very hard to cover private parts. In the end, it all becomes a matter of drowning pain in grief and living with death without any resistance.

"Did you know that I hunted one of them down with my rifle?" my father asks. "Of his own free will, he came to Abu Gamus, the place they had devastated for years. He was standing on the opposite shore. Maybe he thought it would be safe to bathe in the canal assuming we were nothing but resigned ghosts. I killed him with one shot."

Although they can be imaginary gates to worlds of harmony, words cannot describe my father's smile. When he forces us to leave without him, my mother declares terrible wars on him and on me. She cries out from the prison of her fear of death: "You want to die for no reason except not being able to leave."

All of my father's attempts at humor fail; she responds to them with a smile that stifles my tearful, joyous laughter. Her smiles are not so much fake as they are distracted. They emanate from her own private world, a world with green lawns she could barely touch with her feet, pure blue skies to stare at, and various other things I could not comprehend. She would wander around wearing a green shawl and pants made from the same fabric, which took my father two hours to sew. She put them on saying, "These clothes are more appropriate for the countryside; modesty and elegance are what we need so that people know we're special."

She would come up with apt figures of speech following her long meetings with people who returned after being endlessly humiliated during their immigration. I would feel terribly guilty as I tried to dissuade her from departing to these dark regions, which colored the spirits of our friends and neighbors with the gloom of loss and disgrace.

"We won't be like them. I know what I'm doing. You'll see in a couple of days. A real life. I'm not rootless."

While my mother inherited my grandmother's mirror, my uncle Atef took over covering up my grandfather's scandals and looking after my blind grandmother, who did not know if her husband was dead or alive after he ran away with his young British lover. He secluded himself in a distant village where the family owned several acres and a country house in the old Victorian style. One year we visited him and the most I could remember was the peasants' joy to see us and their friendliness toward me mixed with a formality that made them bow down. I did not understand then that this was because my uncle was connected to a formerly wealthy family and was a student in the Police Academy. I did not understand either why my uncle used to tie his cat to the bedpost and kick her on his way in and out with the tip of his shoe. Now that he did not have his cat, he was aimlessly marching up and down the long hallway in our house with the self-assurance of a police officer.

"Don't think that you are emigrating or anything like that. You are just moving in with me. Did you really think I was going to let you live in a coop or in some camp? You are my flesh and blood, Suzy. Do not listen to your father or believe what he says."

This was the extent to which I knew my uncle Atef. He was close to my age and could therefore be my friend; there was so much I could learn from him. But a world of chaos and disorder invaded my life from the moment he walked into our house and arrogantly shook my father's hand. Once that quick gesture was done with, he lifted us up with the same hand from our familiar world. "Quickly pack up your stuff, we're leaving immediately. I don't have time," he said with both his palms turned up.

We sit squished in a cab. There was not much protest in my father's soft kisses on my cheeks or in his reproachful glances to his wife who was too busy to say goodbye in the last few minutes. Until we left, she was helping Asaad and the driver with taking down our stuff to the small pick-up truck. I kept my head turned back until my father and Asaad vanished along with the whole city. Its devastated face disappeared behind a line of broken trains surrounded by blown-up tracks. The cracked concrete road receded into the desert. We proceeded through its vast expanse under a dark sky dappled with distant silver stars, flashing with a playfulness missing from the sky of the eternally dark city we had left behind.

The truck receives signals that seem friendly. The driver slows down as a convoy of armored vehicles covered with thick cloth the color of seaweed approaches. Toward the rear, guns are propped up between two rows of soldiers; their points penetrate the tight spaces between the vehicles. We are approached by a giant soldier rigidly standing in his military uniform. The formal greetings my uncle exchanges with him exempt him from having to explain our nocturnal trip to Cairo, our first stop on the way south. When my uncle returns to his seat, we line up behind him while the driver stares at him with awe and turns quiet for the first time during the trip.

Previously, he was chatting about how the city used to be, about the nonstop exodus of its residents, about his grocery store, which was completely destroyed in a night raid and had its contents hurled to the middle of the road. For days and days, he tried to separate sugar, flour, tea, butter, cheese, bottles of alcohol, bottles of local drinks from dust and debris . . . uselessly. "This used to be a rich city for decent people. What a loss! God help us."

When he senses my uncle's important status, he starts talking about how serious the preparations for war seem this time compared to other times in the past. "This time it must be for real. If you saw the weapons that keep coming through, you would believe me."

In exile, one life recedes and another one begins. One world is evacuated and its tenants are replaced with new, extremely nosy ones. I'm now half an emigrant stuck between the green highway and the irrigation control building. Our family house lies in the middle of this small stretch of land, which extends to the only building with a phone in town, the last connection I have with my father, Asaad, and Hamida. Loneliness is my only companion as I wade in cow dung at sunset completely alone.

I bump into a woman who has just jumped out of my uncle's bedroom window. She tries to catch her breath as my mother calms her down and straightens her dress and the strands of hair that show under her thick black head cover. The minute my mother is done, the young woman attacks me and slaps me on the face—a small act compared to the magnitude of her desire for revenge against my uncle. My uncle is lying down in bed thrilled, shaking his feet, and smiling at my mother as she screams at him, "You're crazy! Do you know whose daughter and whose wife she is? Do you understand what they are going to do to her and to us?"

"She came here of her own free will."

"So that you make love to her, not burn her with your cigarettes and bite her flesh with your teeth, son of Selim Bey. She loves you, fool."

"She loves me? Ha, ha, ha. Are you stupid? She loves the uniform and chases the police officer, a real whore. The only way to show her respect is to let her clean my shoes."

At the beginning, it was difficult to pronounce the new words in the rural accent that drawled much like the cycle a loaf of bread made from kneading to being thrown into the depth of the clay oven, which suddenly hissed waves of smoke that dissipated once the thin loaf surrendered itself to the hot surface. I used to ignore this accent and to repeat the same words correctly according to sound or order of letters, at least as much as I spoke them with my mother and my uncle, who maintained his upper-class way of speaking when no one was around. I used to stutter when he insisted that I say the words according to the wrong way he heard them.

Our stay in the family house often gave gossipers and snoopers the chance to come in the house under the pretext of performing small tasks for my mother, whose life here was very different from her life before. The name of our hometown by the shore would come up in the stories told by the elderly who encountered it on their pilgrimage. They spoke passionately about its gorgeous red brick houses, which were lined up on both sides of the road and resembled the train stations built by the British, except that they stretched out at equal intervals, displaying their gates and wooden porches between the trees. They also wistfully spoke about the enormous ships that sailed through the tight strip of the canal and which looked from afar like a piece of the city itself slowly disintegrating into the big sea over the tip of the gulf from the Prophet's Gate which was called Sues, or Qalzam, or Suez.

We have turned into an odd family, seemingly wealthy, enjoying the future power of my uncle, now a senior in the Police Academy. The townspeople treat us with respect that borders on fear, yet with love shown in the attentiveness they give my mother despite the cloud of arrogance that hovers over her as she gives small bribes that fall like rain on the attendants who follow her everywhere she goes. Their solicitude gives her a sense of dignity she well commands with her white, rosy-colored skin, her graceful figure snug in her dark-colored dresses, tight fitting because of the pregnancy she discovered after fits of vomiting she initially attributed to the quality of drinking water. She should have been a lady or a famous movie star, lording as she did over the geography of our new world, whose borders came to a halt at the lifeless mirror she polished carefully before standing endlessly in front of it, oblivious of time and place.

Here I am smothered by the smell of ghee. It reeks from my grandmother's bedroom next to the pantry, which has now become a big storage place for the kitchen and its accessories after the addition of a factory-made gas stove, the first innovation ever in this quiet town. In the evening, the storage place turns into a playground for rats proudly prancing in front of my uncle's fat cat who gets fed and kicked in equal measure.

My mother dozes off, exhausted by her pregnancy, while my grandmother snores in her perpetual darkness. In the perfect silence that exquisitely surrounds the graves, piercing the cold moonlight outside the locked window with their tombstones, I feel completely trapped. My uncle plays my father's role and my grandmother plays my mother's while my mother is gone most of the day at some distant village school, coming home full of dust and aching so much that she spends the rest of the day bedridden and mirror-fixated. She talks to her mirror as she tightens her dress around her belly, which bulges in a way that makes her face cringe under the weight of the baby that was fired at her one scary night when we slept through the alarm of a night raid which, it turned out, never happened. Instead, an early morning raid took us by surprise before sunrise. It killed off the early light, suffocating it with debris, smoke, and the dying cries of more than half of our neighbors. Covering my eyes with my hands, I saw them twisting and turning under the worn-out pistachio-colored bedcover, my own father and mother whom I placed above everything else. Now, instead of revering them, I felt a deep shameful hatred toward them as I tried to close my eyes over their muffled cries.

Two prospects obsessively haunt me: that my father would die in an air raid and I would become completely cut off from the city, and that my mother would die while giving birth and would be buried in the spot I see from my big window where the green grass meets the pure blue sky.

31

Through my imagination, I escape from this hateful place where my uncle inflicts stringent security measures on everyone around him, and where my grandmother constantly curses Nasser and the fate that assigned her to complete blindness. These fears lead me to form friendships with other emigrant families to learn more about the humiliations they ruthlessly receive from every direction, even from the cold wind stabbing their bones as they lay down in the stadium lanes which were geographically divided by blankets and sheets provided by social security. I try to adapt to living away from my city and from the ones I left behind. I look for them in my walks, getting a glimpse of Asaad with his slim figure and the black circles around his eyes as he turns his neck back for a long time to follow me walking with my mother in my compulsory emigration. Memories of Andrea sail through my heart, parting like waves to reveal twilight. I listen to songs about love surrounded by ruins now buried in the foggy village stretching outside my window. I listen to jazz and rock, which Andrea used to play, making the lights dance on the walls and on cheerfully colored pieces of furniture. His house was endlessly energized by the craziness of his older sister, Mademoiselle Rebecca, the schoolteacher who used to tint her hair in vibrant colors which, together with her chic glasses, crowned her extremely sexy body wrapped in Hollywood-style clothes similar to what Marilyn, Sophia, and Jane Fonda wore on the screen of the summer movie theater. Like bright stars in a clear sky, his family shone in my mind. Everything seemed perfect, even Rebecca's gentle shivering as she absent-mindedly smiled during the flag salutations at school in the cold morning, her fast walk on her way out of the classroom like a woman on a mission interrupting my aimless drifting among the classrooms on the first floor.

"Bonjour, Mademoiselle. Comment ça va?"

"Je suis bien. Merci."

"Qu'est-ce que c'est que la leçon française?"

"Je n'en pas . . . mais bien."

"Bravo! Your French is excellent. A tout à l'heure."

She walks away trying to smooth her skirt around her thighs with gracefulness. I run around the schoolyard eager for the bell to ring so that it is time for the French lesson at her home. Her room has the color and smell of roses, a complex network of precious feminine details overseen by her kind grandmother. She walks around directing her Greek anger at sofas, knowing that we can hear her during our private lessons in this amazing house with its wooden porches overlooking the coastline. Its huge, damp entrance smells like the waves, which we can almost hear in our imagination. We walk up the round wooden stairway to the door decorated with Christmas bells; green wreaths surround the small window where Andrea's mother stands, looking like the Virgin, her big eyes searching, "Who is it?"

When she first opens the door, rare scents envelop us and enter our memories before we become used to their sweetness while we try to hide our devouring looks at the mother. Her brown hair is surrounded by the heavy smoke from her cigarette as she curses the fate that ruined her happiness and deprived her of a hotel which was built by her grandfather and had now become a headquarters for the Socialist Party.

We try to win the friendship of Madame Rebecca's daughter who consumes frightful amounts of candy, turning her into a ball of energy and insolence. She draws wild images on the walls of the study room; for example, a blood-sucking butterfly that emerges from its third cocoon into a void, violently attacking me and my friends. We eagerly wait for Andrea's smile, which turns French into a language fit for love poems and fantasies when we hear it mixed with his Arabic.

"Bonsoir, rascals." "Rascals" was his signature curse. "Pourquoi are you late? I have a big surprise for you. I have just received *Last Tango in Paris*, Brando's latest movie."

The white sheet falls over the blackboard; Andrea turns on the movie projector. I spend the whole time watching his face while the movie is playing; knowing that Asaad is deliberately fidgeting next to me to disrupt the inner smile that sets my cheeks on fire every time I see the reflection of Andrea's face on the projector.

Andrea materializes now in the dim lights of the village asleep under the muffled cries she intermittently hears—for the first time the pyramid has crushed the spirit of the girl whose name was Suzy and who loved red grapes. She both fears and loves red. She usually wanders like a lost sheep, but in her mind she keeps an image of a place of harmony and loveliness beyond the foggy labyrinths of war; every time she puts on larger-size shoes and changes the story of her red dress, only imagination takes her beyond her window. Watching the fireworks chase away dark ghosts distracts her. Because she is a child no longer, she leaves her mother's arms to enter a bitter, dysfunctional marriage. In the darkness lit only by moonlight she looks for some meaning. The moonlight draws intricate shapes of sorrow over the souls already destined for suffering. She is lost in pondering those shapes. Her previous life wasted in inertia is sharply dismantled when she stops pretending that everything is fine, that nothing happened, and that what she saw that night was a mere nightmare, even Khairiya's screams, the fourteen-year-old emigrant who is one year older than her and looks much like Hamida, Asaad's sister. Khairiya's screams were not louder than the screams of her uncle's cat every time he kicked her with his shoe. She did not invent the three men who took turns lying on top of Khairiya and the blood that quickly dried over her exposed cold thighs was not simply the menstrual blood that scared her when she was ten. . . .

I was hiding behind the shed unwillingly watching through the dry reeds. Needles pricked my skin when I felt the cold blade of a knife pressing against the skin between my shoulders and my neck. It was one of them but because it was pitch black, I did not see him leave the triangular-shaped shed, which from the other side of town looked like a monster feeding off the reeds. Khairiya was lying down there with three men taking turns in penetrating her after they managed to drag her to the shed to have some fun for the price of two rounded ten-piaster coins, a dramatic detail good for a movie from the 1960s.

"If you say a word, I will slice your flesh with this sharp knife."

"Leave her alone. Don't hurt her."

"Why not?"

"Her uncle is Atef Pasha, stupid."

"But she is better looking than Khairiya."

"If you come back tomorrow, I'll give you twenty piasters."

"What twenty piasters, moron? She deserves a whole pound!"

"Go away kid; leave immediately and don't you ever say a word!"

He pushed me hard so I ran away. I tried to wipe off the memory with stumbling and falling, filling my mouth with the wet sand whose taste Khairiya used to find exciting. The rape party was over; no hero appeared on the scene to relieve the viewers and take the victim home to her bed where he places a noble kiss on her closed eyelids.

We would all feel more comfortable if we could leave our seats believing that what we just saw was the movie director's interpretation. It would be better if I could believe that my insomnia and the stinging in my heart and in my eyes as they keep staring into the frozen eyes framed by Khairiya's terror-stricken face were the result of issues similar to what made my mother talk to her mirror as she went over the mental stages of her life divided according to gates of alienation she had to walk through. She had the problems of being both rich and poor. She was trying to maintain the family's traditions over the land that was taken from her. She only received as much of her inheritance as my uncle allowed. If she could sell her share, which was a little bit over a few acres, she could build her own home and independently raise both of her children, me and my newborn brother.

The train ride was less hectic than the family house. I let my fears slip through the fast-moving posts. The terror that had paralyzed me for days dissipated through the windows. The sky was taking me away from Khairiya who visited me on the third day. She sat next to me on the second step in front of the house's doorway and talked about everything except what happened that night. I wished she would refer to it, if even indirectly, so that I could stop her, but the usual chapters in the emigrants' black comedy took up all our time. When she showed me the several ten-piaster coins she had, I saw again the three frightening faces pushing me toward a fate I was saved from when, after madly looking for me everywhere, my uncle dragged me by my braids and threw me at my mother's feet, screaming, "The girl that you were friends with was found murdered at the back of the market. See who this bitch has been running around with?"

I could not talk because my fear was accompanied by a chronic pain between my shoulders and my neck, and because a drill had been constantly harrowing my brain to cast what I witnessed into oblivion until it seemed that nothing had ever taken place. All I knew was that a poor girl used to keep me company with her visits and with our walks through Water Street, which split the town in two. We would ponder what brought us here and remember the paved streets of our hometown and the smell of freshly baked bread and grilled fish in Shusha's bakery, which baked bread and grilled fish at the same time. We would also remember jumping rope and skipping in the French garden that overlooked the meeting point between the bay and the canal; what else . . . I couldn't remember. This was all I shared with Khairiya. Her father, Amm Kahlawi, was a fisherman who could not feed his family off of fishing in the shallow waters because the fish were rotten, as he would say pouring fresh water on dark-colored fish that twitched in the big pot, perhaps as Khairiya herself did before she was found dead next to her blood-soaked clothes. Perhaps the argument over money was decided with the same knife that had earlier been pressed against my skin when she cried and almost screamed demanding the full amount they promised her. A sharp knife, a scream, and a moon trapped in the reeds surrounding the shed would take her back to the streets leading to the peaceful bay, to Shusha's bakery, and to the French garden.

My eyes are like two cameras recording two scenes: my father is the lead actor finishing the steps needed for setting me free; my uncle is asking him to stay to take care of his family now that he has a son worth living for.

"I can always come over; but if the lady wishes to go back with me, she should feel free."

"That won't work. . . . You should stay."

"I don't have time to travel back and forth every day and I can't live without my job."

"Are you trying to tell me that you're busy working? But there is no one left in Suez."

"How could a police officer know nothing about the work that's being done there?"

"Isn't the war over and we've crossed?"

"We've crossed but the war is not over."

"Okay, then, take your daughter with you and look after her. She is at a tough age and I'm too busy. I'm too busy. . . ."

My uncle leans over my mother and audibly whispers in her ear, "He won't be able to take care of her over there. They'll be back in a couple of days. Be patient."

So I traveled with my father. We took the train for half of the trip. He was trying to be friendly but I was no longer the child who left him over two years ago with her mother and her uncle for a world that completely matched Don Quixote's tale. I felt how torn he was as he tried to convince me to go back to my uncle and wait until the situation changed

36

at home in the city since at that point it was neither appropriate nor safe for a young woman my age. I moved to the seat next to him, rested my head on his shoulders, and burst into tears. He embraced me with a compassion that freed my tongue of fear and paralysis. I told him everything except what happened there: I would cook for you, I would wash your clothes and iron them with the heavy metal iron, I would be careful with the buttons so that they would not melt as they did with my brown school uniform when I tried to iron it. We both laughed until I fell asleep with my head in my father's lap.

The bay is covered with the wreckage of the destroyed homes along the road by the shoreline of which nothing is left but a painful memory. All places try to tenaciously persevere in the face of the air raid alarms, which pierce the air and fill uncovered evacuation trucks with human beings deeply humiliated by fools who do not understand the terror and chilling convulsions of death. Bits of human life are saved in mortuary refrigerators; no one knows why all the corpses are being preserved. For the home country? For God's sake? For the people who will never know what is happening here and what happened there in the labyrinth of the desert, people who will never have to count the mass murders of their army units, who are lucky to never have to learn the colors of the mire of death and devastation—the gray that invokes sorrow, absolute relief in black, the red that runs lost lives into annihilation, and my father screaming at the end of the hallway, "Be prepared for war even in your sleep; fire at your enemy before he does."

Who can contain this insanity and who can prevent its floating into space with its blind assassins? Death, I love you with your cancerous spread through the ghost town. I keep looking for you under debris and between fires and where you lurk disguised in tortured faces.

The pillows made of coarse sandbags mix dreams with the nightmares of the sudden, terrified awakenings caused by the roaring of the cannon at Abu Gamus as it lay in a long coma after being bombarded.

I sleep huddled no matter how big my bed is. I do not dare stretch out my limbs in any direction for fear of losing them. If it happens by accident, a great terror wakes me up, then I go back to falling into cycles of sleep threatened by stray bullets; my father pats my hand according to their number. He takes me on the hump of false courage to the mortuary refrigerators. Together we walk through the long hallway that separates life from death while Asaad follows behind. The tunnel stretches out and the walls glow faintly in the dim neon lights. My father walks over the tiles to point to the shiny doorknobs of the cabinets lined against the metal wall distinguished only by carefully engraved numbers. When he pulls a random knob, terror itself appears in the empty room. It yawns and stretches; my father begs for a little mercy for me and for the dead woman holding on to her child, perhaps the way my mother did a long time ago. I imagine their embrace before they were severed by the evil dropped from airplanes flying over the dreadful mire of chunks of flesh mixed with crushed bones. No personal identifications, no features. I believe that all my senses dried up and shrank at that moment as if the person looking was not me. Half of my father's words were swallowed by the dark void of the refrigerators; their deep echoes woke me up from staring at ugly death.

"You are still a young woman, but you are free. . . . Point, aim, and shoot directly at the head so that both you and your target find peace."

The worst thing Suzy had to do in this charged atmosphere was having to shower after menstruation to resume fasting in Ramadan. The world around her was becoming increasingly complicated, especially after she lost several battles and realized that there was something inherently wrong with everything. The war ended in victory, according to the anthems that were composed in a hurry. In actuality, she returned to a confinement blocked in three directions that intersected on the way to Cairo. A few final raids devastated what was left of a city that experienced all the atrocities of war; now orders were issued for the people and the army to 'fight until death,' but there were outcomes worse than death. That was what my father taught me when he took me to a black hole between life and death, which sucked down all the dreams I would have to ignore from that point on; they were replaced with nightmares that stuck to me by force of the hot air that rushed against my face and made me shiver as I was leaving the morgue, which was on the edge of town and surrounded by the wild reeds, climbing its walls and letting out low moans in the wind.

He took me to the beach to teach me, as he once did with swimming, how to identify my target, point at the head, and think only of my own safety: either death or a good shot. In the meantime, the wounds caused by airstrikes and bombardment were infected so fast that amputation was the only option until the city was filled with limbs and parts hanging even in imagination.

I was taken by surprise when my father shot both of them dead. I sensed the relief he must have felt when he pointed his gun toward the east and aimed at his target with great precision: he hunted them down with two bullets, one after the other, loudly demanding that they die. But our relief dissipated in an instant as if a curse haunted our short-lived victories and made us fear our next step. There were three soldiers hiding on the eastern shore of the canal, keeping watch over a strong Resistance, spying to find out whether we would fight back or not. The third one found an opportunity to suddenly re-emerge, wounding my father and my conscience with a stray bullet as, on top of a sand dune covered with the wreckage of homes and the debris of scrimmages, my father was teaching me how to overcome my hesitation and choose the right moment.

For an instant I was absorbed into the sky that used to resonate with our talk and laughter under the moonlight. My heart was filled with the pure scent of freedom and with the splashing waves drenched with iodine. Nothing could fight injustice more than dreaming.

They were taking a stroll on the opposite shore around the flag that cut through my father as if it were stuck in his own flesh. On this long, terrifying night, the heavy smoke of gunshot filled my chest. One stray bullet and two good ones were shot in a horizon covered with the dust of the early Khamasin, which hid the moonlight and covered the world with dark yellow. Through my father's binoculars, the two dead men seemed different from the third one who suddenly appeared between the two corpses piled on the rough sand. He was one of them but he did not collapse or fall. He escaped my father's gun on that distant night to become an evil ghost, haunting me forever and keeping alive my fears and my regrets over a dull moment that cost my father his leg, which twitched in the blood-stained sheet all the way from the hospital to the martyrs' graveyard where it was buried. The other two dominated my nightmares regularly, vainly trying to break free and aim at my father who jumped up and blocked the bullet's way. He pushed me to the ground fast enough so it would not hit me while he took it, but it did not hit his heart or his head. Either it changed its course, or he remained suspended up in the

39

air so that it cut off his leg at the thigh, ending the dream and denying his wish for death. My heart used to pound every time he walked in like a hero on the stage of my fears after each raid.

My father's khakis were replaced with an administrative police uniform. In the morning, he worked in the police station as a payroll clerk; at night, he worked in the sewing shop to pay off my mother's extra expenses, which included mainly piano and French lessons, as well as the fabrics she cut and he sewed so that she and I could walk side by side wearing the same colors of dead flowers. Whenever he rubbed his chin against my head and my face, my heart would be filled with warmth and peace. I never thought of him as a mythical hero and he never referred to those times. He would simply speak while softly cutting fabrics according to each customer's measurements—no matter how difficult the fabric was, he was precise.

The radio was describing heroic deeds and giving instructions urging us to fight bravely until death. My father deeply regretted not dying as a martyr because he believed he was meant for it but a cruel fate denied him and left him handicapped and trapped. We were rarely hungry or thirsty. Everything we had was spread on the bare floor like a table as we nibbled on stale bread and crouched in the dark. From the outside, we must have looked like giant rats.

We were still under siege while my father was in the hospital. The hospital continued to operate despite lacking everything, even water to sterilize, and which was no longer safe to drink. It came from the ancient pilgrims' wells. In my sleep I was seeing camels following a mirage that turned into a canal through which thousands of conquerors passed. When I woke up with a start, my father's smile greeted me. I kissed his veined forehead and heard him saying in great pain, "Could you please scratch my leg, Suzy?" His eyes widened as he spoke. "It's amputated, but it's still itchy," he added with a smile.

"Your life is more precious than anything else."

We laughed and cried. My tears ran down, mixing with the heavy, sticky drops slowly falling from his eyes. I wiped his face with the palm of my hand. His chest jerked sharply as he tried to get up.

"I would never be treated this way again. This has to be stopped or it would keep happening and justice would never be served."

"I don't understand."

"Your mother now ignores my handicap and pretends that she can't stand seeing me this way. Even if she were the sultan's daughter, she should still be here."

To that extent he loved her—perhaps more than her denial and rejection. She knew him only as much as she saw him in her thoughts; she cared more for her idea of him than for him. This was what was missing between them. How could I not see it before? A dreamy woman and an idealistic man running back to take shelter behind the fence at the top of the bay, refilling his gun and counting the number of bullets—minus the stray ones—the sum of his glorious and patriotic deeds, fighting a people whom he said, like us, had the right to live, but they denied what they knew deep down before their consciences died in the vast desert.

In the name of what should good and evil be equal? In the name of what should it be acceptable that dead bodies scatter the ground and hang down from walls to die over and over, envied by my father whose leg still tingled after it was amputated and buried without ceremony while he lay in the orthopedics department in the Suez General Hospital, on the second floor, first right, second left?

First right, second left. Easy directions, frightening in their hidden contradiction. Assuming my memory was poor, my father kept repeating them: first house on the right of the railway tracks, first right, second left, the house with four wooden balconies. You'll find them there; they all know you. They must be taken out of the station. Best time is immediately after dawn. Early tomorrow, you will take the cartridges from the stash under the button machine; your last assignment, hero, and you must finish it, right? Right?

What could I have said when even my ears were burning with fear over my father's last mission, which depended on my coming of age and being ready to face death? My childhood was over and I was entering a male stage imposed only by my father. War made this rare and unique reversal possible.

"I can't help it, sweetheart. My role is over, but we have to carry on; no outsiders can fight for our rights. You will replace me. In short, be a man!"

41

These were the demands my father made with a power that swept beyond qualifications and capabilities. Was he using me to finish his work, or did he trust me with something he aspired to, something different from what nature and what my mother had prepared me for?

"From now on, you have no time to sleep, hero. Go get ready to return the package to its owners. You will have plenty of time to sleep later."

My mother's wishes and her influence over me were erased by my father's kindness. I took a cold shower with what was left of the water that was used over and over until it changed color. I put on a boy's clothes to assert my rebellious departure from my mother's womb. I broke the cycle that drew me to her and to her mirror without ever being gratified. Fearlessly, I became the boy my father wanted and ignored my mother's instructions, "A girl should never be raised like this; she should be taught how to walk, turn, sit, talk, play the piano. She should be a lady. I'm trying to make you a princess, not a fighter."

My father was looking at me, appealing to my hormones, so I had to reassure him, "I don't want to be a lady. I want to be like Daddy and his friends."

I run into my father's open arms. I stand tall despite my fear of gunshots and airstrikes. Lonely and unhappy, my mother fades under the pressure exerted by the three of us: me, my father, and the boy I pretend to be for my father's sake. Unlike knights in shining armor, he ends up lying down in a small corner of an unclean hospital filled with injured victims trying to figure out the cost of the aid machines they may or may not receive while they are being bombed over and over again.

The bombing went on until the air was filled with the smell of gunpowder. Even dust was trying to escape the debris mixed with random screams that echoed in distant spaces where human remains mingled with gunshots and rockets exploded in the middle of the street, blasting families in their houses. In the end, these were combined in scenes no longer shocking to us as we played inside these homes, touching their melted edges and cold protrusions with our bare hands. I would climb the piles of debris and wreckage and pass through the fields of fire with my neck yanked by the silk handle of my school bag with its multiple pockets, which my father had designed for me. "This pocket is for your pencils, this one is for your sandwiches, this one is for your notebook, the back one is for books, this one is for paper, and a small secret pocket for your allowance."

I used to save my allowance to buy magazines from Amm Hasan, the Nubian, who insisted that I take whatever I wanted and pay later when I had enough money. But I preferred to pay first as my mother had taught me. Was it Abdel Halim's voice I was hearing singing loudly in the morning of another day under siege?

Homes spill out their guts. Bathrooms, kitchens, and rear bedrooms dissolve in the wreckage. A radio in a big wooden frame hangs in a cloth bag off the broken beams, sticking out of the gutted wall, trying to resist falling down. Its white knobs shine in the dim light of the early morning shrouded with the dense fog that wanders through the still devastation. A strong and clandestine compulsion accompanies the fear that used to softly and smoothly descend upon me like an accidental, involuntary death. I try to evade its inescapable grasp over my quest for an early education in the matters of life, death, and shock. Distant lights resist fading. I go up the street and pass by the mosque without paying much attention to the tracks yanked off the railway. The road never felt this long. I used to walk it with my mother on our way to Miss Pauline's salon every Saturday night to take piano lessons; this is also the same road I walked with Suria to take French lessons. My mother used to send me down this road, accompanied by Asaad, to deliver a plate of ashura or eid cookies. I knew he was jealous when Andrea teased me by blocking my way up the stairs and did not stop until I let him plant a quick kiss on my cheek. Now I walk by myself wondering in despair if these times will ever come back. I look around me for an answer: everything has been bombed and now I have to wear sneakers and boys' clothes, fitted by my father when we returned, to match the city's tired raggedness. Two suits with dots the color of sand soaked in heavy oil instead of my dresses, which once fluttered like rose petals in an open field.

I take the first right and turn at the second left. I look for the four wooden balconies, which overlook the Fortieth District police department. The house has three façades. The second one overlooks the Darisa housing projects and the third overlooks the train station where the pilgrims in their white clothes used to pace along the platform, their faces beaming with longing and devotion. They would engage in deep religious debates in the bazaar owned by Ijith, the devout Hindu who used to celebrate the pilgrimage and its pilgrims by helping them out and providing them with gifts of soap, incense, Kashmiri rosaries, and Indian turbans to take home before they went back on the train. Why can't memories bring a thirteen-year-old child joy instead of pain and a lump in her throat? The memories were turned into fantasies by my father who was shaping my mind with his war machine.

The signal was the dawn call for prayer once it was heard over the gunshots.

"Prayer is better than sleep." A call now made redundant by the insomnia of the city under siege. I remove the metal prop from the two big panels of the wooden door. I walk by the counter my father uses to spread out the fabrics he cuts with the big scissors that no longer shine when they are held without hope open over an old, faded piece of fabric. I drag the worn-out wooden box from under the sewing machine.

"My heart will show me the way. . . ." The radio was singing, still hanging up in the air; anyone could have easily climbed up, undone its noose, and put an end to its cries. The doors of the houses were tightly locked behind the blocks of rock and concrete that punctured their walls. How easily my playmates and I used to walk in through those holes to toy with people's possessions, sometimes eating out of the dusty plates randomly strewn over marble shelves by earthquakes. We would look at the photos barely clinging to the walls and allow our imagination to go beyond the years of attrition. We would act out the lives and the struggles of the houses' owners in shabby theatrical shows created and produced by Andrea. They always consisted of the same cast: a father and a mother, a daughter and a son, a lover for the daughter, a mistress for the son, and a stranger showing up to complicate the plot. When nighttime came, threatening more air raids, we put everything back the way it was as if the owners were returning home as soon as we rushed off. It never occurred to us to swipe some souvenir. The homes were our half-dilapidated theaters, which we brought back to life for a few stolen hours.

My father reaches out toward his amputated leg trying to scratch it. When he does not find it, he quietly starts crying. I tighten the bedcovers around his waist, staring at the bandage wrapped around the stump where blood has drawn a map. I stir the hot air with an old newspaper, which makes the red ceasefire headlines dance in the air, but the ceasefire does not put an end to the wounds covered with blood-stained bandages.

They insistently haunt my short naps and leave me helpless under siege in a war the newscasts declare over.

Gunshots and sandbags are signs for the backdoor. No one cares to remove the debris. I climb up heavy with the weight of the mission my father's handicap has imposed on me.

Today a new Suzy is planted in my memory as she climbs up the ruins of what resembles a stronghold with spilled-out guts randomly scattered everywhere. I sneak between tanks and partly operating armored vehicles to deliver cartridges to the men, including Asaad, who was two years older than me, one year older than Andrea, and two years younger than Ijith. When Suzy appears on the scene, guns almost fire at her. My father forgot to give me the password to protect my unannounced entrance.

When I shout an improvised password, "I'm Muhammad Galal's daughter, I'm Daddy Muhammad Galal. . . . I'm Suzy," the men burst out laughing; their laughter echoes louder than the gunshots on the balcony.

"This is your day, Suzy," Asaad whispers. "Remember it well."

Of course I remember well. I remember their eyes and their chests lined up behind the rifles that had previously accompanied the wounded and dead soldiers and their remains to the General Hospital. The weapons were treated with extra care and stored in medicine cabinets until my father and his companions decided to recover them from storage where they were in perfect condition and bring them back to life without permission. When they held them with trembling hands, their bodies shaking, sweat covering their faces like masks, they all looked alike. When the echoes of their gunshots were heard, the world took an interest in the deeds and tales of these few unwavering locals not driven out by the autumn rains of death or vanquished under long months of siege without aid.

I watch through a half-fallen wall in the revealing morning light, speechless, quiet, lost in a fog of dreams. I see an Israeli soldier sneaking in behind them, carrying a gun unsteadily pointed toward their backs, which are glued to the porch and the windows. I stare at him in panic and open my mouth to call Asaad's name, but he hears me before I even say a word.

"I heard her saying 'Daddy' so I turned around and found a gun pointing at me and bullets flying everywhere. But with my rifle, I had the guy pinned to the wall," Asaad says.

According to the testimonies of Amm Salama, Amm Khabiri, and Amm Abdel Mungi I did not make a sound. Later that same day, Amm Abdel Mungi was shot several times and fell off the fence so that his upper half was stuck on the wall and his lower half dangled. His last words to me still pierce my heart, "You could have screamed, jumped, thrown a stone at him, or done something instead of giving out one cry that made Asaad turn around and kill him before he could shoot the rest of us. Because of your laziness, we could all be either in the hospital next to your dad or bottled up in containers."

But Asaad defends me, takes me back, rewards me.

"You saved my life, Suzy. I have good news for you. Andrea is back."

All is perfect! Andrea is back.

"Could I see him right now?"

"He'll be here in a just little bit. It's not eight o'clock yet."

I did not know it was Andrea who delivered food to Resistance camps in the Fortieth District. I always thought this task was carried out by a poor woman named Asmaa. She delivered messages, news, and food protected by the innocence of her pretty face. Her role was immortalized and she married one of the heroes.

"It's not like you could just stand on the shore, hold a gun, and start shooting."

"Please don't remind me; I wish it never happened. My dad would have been fine now."

"Don't blame yourself. We should never think that all bad things happen because of us. You look a bit taller."

"I am although we have nothing to eat."

"I didn't say you looked fatter. You're older, Suzy. Could two years change you so much?"

"And much more if you only knew. . . ."

The lighter a substance is, the more powerful and beautiful it is: an old fact that for some reason now crosses my mind. My memory will inevitably fade over time. For short periods at least, I may be able to forget the events that shocked me and robbed me of the confidence my father instilled in me and I treasured somewhere deep in my heart.

I briefly pass out and dream of my mother. She is walking with the poise of a queen but with a bit of gentleness, accompanied by her maid, some unattractive friend, an odd daughter, and a porter she knows will spread the story of her arrival embellished with details of her generous tips. These tips will pave her way with other unscrupulous people, who have no qualms about accepting bribes. At the end of my nap I dream of Khairiya.

"These evacuation trucks are frightening, Suzy. This unusual cold in the countryside combined with living in the wild crush your bones as you shiver lying down in a bed with loose nails. You wait all day for a gift that may come from a rich merchant, hoping that he is only doing it for charity or as a chance to view the bizarre memorials of the disfigured people who escaped war and death. They don't know anything about us here. They have no idea about how much older we are growing every minute because they have not seen the dead or smelled the bodies burned with napalm. They have not seen my brother's head catching fire when he was looking for food in the army trash cans. I was waiting for him on the opposite side when he was hit by a bullet that made his blood gush over the round containers of Nesto cheese and the boxes of the cumin crackers he loved so much. . . ."

She sobs and turns red as she continues in anguish. "I loved him more than all the cumin crackers that were covered with the blood that splashed me when I stood there watching. In a moment, his body became a pile of mangled flesh burning on the asphalt right in front of the peace-keeping forces. What peace? My father was crippled with sorrow when our house fell down and we had nowhere to go but the streets where we were sure to die. But the streets here are not like the streets there; at least there we could turn either to God or to the enemy. Here we have our own people and they make us feel guilty all the time, even in our dreams. For them, we are the weird, ugly creatures that constantly remind them of war when they are removed from it and don't have to even think about it. I do feel bad for them. Not much has ever changed in their lives— whatever happens has no effect on them. Don't you feel when you walk through the fields that all the peasants look exactly the same? Even if their educated sons were to sit next to them, they would still look the same with their hands stuck in the mud."

Why did the great struggle turn into a love story complicated by absence? Was love the purpose of all heroic deeds? My life was changed and I became deeply afraid of death. Exalted notions about the world started to enter my head. Soft words moved me like a warship buried in sand. Guns were devastating my city and destroying monuments too magnificent to have been created by humans.

We were engulfed in bullets aiming at every little chance we had to escape. We lived in hell where we understood that our suffering was preordained. Only running undercut despair.

"Run, Suzy."

"Run, Andrea."

The fires behind us climbed high walls and sneaked around corners. We would run until the dark tunnel of sudden bombing came to an end. My heart would cry out in sweet agony, "I love Andrea Georgiani and he loves me." Breathlessly he would tell me, "I . . . lo . . . ve . . . y . . . ou."

Here was my hero who could bravely confront Asaad. When he arrived, he left the metal containers of food and the bread at the doorway away from the porches where the fighting took place so that they could have their breakfast in the peace they craved but were denied even during a meal. They could not sit down properly; instead, they crouched like the peasants used to do when they came to sell their goods to my mother in our backyard with its mosaic floor. For Andrea, I was a mission like carrying guns was a mission for Asaad; I was my own homeland as Andrea used to tell me.

"I will never leave you again. Can you forgive me?"

He was dancing and jumping up in the air while bullets were flying around him in all directions. As I ran next to him, holding my school bag over my head to shield me from bullets like an umbrella, I was thinking if he dropped dead right then and there, then this beautiful boy with brown hair falling over his forehead would be gone forever, leaving me to my loneliness. These were my thoughts as the bullets chopped bigger holes in the walls and flew like splintered rainbows. Andrea stretched out his hand to me, and I ran behind him as if his hand was going to stay there for thousands of miles. When our fingertips touched, we became undeniably happy, a happiness that erased my sins in those early years and broke the siege that held us without shelter or water or news of the outside world.

I walked alone through the big gate of the hospital while Andrea stood looking at me through the fence as if I were a gift he was sending away. I gracefully walked up the path that led to the massive building with its five floors. The fourth floor was the orthopedics department where my father lay. I entered the building and ran up the steps of the spiral staircase. I threw myself in my father's arms and burst into tears.

January 1974. The siege is over and the road to Cairo has reopened. We go back in a truck: my mother, my brother, my grandmother, and I. We sit in its dark box with no windows to show the surprise in our eyes. It rushes forward regardless of the hopes and ties the small family gradually loses along the way. Along with the old furniture carefully stacked up, the box carries the old wounds that stole the light from our eyes, the smiles from our lips, and the truth from our words.

Here we are, going back loaded with the deep feelings of injustice that ferociously eat my mother's heart out. Even in her sleep she looks annoyed, like something is tearing at her heart, forcing her anguished blood to gush forth while she is frozen, unable to move. The pain she carried in her heart meant nothing to me even when it felt as if she was pounding my head with a heavy hammer made of violence and refusal and constant screaming, things that made my head swell with revulsion until I could no longer stand her. This hatred was not cheap—it came at a high cost. It was like a drug I was injected with every day and every minute until a final nightmare numbed my brain and I became nothing but filth to my mother despite my own overwhelming suffering and my despair of ever escaping the grinding machine that was waiting for me every morning.

Instead of the reflection of her face in the mirror, a monster made up of angry blotches appeared. Anger was an acid substance that did away with any chance for contentment, joy, and love. She must have lost her mind and breastfed my younger brother insanity. How else did he enter his third year, under airstrikes and destruction, completely neutral, like a sunflower that follows the sun in any direction regardless of where its yellow shade would fall?

In a random ceremony held to honor the heroes of Resistance, my father received a medal that decorated the suit he wore only for that occasion. Later on, it collected soft dust on its old wooden hanger like burns on stretched flesh, rust corroded his medal, and no one cared enough to listen to the trials and tribulations of his life. Every day he woke up with the feeling that he had lost everything, especially when he put both his socks on one foot—one over the other—so that they would wear out at the same time. He was given a metal crutch with a black cork pad that gave his left armpit horrible bruises. Because he was left-handed, his right foot could not handle the job of two feet and it deteriorated rapidly. He would lean with all his weight on my shoulder, the one with the old injury. He would try to lean lightly but fail. I would keep encouraging him to get used to the crutch.

"I'm sorry, Suzy."

"Don't worry about it, Dad. My shoulders are broad and strong. I can carry twice your weight."

We repeated the same routine over and over until he finally collapsed next to the mirror, studying my mother's face. If he talked, he did so in a low, agonized voice, restrained by trying to avoid invoking any memories.

I moved my few possessions to my grandmother's bedroom on the first floor. Every night she shared her bed and her stories about everything, except the present, with me.

A mass service was held at the gate to the city where trucks loaded with construction workers and handymen coming to rebuild the city were passing by. They came to our house to fix some of the small cracks. My grandmother was screaming because the construction materials were hurting her eyes. My brother's mouth drooled as he tried to drag my mother away from the mirror that used to stand at the entrance to the family's old house (which was nationalized by Nasser and turned into a headquarters for workers' unions). My mother's day could not start until she stood in front of the mirror, talking a bit to herself, and fixing her hair and her shoes. In the meantime, I would be confined to my grandmother's bedroom bored with her stories about the old mansion, "an epitome of wealth and elegance." I would fall asleep hearing her deep sigh, warning of the future, "Those were the days."

My mother completely loses her mind when she finds out about the bottle of wine I bought for my father. She starts slapping my face and screaming out loud, foaming at the mouth, and looking like an eagle that lost its eyes until we both fall down motionless on the floor. I get up feeling more rebellious while she recedes back hundreds of years until she becomes . . . nobody . . . no more than a specter that speaks with an awful calm to cloak flames of anger impatient to erupt. I never felt any pity toward her when her face shone with that glassiness that seemed to smack me every time my eyes met hers with the bottle hidden behind me. A perpetual sunset witnessed my withdrawal from my family into Andrea's enchanting one. Their windows overlooked an overturned tank that had a white star that looked like a skull with two crossbones. It was carefully drawn over rusted tin plates as if to draw a line between us and the dangerous spots. This tank hit one of my father's friends. He was dancing in the large square when he was surrounded by army units. The holes in his body were large enough for the air to lift him up and drop him down on his knees, dead, on a narrow strip of the wide street where he defied the siege like an ancient winemaker, his blood streaming in all directions.

My love for Andrea and his family cost me many slaps, bruises, and curses, usually invoking my father's name. When he had too much to drink, he confronted everything with the same sad, sheepish smile and weepy apology. Every time my uncle Atef came to visit, my mother took him aside in the guests' room at the far end of the house to tell him about the family's bad situation, which somehow always revolved around me. Her report would begin with Asaad, who was "nothing but a hired hand working for her father" and my long walks with him by the shore. The coast wrapped around the city like a ribbon around the heart of a young lover. I would walk next to Asaad, trying to reach out to his kind and thoughtful mind as he walked me through Balzac and Natalie, Freud and Virginia Woolf, then Sartre and Simone, the history of Egypt under Mamluk rule, their horses' stables hiding underground rebels who lurked behind fancy balls—rich worlds unfolding new vistas of knowledge and wonder in my eighteen years—then Marx and Lenin, Mao and Guevara from Andrea's library until a new rebellious mind emerged against all the suppressors of an evasive freedom. I wished then that I had known all the names because life seemed to offer something far more profound than what my mother was preparing me for. Sometimes I had to say no to my father when he asked me to buy him alcohol on credit from Amm Ishac's grocery store because the receipt would be written on my body with his sharp, ravishing eyes. This made me fear all store owners and ultimately despise them.

My mother would also complain about my constant absent-mindedness and my habit of staying up all night to read obscene books and, of course, I did not help her with the housework. As a result, I had to finish reading

The God of the Labyrinth in the bathroom because my uncle's physical abuse increased every time he found a book other than school textbooks with me during the search campaigns he held at the beginning of each visit. These visits were frequent because he was temporarily stationed at the police headquarters in Cairo and was able sneak off work to come over anytime he had a craving for fish. While waiting for the pink parcel of fish to arrive from Shusha's bakery, he would try the force of his leather belt as it lashed my body.

"What are you reading? You're nobody and you should just do your homework."

I would have to stay at home for at least two weeks after until my face healed. The pain would drive me to Asaad, whom my mother used to refer to as "a handyman, working for his brother-in-law, who came here with the construction people, barefooted, hungry, and dirt-poor. Now he is a filthy-rich contractor with piles of money he made out of the debris of devastated homes."

When she met my dear Andrea, he got his own share of her disapproval: "A punk, in love with himself, who cares about nothing but his movies and his music and his travels and all sorts of nonsense that draw losers to his side."

Andrea gives me D.H. Lawrence's *Lady Chatterley's Lover* to read so that I learn how the world turns around after it seems to fall apart and how the proletariat push forward the peasant revolutions.

In the solemn Orthodox cemetery across from the tall Jewish tombstones standing over the victims of the Second World War, I sense the deep sorrow behind the transparent black veils and the formal suits. They were especially made for the sacred funeral rituals of one of the last icons of this family of ancient lineage. I'm at the grand funeral of Andrea's grandmother. I offer him my condolences with my eyes as I stand behind my mother, who resembles his sister Rebecca in every way, even in her bad luck. Rebecca, as my mother said, "used to date teachers who kept their illnesses hidden under their heavy winter sweaters until she married Monsieur Adel, the science teacher, who turned her home into a meeting place for socialists. He stole her money to build a big house in his village for his cousin, a peasant who made fertilizer out of animal dung with her bare hands."

I remain silent to hide my confusion, embarrassment, and fear of my mother. Surreptitiously, I insinuate myself into Andrea's dignified mourning. Like a new branch in the family tree, I gaze at the old undertaker. Leaning over the graveyard's high fence, he appears to be listening to imaginary music filled with death.

At midnight, I climb back up to my grandmother's bedroom still feeling the magic touch that penetrated my heart. My grandmother is blind but her deep insight into my soul unveils my mythical journey. Despite the sharp scent of her own disappointment that involuntarily fills her nose, she can still smell something new and suspicious coming out of me as I lay fully dressed next to her. She must have guessed that Andrea was my Prince Charming because of the French perfume that he liberally poured on me. Several toasts were made in honor of the departed family head, whose presence was still felt as if bestowing her love and blessings on everyone as they crowded the few rooms and the big reception hall in the apartment. Their loud Greek shouts and nervous conversation pointed to the necessity of returning to Greece before things became even more difficult for them as a minority. They were no longer viewed as part of a society that was now taking reactionary measures under a government that did not hesitate to slaughter all kinds of leftists.

"Did you hear what happened to Ijith and his father?"

"Of course; he converted to Islam."

"He had to change his religion to make a living. They used to stand in front of his shop and bully potential customers."

"If they went in to buy something, they would be beaten."

"They persecuted him until his hair turned gray in the prime of his youth."

I kept my head down feeling sorry for Ijith. I found out from Asaad that he and his family left Egypt for good and that he told Asaad the following: "The war with the Zionists is over and now our turn has come. I'm going to catch up with Reena in America. We'll get married. How I respect this girl, a descendant of Gandhi's, who has to keep running from one country to another. She asked me to leave her alone because she could put me and our children, if we ever have any, in danger. She wanted me to forget about her before she left Suez and revealed to me the secret of her lineage, which constantly puts her under the threat of assassination. I may give up my religion but I will never give up on her.

I love her and I have tied my fate to hers. I wish you could see her when she knelt down to touch my father's feet, then stood up to kiss his fingers, like a queen patiently bearing the weight of her crown bejeweled with great dignity and history. Then she would come down to earth to feed poor children rice and lentils out of her own dark, sensitive hands. . . . I'm deeply in love with her, Reena Kabul, this Hindu peacemaker."

Surprise grew inside me like branches blossoming into happiness as I danced with Andrea in the balcony that overlooked the police station with its wooden scaffolds. I was in the arms of a Greek god melting with the clouds over the legendary heights of Olympus. I had two glasses of Andrea's strong red wine, and it made me feel as light as dust softly falling over a war scene where fear is conquered with imaginary guns firing without causing conflict or discord.

Can this world put up with me, with my legacy of my mother's insanity, my grandmother's blindness, my father's alcoholism, and my brother's nihilism? Andrea takes me out to the ivy-framed balcony awash in bright moonlight. The same moon that used to seem so agonized now turns my being into pools of warm luminescence and shade that extend over the wooden balcony floor. He pours love pleas into my ears, the deep line between my shoulders, and my neck; his breath burns with a mythical glow through my senses. Mine is a small world shielded from the big world for one night in which I'm a princess and he is my master and slave, the composer of my favorite songs, the dawn's muezzin and the player of church bells. His broken Arabic contains the secret of the universe. He is the bright star in my night, shining over palm trees blooming and casting their shadows in seasons of drought; he is a smiling hermit in my shrine. He was my hero, the center of our hopes and travels and parties, including our visits to the movie theater where we would circle around him after Ijith was gone and we began to miss his dark skin and the layers of his soft black hair.

"India. We want a trip to India, Andrea."

"We want India . . . India."

"No problem. Let's go to India then. We should start saving by cutting back on movies, beer, and fishing trips to Ain Sukhna."

On our last trip to Ain Sukhna, Andrea was still sad over his grandmother's death. Filmmakers no longer went there. Our trips used to coincide with their filming schedule, allowing us to lovingly follow the acting while Andrea played small roles in single shots where only his back was shown as he walked along the shore like a vanquished leader.

When he rejoined us, he smiled at his inability to accomplish his dream of being a big director. He liked to walk back and forth between the director and the photographer, advising the actors to relax their muscles even during painful scenes. Instead of thanking him, they would politely ask him to leave the area where the work took place, work he loved perhaps even more than me. He used to tell me, "After India, we'll immediately go to Greece, then Hollywood; a brave new world with no fake gods made in trashy movies. No, over there success is granted those who deserve it; only the kind of success that allows one to stay on top. You'll see me making the greatest movies."

That was a short break filled with abundant and rich tastes to savor. Meanwhile, the voices of others were as magnified as headlines for Suzy. But she was trying to learn, from studying grammar, the connection between the meaning and the structure of a sentence. This was harshly noted by her retired Arabic teacher, Mr. Naguib. Her mother could not trust a young male teacher or stand a gullible female teacher. So she hired a retired senior teacher whose worn-out jackets and usually loose tie drooped over his large belly. His ideas were strict and unwavering. When he heard her opinion that grammar depended on consistency whereas language use was situational, he decided that she was an idiot: "This is nonsense! There are no 'situations' and no rules on demand. Everything is already in order. You cannot change anything because this is the language of the Quran; any modification is heresy. You do pray five times a day, don't you?"

Only a few weeks earlier no one was asking this question and certainly not in such an accusatory tone, but I often encountered it afterward from different people and always with the same tone.

Andrea's world was the only one that remained unvanquished. He opened the doors of imagination wide and seated me on its highest throne. A generous kiss from his lips on the back of my hand would make us both feel the same agony and longing. Then he would whisper into my ear, "You are the greatest reason why I love Egypt. You are the most beautiful person here. You are my life's camellia, blossoming with kindness, intelligence, and power. This is you, love. This is you."

The prince had a smile that filled me with all his magnificent beauty. I was entering adulthood in those days and trying to use the fleeting moments I shared with Andrea to resist the madness that incessantly enveloped our house. At the same time, I wished I could stop because my love for him was accompanied by feelings of guilt toward my family, who stood stubbornly on the desert side and would never forgive me if I really ran away with him. Our plan was to try to convince them by any means whatsoever that my trip to India was not going to harm me in any way and that I was going to come back exactly as I was when I left, especially since Asaad, whom my father trusted, was going to be with us. But this was not the case. Asaad's sympathy and support forced him to lie for our sakes.

He told Andrea, "Congratulations. You deserve Suzy. Take good care of her. I will visit you at your new home when things settle down. Don't forget to send me the new address, Suzy. Keep me posted and don't worry; your secret is safe with me. Don't forget about me."

All the time I felt that I was a thief about to be caught red-handed. I would stare into the faces around me trying to see if they suspected anything about my plans. I was also hoping to save those faces in my memory. But even then I realized that I was not going to miss them because they had become so horribly tiresome: my mother and my father, my grandmother and my brother, and the old Arabic teacher whose lessons replaced Madame Pauline's piano lessons.

As usual in Arabic movies adapted from foreign ones, this one took a tragic turn: a gloomy outcome for the beautiful dream that was supposed to begin with our going to India. But Andrea could not take anyone anywhere because he was savagely attacked and beaten up. His bones were broken and he lost a lot of blood before we had enough money for the trip. I used to save money in my cloth bag. It was the color of molasses mixed with tahini, my father's favorite dish. I now carried my wounded heart in this same bag that was once filled with bullet cases. In the end, Andrea's blood was shed behind the Franciscan School on his way back from the Gharib district. But he kept crawling, dragging a bright, winding trail of blood all the way to the wooden gate of his house. He left bloody fingerprints on the bronze knob that dangled from the mouth of the stone falcon attached to the wall.

A similar party took place with the same list of guests but to observe different rituals. This time anger was directed at the regime that did not offer its citizens protection and did not respect civil rights. Their eyes kept accusing me until they glared with hatred. In the meantime, I was wondering, what about me? At whom should I be angry? At myself, or at my own horror for being part of this? I saw reproach and disgust in those strangers' eyes as if they were holding crosses to burn me with the fire in Andrea's mother, Aunt Viola's words, "This is all because of you. . . . All because of you."

I was waiting for Andrea to wake up so that I could confide my weakness and helplessness in him but he was lying unconscious in the narrow tunnel between life and death. I still envisioned him gathering the dark night off my soul and weaving poems of solace with his fingers. His departure left my spirit in perpetual winter. Rain fell on my conscience like a whip lashing out at me for no reason other than that I was different. I shared, thus, the fate of many other outcasts whose difference brought about the early demise of their existence.

So time passed as I struggled to finish my senior year of high school with the added pain of missing Andrea. Something inside me was heading toward a permanent disconnect from my soul, a soul that quivered like a glass pane, a soul that could already feel the cancerous spread of old age and neglect. The question came up again: where would I be next winter?

Act 2

Marxism:
At First Sight

I did not expect that my life would be so empty and that I would be referring to Andrea as the one who 'used to' do such and such. . . . A memory smeared with his own blood, blood spilled over bright yellow sand as long as his last journey. I lost trace of him after I saw the last drop of blood fade in the light coming out of his window until it evaporated and disappeared in the darkness.

The same darkness enveloped me and my mother when Andrea's door was gently closed in our faces. That hurt her so much that something akin to insanity began welling up in her face, a look glowing with anger and hatred. Her feelings must have been intense because she mumbled through clenched teeth that I must be the cause of all her sorrow— that because she gave birth to me, she was stuck with my father, no longer the same large-framed, dark-skinned boy with whom she platonically fell in love. He used to walk by her house, beaming in his military uniform, hiding his anguish in a soft song he whistled wistfully. Her cheeks would burn and she would feel like opening the gate and running after him before he completely disappeared. Instead, she would simply wait for him at the same time on the following day and so on and so forth until it was all over so fast. He became someone she wanted to get rid of just as fast, but I tricked her and insinuated myself into her womb so that she did not know I was there until after two months when I began to stretch the skin around her belly and make her faint several times a day. She was a very lonely woman. While her mother suffered the pain of abandonment and need that her husband had left her with, her younger brother dreamt of becoming a police officer. As for the rest of the family, they were hopeless.

I still believe that in many ways love is similar to hatred. Both hurt and fluctuate and do not mean what they say. In my case they join forces to create a third type of being, one that grows over my own features. I can hardly recognize myself, and when I hide my face in my knees and squeeze my hands between my legs, I look like a human pile of fear and anxiety or a dark bird burying its head in its wings in the sand. I try to hide my claws so as to maintain some of my humanity, but I could care less about determining my gender. My mother does not teach me how to act male and my father does not care whether I become one of his honorable women. As a result, I am what I am now: a fluid, frantic soul under a scaly carapace sometimes scraped by an old love song, music from a small radio carried by an old man, a man who is roaming the city that looks, behind him; like a black monster vomiting yellow flames. Deprived of mercy, the old man sits on the rocks facing a bay at sunset when the low tide reveals the red color at the slimy bottom covered with dark green sticky moss.

Oh, love
Love is my survival
Oh, love
Love is my death

The sudden spring breezes carry me home to my mother's mirror which everyone invades as they walk back and forth through my life. I always have to defend myself. Andrea's smiling face appears in my fitful dreams as I move into my twenties trying to be pure by lighting a candle to set my soul free from the heathen manacles that devour my weak wrists. Self-disgust forces me to take a hot bath and to stand bare-footed, my hair dripping with pure water as I try to dry my fears.

60

At any rate, I find solace in the miserable state that never leaves me. Even when I laugh, heavy teardrops fall from my eyes. I end up dividing the future into distant stations so that I can keep traveling from one to the next.

My fate is now tied to my uncle's because I have to move in with him. He is finally transferred to the same town where we had to live a few years ago. My mother's family owned a house there. Besides, he is a successful intelligence officer at the university that was my first and only choice on the application forms filled and submitted with his help. He becomes the donkey and I become the cart that carries all sorts of alienation and accusation, but with the expected graciousness of a new student at college. This gracious attitude stems from my belief in freedom of expression and in human nature that gives every person two sides—good and evil, black and white, and so on—therefore, I forgive all insults without expecting an apology or even a concession that I'm wronged.

That was exactly what my father did after years of uselessly trying to drag his one leg along and after the epiphanies he had when he had too much to drink. In the end, the war was fought for a privileged few who received all the recognition. What he and others did, whether they were dead or living, was a patriotic sacrifice incommensurable even in terms of the price of the imported prosthetic leg that replaced the old wooden crutch that made him look like a scary figure in a children's book.

I see myself holding my books and notebooks wandering through the university campus. Its lecture halls and corners fill me with awe and a vague longing. I oscillate between despising kindness and viewing it as goodness that may prevail and become the main moral value for everyone.

Even Asaad started to give me hateful looks that he quickly toned down when I confronted him. Why not? Hamida told me that he thought I was the reason for what happened to Andrea. "Had I not loved her," Andrea told him, "none of this would have happened."

Nothing but evil thoughts and hard feelings. That's what I find when I write the biography of the female I once was. My face turns a different page in the mirror; it reflects so many memories and faces smiling wickedly to hurt me, reminding me of my failure to mourn even losing my mother forever, reminding me that I did not have a chance to help her make up for a miserable life that vanished like a drop of water in the sand of which nothing is left. Nothing is left of her except the mirror and the few pieces of clothing that had been wrapped carefully around mothballs and black pepper kernels for years until my first day at college when I put on one of her dresses. They were made by my father a few days before their wedding; he had toiled day and night to finish the task of making her twelve different dresses, which he piled at her feet before he collapsed from exhaustion.

My mother discovered that I had no suitable clothes for a college student so she gave me those dresses, except for five revealing ones that she said were inappropriate. But now I was trying them on and learning to walk like a lady in the way she had always hoped to see me. That made me rebel more and insist on wearing walking shoes. I fought hard to appear like the rest of my classmates for the simple reason that I was one of them. At least I was for Siham, who was the first to befriend me.

"Is it true that your uncle is Colonel Atef?"

"Yes, but I have nothing to do with . . ."

"Could you please ask him to marry me?"

I have to hurry up and leave before the sun becomes burning hot, as my mother is telling me. I try to take my suitcase from my brother, who is trying to ride it like a horse across the window. He is yelling at it to dash through the window through which a humid day is beginning to appear. I carry out my father's last instructions in a hurry. I kiss my grandmother's hand and she graciously smiles at me when I tell her, "Goodbye, my lady; I look forward to seeing your sweet face again." She shoves some money in my hand in addition to my allowance, which is mostly spent on sneaking in alcohol for my father as if my mother does not know. But her silence is becoming increasingly hostile. I finally make it to the main entrance, dimly lit and awfully humid, where Asaad stands fanning the air with a book as he waits to take my suitcase to the train. He makes sure that it stands like a wall between me and the intrusions of my travel companions so that I don't have to chitchat about my trip just as I'm doing now, telling him how I hugged my brother Selim so tightly that he wanted to run as far as my mother's control allows him. She won't let him play with the other kids in the alley, claiming that "things are no longer the same. Strangers are filing into the city and I don't want him to learn their filthy language."

"Go do your homework!" she yells at him, ignoring my impending departure. I hurriedly say goodbye to my father after I pour the beer my mother is hiding from him into the big soup bowl set aside only for his use because he prefers eating by himself. I give my grandmother a quick kiss.

"I'm sorry to keep you waiting in this oppressive heat."

Asaad responds with mocking enthusiasm, "How can I get tired when I'm waiting for you?"

Despite all the books he has read, his language still resorts to the classic idioms that he means literally.

I regret complimenting him by saying, "If you go on like this, I may fall in love with you."

"I sure hope so!"

He stops pacing and faces me. Then he lifts me up and firmly seats me on the low wall, which is engraved with beautiful fish. It separates the city from trucks with giant tanks that leak big, dark streaks of oil. Neither one of us knows where these trucks are going but they seem to give the locals an ultimatum: either be crushed under their wheels or fill their bags with the gold that drips from the oil fields along the borders.

"Asaad, I already love you."

"Suzy, I can't keep up with you."

"No, I'm the one who can't keep up with you. You are my friend and my brother and sometimes my teacher."

"Me? Your teacher? I learn from you and sometimes I even envy you. You are stronger than most people I know. Don't you know yourself? Your unique genius comes up with the most brilliant propositions. You are impossible to attain. You make me feel ashamed of myself. You may not believe what I've done out of love. You are the miracle that happens only once in a lifetime. I only ask that you remember me."

Of course I remember when I'm tossed from one bottomless abyss to another and when I can no longer distinguish voices: wailing from prayer and heartbeats from love pangs. Everything is mixed up. Truths melt in the glow of fantasies. I no longer know how to avoid the deceit that cuts like a knife through my duty toward myself when I feel the same affection for Asaad even after what his sister Hamida told me.

Hamida's husband was marrying his sister off to a government employee. "My husband and the groom do business together," Hamida told me while we were dancing at the wedding. "He would have loved for her to marry Asaad, but Asaad loves you. He turns down the city's most beautiful girls for your sake. It was Asaad who talked the religious fanatics into beating Andrea up so that you wouldn't go away with him. He was afraid that Andrea was going to break your heart and leave you all by yourself away from home. He didn't mean to hurt him. But the bullies did what they did and almost killed him. It was terrible."

Drums were beating inside my heart and my veins were trembling as I watched Hamida's frozen dance. I wanted to dance to the rhythms of the universe and its fateful coincidences. But my brain was numb, unable to send any message to my body. I was furious with Asaad, who tried to protect me by thrusting a poisoned arrow at my heart. My feet were glued to the floor feeling the echo of the drum. I was both the sticks and the dry, stretched skin. I had feelings of guilt toward everyone except myself. I could hear the melancholy in the sounds of the flute while other girls were taking turns on the dance floor. Unable to watch, I disappeared into the darkness behind the strings of lights that surrounded the bride's chair and the circle of her female guests as well as the opposite circle of the groom and his male guests. But I was terrified by my loneliness, so I rushed back. Wedding songs were playing loudly, touching the chords of girls' hearts, making them dream of the wedding and the white dress as a promise of happiness. I believed all love songs.

Asaad used to sing Halim's song, *"My dreams are big but I'm helpless, princess."* Andrea used to sing Neil Diamond's song:

Red, red wine
Go to my head
Make me forget.
Red, red wine
Stay close to me
Don't leave me

Maybe Asaad and I deserved to be punished. Justice falls on even the toughest—at least poetic justice does. When my ability to defend myself is so weak that I forget who I am and on what ground I stand, terrible shocks can have the power of turning me against myself.

At twenty years old, I had to sort through the chaos. This should have meant simply putting everything in place and rearranging every sentence that consisted of a subject, a verb, and usually a helpless object. This went on all the time in my mind, operating under the assumption that language controlled the entire world with its rules and its idiosyncrasies and even its far-fetched meanings.

It was Asaad who hired the young men to beat Andrea up.

It was Asaad who had Andrea beaten up by the young men.

The young men were hired by Asaad.

This went on forever, and in all cases I remained the object and the subject and the verb.

This type of wordplay made me fall in love with language and try to carefully study it. I wanted to emulate the Nasserist professors who were not considered for promotions whether as directors of cultural relations in Egyptian embassies abroad or as heads of councils at home. Of course they were not considered for positions in state departments either. As a result, they preached despair inside the dim lecture halls of the new college. They tested the power of the language to give commands, to impose prohibitions, and to express desire. Their words would echo in my ears like musical instruments.

"Don't compromise even if they give you a crown."

"Where is the city of Atka. . . ?"

"You can either learn and suffer or enjoy the bliss that comes with ignorance. These are your options. Exceptions are for the lucky few, so do not expect any."

This was the wisdom that made me rely on myself, but it was molded by Asaad's opinions and hidden vices, which still festered even under bandages. My obsession with revenge raged in the depths of my aching soul and unconsciously hurled me through imaginary miles across vast spaces of black pain. Anger forced the words to fly hysterically and uncontrollably out of my mouth at the sight of his face, words like wounded victims who always turned out to be me. "Asaad, my dear, what Andrea has given me is very different from what you can give me and much more than your words. Therefore, I cannot replace him with you."

I take the train across the desert along with weary soldiers. Some of them are running away from the military police with the red stripes on their strong arms. These arms snapped them out of their sleep and deprived them even of their dreams.

I pass the time while waiting to change trains by walking around Ramses's statue. In the middle of the square he sheepishly stares at the crowds through beams wrapped with coarse ropes. The square is about to lose the significance of its name as Ramses Square. Present mixes with past. Nothing lasts and nothing remains the same in this world of stifled metaphors. Everything floats on the river that runs by the side of the cars racing against the Upper Egypt train which carries Suzy Muhammad Galal, a sophomore at the College of Humanities, on board. The only choice she has to finish her degree is to be under the care of her uncle, who works in the college security forces.

Isn't it normal to lose some of my memories for a while and forget the shocking knowledge I was forced to find out? I harshly drown these memories in the small stream that runs along the railway. I try to lose my ability to predict the future, which I acquired through years of nihilism and hell, years that flew by from one moment to another revealing a world of eternal chaos and despair. I fall asleep while reading Simone de Beauvoir's letters to Sartre.

In a nightmare, I see my father on the train taking off his prosthetic leg and throwing it out of the window, "Don't worry, a small price to pay. I will sew it back on."

Amm Abdel Mungi floats outside the window with holes in his body, "You should have run faster and left before your father lost his leg. Your laziness caused this."

I wake up to find Andrea's ghost next to me, wiping away my guilt and encouraging me: "You did the right thing, so don't be sad and don't let them go after you. They won't be able to control you forever."

Then he leaves.

My footsteps glide in the soft sand and my body fails and wobbles. Everything stands still under the scorching sun. I hear my name being called but I don't make the slightest movement. I'm practically gone. I hear myself panting while my name rolls down my shoulder with a sharp tapping between my shoulder blades and my neck, reminding me of the edge of an old knife dripping with sweat.

"Suzy! Suzy!"

"Yeah? Oh, hello. Sorry, Uncle, I wasn't paying attention. Have you been standing here for a while?"

"What's wrong with you? Why are you so confused? Are you sick?"

"No. I'm fine."

"Get in the car, I'm taking you home."

"I have an important lecture. I have to go to the . . ."

"There is no school today. There may be a march organized by the students. They can all go to hell, useless sons of bitches, no more than herds of sheep."

I stand in front of the security vehicle, which has an open compartment attached to it with two long tables. Two soldiers sit at the tables, resting their chins on their automatic rifles. They look like the statues of the two lions on Qasr al-Nil Bridge, surrounded by neon lights and soft breezes from the river. I deeply miss Andrea and look for him in the corners of my fantasy.

In actuality, my life with my uncle is void of nuances. I cannot question any of his instructions and orders or even attempt to do so. The best thing I can do is to master lying all the time about everything I do, including the most innocuous activities such as eating, sleeping, putting on clothes, walking, and so on. Even talking about these things almost definitely leads to me being brutally beaten due to the implied perversion of every-thing I say. Of course, there is no sense of humor in this unobstructed flow of earnestness.

"What Students' Union, child? What posters, young lady? What political organization, bitch? What am I, your cover? Well then, you're not taking your finals. I will break your bones with my own hands so that you will have an excuse to give your 'comrades.'"

Consequently, I went to my finals in the sophomore year leaning over a crutch and hiding under a heavy black burqa that covered every part of my body. Siham borrowed the burqa from Khaled's sister. Khaled was now an active member in one of the religious student organizations. One morning he showed up with a long beard and declared his resignation from the communist party with a dramatic gesture. It took us all by sur-prise as we gathered around our posters with their bright headlines and photos sent by Essam from the party's newsletters. My disguise enabled me to watch my uncle without fearing that he would crucify me at the main gate to let everyone know that I belonged to him and that he would bring nothing but harm to anyone who tried to approach me.

Essam joins the ranks of Asaad and Andrea with a systematic regularity. At first, my mind registers his presence in a vocabulary that indicates nothing alarming or unusual. He sends me short signals that linger in my thoughts and my feelings, but always in a sharp tone that makes even Siham ask me, "Why does he pick on you? He always seems to be watching you."

He seemed to always have me under a microscope, this skinny fighter whose long hair was divided into carefully groomed strands. In the meeting room he showed his emotions in the way he smoked, spreading his cigarettes over the table next to his right hand. He would fumble with them until he decided upon one, then he would pick it up, smell it, and quickly light up. Sucking constantly, the cigarette would glow like a coal between his lips. He was an ideal communist in his poverty, which showed in his oversized shoes. He had only two pairs. He was obsessively paranoid with me perhaps due to my supposed connection to the intelligence forces through my uncle, who symbolized, in a way, Essam's other face. I had the feeling that my fate was irrationally tied to his as if he were an important figure in the process of making history. No better option seemed open to me.

I read Trotsky to learn the concepts that were preventing me from following the conversation about things like the commune, the capitalist world, the Red Army, how massacres were committed in the name of revolutionary ideals, how to export ideas across borders. I almost lost hope when I learned that Stalinists killed Leon Trotsky in Mexico. Since I was one of the virtuous, pious, penitent women, as mentioned in the Quran, I was given a small role in presenting some of the theoretical underpinnings of revolutionary work. But during my presentation I was thinking about Oscar Wilde's opinion that struggle was the virtue of the evil-minded. I was in two minds: believing in the gravity of the current situation for one minute and regarding it as inconsequential in the next.

I hated my comrades when they made fun of me and regarded my theories as a mental break from their 'serious' work, which I viewed as unwise. I was like Don Quixote in my debates with them, arguing that individual revolutions are bound to fail and harm the innocent, and that now was not the right time for secrecy. If in the end we could win parliamentary seats, why not take advantage of this opportunity to unite all factions of society? I was thinking about a statement I read in a novel, "When there are no banners in the horizon, where do the horses go?" I pondered with a great deal of emotion whether the fighter should first search for banners or keep moving forward, regardless of his personal crisis. Why couldn't people see me for who I was instead of who they thought I was? For Essam, I was a token of the old bourgeoisie, an honor that could not be defended or protected, a dead fish sliced open with rusted fishing rods. For Andrea, I was a kiss buried under soft sands.

I judged the comrades according to what they professed and never looked beyond those performances of theirs, theatrically delivered with perfect pauses and breaks. As a good-hearted woman above progressive ideas, I was responsible for making coffee for the leaders of the round Formica table in Amin Hamid's house where his mother treated us like immature losers. Essam took three sugars in his Nescafé. Throughout an entire meeting around the table stacked with textbooks, Amin's mother would sit on the large sofa, which had no cushions, right next to the door to Amin's room; his room had a small window and wallpaper with the picture of an artificial field over his bed. I would be in there with them, the door to the room behind us unlocked, but hard to push open, making a long squeaking noise when the winter dampness swelled its wood. My seat allowed me to easily see the window and the cigarette smoke flying through its shutters. On the other side, I used to stare at an old painting with faded red and green colors under a pure blue summer sky.

Occasionally, I had to leave the room to make Nescafé and tea and a special cup of coffee for Amin, whose task was to provide safe places for our meetings. Those meetings often turned into dinners of soup, rice, vegetables, and whatever food was left over from the family's meal. But I always left the party even before the ceremonial 'in the name of God' delivered at the beginning of each meal because my uncle was sure to yell at me for being late. On my way out, I would overhear laughter coming through the window, the same window that allowed Essam and another friend to see Siham and Amin making love on a small iron bed. How could language change so radically just because someone left the room? Overhearing parts of my male comrades' conversation made me ponder this because they sounded like older men disrespecting females.

Every lover has a sin that destroys love; I was Andrea's sin. He used to tell me with his eyes fixed on the waves of the bay, "You don't wade in the river twice, therefore, our feet have to be grounded in the struggle until justice prevails."

Would Essam turn into another one of my victims? This heart-wrenching thought was the result of a conversation I had with my uncle on the front porch of the house after he had smoked at least two joints. The house could not be sold because of family feuds. The rest of the family wanted to sell it as well as the adjacent plot of land to help them financially. Only Mother stubbornly stuck to her opinion that a heritage should stay in the family. My uncle was the only one who benefitted from the house where he kept me like an amusing prisoner because his wife, General Said Ghunim's daughter, could not stand living there. Her father bought her a luxury condominium on Faisal Street. But my uncle still had to use the revenue from the land to make the last few payments on the condominium. His own salary could hardly pay for his cigarettes and his weekly trips every Wednesday and Thursday nights to be back on Friday. He would drop me off and pick me up at the Suez train station like a piece of luggage.

"You know, Suzy," my uncle said, "I'm really terrified by the look my father and my mother give me in their photo. They always seem to reproach me. Why is that? Tell me is there something wrong with me?"

This outburst of emotion would usually initiate a long night of listening to his long, sorry tales. That meant I could not finish the small-sized book about constant revolution that we were going to discuss at a meeting whose time and place were still a mystery to me. While I was trying to come up with an excuse to leave, my uncle continued with an affection so ephemeral and yet so deep that it should have earned him an award. However, once pot could no longer hide his resentment toward me, he was sure to resume imposing his emergency laws on my life.

"You don't have to fight for anything even if I don't already have it. I have complete control over people's lives. Unless they have my permission, I can kill even their joy in their hearts. I can drag them out naked in the cold winter and deprive them of everything so that they become powerless soldiers in a lost battle. I hate it when I withdraw before I finish testing the torture methods I have invented to continue the battle that asserts my power over them."

70

"By the same token, there would be no function for someone like you in a just world where socialist ideals prevail." Of course, I say these words only to myself. To have my uncle overhear these thoughts would be like asking for a beating. Even if he did not fully understand me, words like "just," "socialist," and "function" were a recipe for disaster. I was no longer willing to argue, which brought me nothing but hard blows and kicks, because I was already a junior in college. I was also beginning to recognize traces of Andrea and Asaad in Essam despite the way he sharply differed from them. At the same time, my uncle was holding me accountable, using his unasked-for protection as an excuse.

"Does Essam still bother you?"

I was shocked and said nothing.

"I know everything that takes place on your campus and I know the real motives of everyone waxing patriotic over there. A little bit of cross-examination yields remarkable results, especially when there are witnesses and evidence. Am I right, my dear heroic niece?"

"But Essam hasn't done anything. He is no more than a classmate."

"My sources do not miss a heartbeat and they tell me everything he says about you, that is, everything he says about me, since we are one family. Have you heard the latest joke about me? Did you laugh along when you heard them saying that I was an officer back in the days of al-Hajjaj ibn Yusif and that I tortured their great-grandparents while the Suez Canal was being dug? Of course, you did not think it was funny and you may not even have heard it. They can't use you against me, do you understand, bitch?"

Thank God and praise to genetic engineers for not having yet provided codes for mind-reading. My uncle would have used them to exterminate the entire class of the junior and senior years and maybe even the first and the second at the schools of liberal arts, law, and library science which were under his charge. His spite would sweep over the fence and around the verandah, where darkness would have drawn a skull and crossbones and an invisible sign that read, "Beware of the filth in this house!"

A conspiracy was being drawn against me now. I was the princess who had stones thrown at her so that flies would not bother her. . . .

"I'm your last chance. You are only safe on this old estate where no one can harm you. Go out if you wish, knock on doors, but none will open for you. You will keep on ringing doorbells until someone answers non-chalantly. You would be given wrong directions until you get completely lost in the crowds. My poor niece, you pursue your illusions with great determination like your hero of a father who has lost everything. But don't you agree with me that the world is in chaos and that God is showing us his wrath? Only violence stops violence and death stops pain. At any rate, go to sleep now and I will take care of that kid. His file is already full with countless offenses, secret meetings, girls walking in and walking out. These are his only claims to leadership."

All morning I had a sense of lurking danger. My uncle had stopped me at the door to object to my outfit although he had checked it several times before and approved of it. He was making up excuses to impose a curfew: because I was a slut wearing revealing clothes or because my eyes had a defiant look, when they were only begging him to let me go to school to attend Dr. Nasr's very important lecture that day. How could I break the curfew when constantly subjected to emergency laws as the only way my uncle knew how to live? The whole day passed with me sitting around fully clothed, clutching my bag, waiting to be released. I was not let go until the following morning. I first ran into Mahasin at the gate. She told me that the police busted the group's meeting the day before and arrested Amin, Essam, and Siham. After that, she took a few steps back to let the rest of the group ruthlessly lash out at me although I had no idea about what had happened. But how could I explain my disappearance the day before without getting my uncle involved? How could I justify always missing the turning points?

"Of course you couldn't be there when you were the one who turned them in."

"A traitor! A spy!"

"Where did you take them?"

"Who is next on the list?"

"You're attacking her because you can't confront the real enemy! What has she done? This has to happen and will happen again regardless of whether Suzy is with us or not," Mahasin yells at them, shaking her head and standing between me and the fingers that were jabbing at my shoulders. She takes me aside and asks me accusingly, "Did you really not know?"

"Even you, Mahasin?"

"I know, my dear, and you don't have to say anything, but . . ."

Naturally, she believed me because she was the only one who knew about the simple and innocent scene Essam and I played like many other lovers using the same lines from an old movie script: the spacious Nile, the moonlight, the endless stories evoking what people called 'a budding love,' Fairuz's voice moving our hearts, Essam's eyes opening wide to take in my world as he shares my admiration for Andrea and expresses understanding and support. When I was alone at home, I conjured up visions and dreams about Essam to ward off my loneliness. I talked to him all the time, my voice echoing in the hallways that I had immaculately polished so as to reflect the light in my eyes. I tried to sit as he sat and wrote his name over and over until I almost forgot how to write 'Andrea,' from whose memory I had somewhat intentionally turned away.

Mahasin was the page upon which I tried to inscribe my strange feelings toward Essam—even when he teased me at the meetings, as if he were not the same person fondling my fingers just a few minutes earlier under the plastic tablecloth with its cracked flowers. We seemed to have made a tacit agreement to meet a few moments before everyone arrived for the meeting. During that time, Amin would be talking to his mother, trying to impress upon her the importance of our work and to convince her that it did not distract him from his studies or from her dreams for him. Essam's fingers would run through mine as I heard Amin's voice, muffled as if sinking deep into a well.

"You wanted me to be a doctor and I'm going to be a doctor, but at the university, not an opportunist who chases after money everywhere and ends up sitting on his fat butt in some private clinic."

"But I can't stand that girl, Siham."

"Siham is one of the best young women I have met in my life."

"But she keeps you away from your studies by talking on the phone all day."

"Mama, you know that I always manage to catch up right before finals."

"Waiting until the last month is what deeply worries me. You should plan on giving yourself more time in case something bad happens."

"Nothing will happen. Bye now. I have to talk to my guests."

"Your who?"

The last question was directed at me. I knew she regarded me with suspicion and distrust because every time she saw me, a fake smile appeared on her face. In vain I would wait a few moments for her to shake my hand. I became obsessed with her little white hand, which seemed so soft when I watched her gently caress Essam's forehead and pray, "May God keep you out of harm's way, my son."

Essam would beam as she and I knew that I was the only "harm" in the room. He continued to belittle me in front of everybody, perhaps to please her. "You're completely safe," he would say. "You can move freely without raising any doubts. Your innocent features would not make people suspicious. Even I don't understand why you are here."

I try to control myself in an attempt to understand the person who is attacking me. But a sudden anger seizes me and sets my face on fire. I stubbornly stare into his eyes and say, "Why do you always treat me like that?"

He was like my uncle's cat when he refused to eat—he became sullen and sluggish. He tried to soften his tone by cracking a joke, but no one was amused.

"The truth is you are hard to read. We all know you and know your father's history and sacrifice, but having your uncle in the picture throws everything off balance and raises all sorts of doubts. We are not stupid or naïve."

This lashing-out routine was useless and a waste of time. My face froze as I lost my desire to defend myself against his criticism.

"Also, what is your connection to the Brothers?"

"I don't have a connection. I only talk to Khaled, our friend. We have to stay friends. He is a good person regardless of . . ."

"Khaled has joined the Brotherhood, which means he is no longer one of us. Do you know how he sees you now? Trash."

"I'm trying to understand so that I may be able to help him."

"So you may even start wearing a hijab tomorrow."

"Appearance does not matter. What matters is what I'm doing."

"Appearance, style, and substance all have to fit. In addition, Suzy, it must be hard to have Atef Bey as your uncle while you support us and interact with Khaled and his group. How do you balance your relationships like that?"

"Don't we always say that we should be one step ahead of the masses? This means we should stay with them and should try to know them better. How else would they follow us? Especially given our distorted image? They know nothing about us except that we are a bunch of anarchists who believe in communism. We have reached a stage in our work at which we have to pause to reflect on our mistakes, weigh our options, and draw attention to our real philosophy so that we can gain new members. We have to make everyone respect us."

I see Mahasin smiling to encourage me, Baligh nodding his head with approval, and Essam lost in thought. Siham signals to Amin to end the argument, so he bangs his empty teacup with a spoon and starts singing, "*A fly is standing on a bottle. I try to shoo it away, but it tells me to mind my own business!*"

We burst out laughing and the case against me is closed for now without resolution. But Amin's mother accuses me with her eyes and engulfs me with her fears. Mahasin tells me not to misjudge Essam because this bickering means that he loves me. I feel like I'm bouncing over uneven chalk lines while my heart is like a box filled with soft sand. Essam plays his role with great conviction. He tells me all about his history and shares his dreams with me. We walk by the great river. The Nile, stretched out under the sky, is like a legend still being born. Essam fumbles about for my hand and puts my mind at ease.

"I love you, that's the problem. But you are unattainable. Your absence is abandonment: your presence brings order to the world and infuses darkness with light."

He fills me with joy, banishes my loneliness, and follows my dreams, one by one, until a chain is wound around my neck.

I walk through the gate by myself. Everyone sees my vulnerability. I walk away from the noises that pierce my skin with accusations as sharp as needles until my face loses color. I imagine Amin's mother slapping my face. There is no doubt that I was behind what happened because my uncle masterminded it. What should I do? My lucky charms do not confer any magic power. My uncle takes great pleasure in seeing me suffer. He revels in the pain caused by the chains he has bound around my wrists through decades of brutal beating. He dumps another load of refuse into the stream of my life. I try to fight back with something made of pure hatred, much stronger than love. Angry and hurt, I try to shove evil away with my fettered hands.

I pick up a pen and a sheet of paper from the floor and start drawing the dancer I used to invoke whenever I felt intolerable pain: her once-beautiful long hair is disheveled, her tight-fitting costume is loose and its colors run, her round belly wiggles like waves, gravity pulls down her thighs and dissolves her waistline. I cover her aging upper half with red and blue reptiles attacked by black monsters. Her skin is no longer soft. My dancer is quite old; her face shows nothing but pain painted over with a drunken smile. Her long career of holding on to one stage curtain after another has drawn a circle of misery around her like an invisible electric fence. Her dancing is an agitated quiver. As for a smile . . . hopeless, not even a chance. In the end, the pen circles a big zero around my pain, making my desire for revenge stronger while my uncle seems to grow larger with arrogance and triumph. With forced neutrality, I have to squeeze my anger like a rubber ball because I dread the control my uncle has over my mother for running her share of the estate. She only receives a few pounds at the end of every season after he subtracts the money he allots for my expenses.

"Your daughter eats like a cow."

Eating becomes my secret habit in my deprivation. Instead of the support I crave, my family, who superstitiously controls my fate, deals me another blow. Should I ask my uncle why? Or should I wait until the end? In my mind I confront him with terrifying words, but my mouth remains shut and my heart sealed over the rotten aristocracy of my family. When he catches me daydreaming, I jump as if stung. I quickly take my feet off the old desk, shut the windows, and look like the photos of dead people in frames marked with black ribbons. My shadow creeps around like the wrappings of a mummy unfolding with great pain. I pack my suitcase and prepare to walk out on this horror, on the emptiness of this deserted house, on my uncle's secret files. A sudden departure that breaks my uncle's siege and escapes from his dungeons where not even reptiles can crawl. I catch the last train without a definite plan. If I go to Asaad, I will receive the same pitiful yet reproachful look. When I finally rest my head on my father's shoulder, I do not see an end to my pain. I cry hard until my father's wet gallabiya sticks to his chest.

"Where is my little girl who makes me feel as boundless as the sea waves?"

I was like a seashell hiding at the bottom of the sea, its sands guilty of nothing except reflecting dark shadows. . . . This was what Suzy who was buried in deep waters saw. Everyone was running from everyone, throwing stones at each other, and gloating over each small misfortune.

Dear God, why did you make me see with such clarity only to take my sight away, leaving me with a blindness like that which afflicted my grandmother all of a sudden. She offered no resistance, knowing that all grandmothers before her had also ended up blind. "The mirror is the family's heirloom," she told me. "It is now mine but it will belong to your mother and later to you and to your daughters. Keep in mind that mirrors have to be passed down early on before they lose part of their significance."

Why then does she not give me the mirror? Does she forget? Or does she hate seeing my reflection in it so much that she completely avoids me during my visit? I feel ignored. Maybe she does that because I don't look like her. Or is she afraid of me? This must be it: of course, she is afraid of me, just like Amin's mother used to be. I'm an evil spell only detected by mothers who know beforehand that it cannot be broken and that prayers cannot change fate. They only fight the curse with silence and avoidance. How can I break this pattern? Why should others' love for me always turn into hatred? I have a "noble bearing" as Andrea used to playfully tell me, but I have to live up to it.

Selim was standing next to me, smiling feebly. I was smiling back at him and crying while I listened to my father trying to keep both his and my uncle's voices low as my uncle was delivering one of his sermons: "Your daughter does not go to school to learn, but to be loose. I don't have time for that. You should keep her with you. She doesn't need a college degree to be a housewife."

"She is already a junior. After one more year she will earn a college degree. At least her education will make her a better mother."

I was watching the same scene again with my uncle playing the same role. My father did not stand up for me. Instead, he begged for mercy. I watched quietly and smiled submissively. Had my father stood up for me the first time, this would not have happened again and I would have a different role model to follow other than my father's meekness. I strongly wished to stay in exile, but I suddenly remembered the challenge that we all agreed to undertake when Amin said, "Either we all get PhDs or commit group suicide."

"I must be a doctor of philosophy," Essam said while I remained silent. What would that accomplish? But now I was determined to be a

77

college professor. This was beyond my father's dreams and my mother's expectations. Putting up with my uncle was the price I had to pay. Therefore, I was hoping that my father's pleading would succeed and my uncle would let me go back to finish my studies despite all the hurt he was causing me.

"The kid is feeling guilty. She can't face her classmates, which means she won't be talking to anyone."

"She is a loser and she made up this crisis to skip her finals."

"Please, for my sake."

"Okay, but one more mistake and there will be no more school. I'll see to it that she never sets foot on campus again."

Essam will sure be proud of me when he finds out that we are in the same department. Together we will write dissertations different from all clichéd ideas. Whenever I imagine us debating some concept, I see him with his skinny body, his rosy skin, and his shaved head, but he is always naked in my thoughts, chained from the neck down, his ideas falling on the bare cement floor of the torture room.

I am sitting next to the torturer on the train of the dead. I rest my head on the suitcase between us, pretending to be asleep, to avoid a confrontation that might in the end cost me the chance to forge my future. I have to play by his rules all the time. I have to stop feeling guilty toward my friends who ignore me as if my uncle is a stigma. Now puffing on his joint, he begins talking about putting me under surveillance.

"If you are now feeling sorry for your friends, prepare to feel much worse in the future. We have orders to crush them. No one should have to deal with them and they make a lot of unnecessary noise. The world is changing fast and most people are living in poverty, ignorance, and deception. No one is paying attention, and even if they did, everyone is used to being let down. You must think I'm not patriotic. But I'm more patriotic than you and your nonsense. I have voluntarily given my country everything I own. I contributed to the nation-building with my father's house and my ancestors' land, which were confiscated. I'm a stone in the big wall of the nation. But I can't be powerless. I need handcuffs and retinue to be a leader. I want my people to be useless trash like your and your friends. Don't try to intimidate me by looking so dignified. The map is not a piece of paper; the map is in my head. It's been a while since anyone fooled me. Even ideals are lies: security and well-being for all equally; justice on a flawed earth. But can you make a cat and a mouse live in peace as equals? Do you still buy into that?"

"No, Uncle, I don't. I just want to finish school."

I had decided to act with some wisdom when I watched my father beseech him. I needed to make peace with my uncle, who was as cunning as a fox, until one of two things happened and until I could be completely independent. While I looked around the house, I was trying to come up with a plan. I would organize the neglected white files on his desk and maybe I would secretly read them in my spare time. I would not let myself be as frightened as the cat who was trying to be too quiet to be noticed. Some of the things I saw reminded me of horrible incidents in all their humiliating and painful detail. My eyes kept switching between my uncle and the cat as if my gaze were screaming out my failure despite my silence. Then I stared at nothing. Tears calcified in my bulging eyes until they fell like black stains, spreading out, repeatedly vanishing. My father's words rang in my ears, "I'm waiting for you to come back to this house a strong woman armed with her education and making me proud."

Now, Suzy, you live in your nightmares and wallow in misery. You try to wipe away the traces of beating and kicking from your uncle's house. Your hopes turn to ashes in the cold winter. You're helpless and unworthy; everyone walks away from you. Even Amin decided to avoid you when you visited him in his home after he was released. His mother talked to you through a door only slightly ajar. She dismissed you by saying he was not home . . . goodbye.

But, through the dark crack in the door, you could hear him singing, *"Give my greetings to the prisoners across the city; wish them good morning in your animated voice, the kind of morning that feels like a holiday."*

· For a while after, everything becomes so quiet.

I had promised my father a new manual sewing machine with my first paycheck from my teaching post at the university. This motivated me to graduate with honors. During my senior year, everything changed except Essam's absence. For some reason, my uncle was transferred to Upper Egypt, but he did not take it as a punishment. In fact, he seemed grateful because this was the least sentence received by an intelligence-gathering force that included him and his father-in-law. The resignations and transfers were carried out quickly, no questions asked—unnecessary, perhaps, at that point. On the other hand, this punishment came like a reward for my good conduct during the period of minute screening of every breath I took and every page I read. This release from my uncle's prison enabled me to take down the old dark curtains and replace them with glass panes, allowing chunks of light to fall on my gloomy spirit. I decorated the concrete walls with pictures of healthy children licking fluffy cream.

I left the house that was a prison for both of us. I closed the gate behind me and walked around the campus walls where I was no longer a student. My job appointment letter was now my passport to something grander than a student ID. In the last few months of my senior year, my mind tried to figure out the reasons behind the hatred I encountered. All my friends avoided me. I became more lonely and estranged; no one had time to listen to my reasons for keeping aloof. My father's sewing machine now seemed more real than all the secret plans of the secret party. It materially existed in Anas's shop for repairing, selling, and buying Singer machines.

I saw Hamida and her daughter off at the train. After Hamida stuffed money into my hand, the train departed, leaving me in an empty space.

"Pay them back," she said, "when you get your first paycheck."

She made me promise to visit Asaad to change his mind about marrying Rebecca.

"The age gap is not important, but she is not normal."

I thought about it on my way home. How could Asaad and Rebecca get married despite the vast distances between them? No matter how much I thought I understood others' motives, there were always things I could not comprehend.

I stopped in front of the shop window across from the train station. I stared at the sewing machine and thought of my father using it to make suit jackets and white shirts. I would have him make Essam one when he was released from prison. I softly touched the two marble columns of the hotel and felt a familiar chill; it reminded me of Andrea's touch. When I pressed my body against his, there was a flame that lit up the gloom in my soul. Rebecca often ruined the moment by abruptly coming into the room to mention something she just remembered.

Rebecca was the only one who did not leave. She alone tried to take back what was taken from her: the hotel and the money her husband, Monsieur Adel, the science teacher, swindled out of her to build a house. She converted to Islam and started wearing a hijab-like head cover, which used to slide back and reveal strands of her beautiful hair. When she was eventually able to retrieve the hotel, she started walking around its empty rooms trying to exorcise the evil spirits she believed were lurking in its corners and under the heavy rugs. She was trying to wipe away every trace the ruling party members left when they used the hotel as their headquarters.

"She is definitely crazy but you know how magnanimous Asaad is. He thinks he can help everyone and he wants to fix the universe, but he has it all wrong," Hamida was telling me as she filled me in on what I had missed. How different it all was from the prophecies I made one night while I lay down on the sofa in my parents' bedroom, eavesdropping on the complicated details of the relocation plan my father was making for me and my mother. As they exchanged advice, I thought that everything was going to be fine: I would marry Andrea, and Asaad would marry Madame Rebecca even though she was older because he was mature for his age and because he could not hide his infatuation every time he caught a whiff of her perfume. I foresaw, as I walked through the almost-deserted city with Khairiya, that my mother was going to die while giving birth and that my father was going to be killed during the war. My father was indeed almost killed because of me. My mother squandered our money on pretending to be wealthy in the village we moved to and ran out of all her valuables by bribing nosy women. My uncle kept trying to convince her to divorce my father. She should have married someone with fortune and class because she had her own income in addition to being from the Selim family. My mother did not die, but she fell into an abyss of fears and obsessions let completely loose once my brother's umbilical cord was cut. She insisted on covering his small face with a black veil as she carried him in her arms or laid him down in her lap and had my grandmother do the same.

As for my prophecy for myself, I did fall in love with Andrea; I was "the light in his eyes," as he used to lovingly tell me. My eyes lit up with joy whenever I saw him. We enjoyed each other without doing anything that could dishonor us. Although Andrea was sure that in the end we

81

belonged to each other, he was careful that I remain a virgin. Despite his liberal and progressive ideas, he still believed in male honor and female chastity and was proud to be the first one to ever explore my femininity, which was simultaneously as deep as the ocean and as high as the mountain. In my young body, he uncovered a river of goodness that ran through my heart and filled it with a moist creaminess. He declared that he was the first to climb to the top of the mountain and to dive to the bottom of the sea and quoted the poet killed by silence—Cavafy. "There are too many poets to count. But I am a historical poet. I could never write a novel or a play, but I feel inside me a hundred and twenty-five voices telling me I could write history. But now there is no time."

"I, Andrea Georgiani, declare that regardless of the passage of time, I will never turn away from you. I will always be there when you need to talk or be in someone else's company. I will never burden you. You are the shore I land on, Suzy. Just be happy with me; I miss having someone be happy with me and I don't know why just seeing me makes others sad. Feel safe in your sleep; I will tell you stories all the time. I will keep your candle burning. You are the best companion and the most beautiful loved one. Your beauty is enhanced by your wisdom and your goodness. You're even more beautiful than my sister Rebecca who wreaks havoc every-where she goes. I will build you a sanctuary to find peace and happiness so that we can bring together our torn families under the guidance of God's words. God, where do words go when I try to describe you? You are beyond words; you must be experienced. Oh how you dominate—with the irresistible twinkle in your eyes, the roundness of your shoulders, the largeness of your bosom and its loftiness, which makes me want to touch it and stay in its embrace forever. Nothing compares to you."

The riffraff withdrew from the city and the construction resumed; everyone expected things to go back to normal. Andrea still joined Chekov, Tolstoy, and Abdel Rahman al-Sharkawi in shaping my thoughts. These thoughts did not require an open war with a bloody government because they were simple but profound enough to provide a glimpse into a just, egalitarian world. Through a small love experience, I accomplished what millions could not: being me, Suzy, the woman forever playing the leading role. Andrea used to think that second-rate actors were bound to remain second-rate actors no matter how successful they were because they would always fall back to their old habit of believing that they had an acting career. He gave me Henri Bergson's *Creative Evolution*; I read it the same night lying down next to my grandmother who could smell Andrea's scent on my breath. My breathing became regular and I fell asleep with the open book in a wistfulness that my screams and my nightmares interrupted. Small frogs are jumping out of my throat and crashing into my legs. Black snakes are crawling out of the cracks in my heels. A sudden feeling of loss wakes me up: Andrea would not be sitting there in his favorite chair in the corner, pensively smoking and asking me to keep quiet while we watch *A Tale of Two Cities* or *The Godfather* together.

His blood was shed because of me, because I'm Muslim and he is Christian, but they did not wait. He was going to convert to Islam and sign the paperwork because he believed that every religion had the same message although it was not to be realized on earth. He was going to marry me because he thought I was as pure as the Virgin. Why? I never knew and I was never able to locate the source of his faith in me.

For weeks I was bedridden trying to confess a sin I did not commit. I had no sleep or food until I gave in to devastating feelings of guilt toward everyone, even Andrea's family, who slammed the door in my face. Yet, according to my fantasies, we were still going to be married.

"Don't feel bad, Suzy. Andrea's wounds will heal before your tears dry up. I love Andrea, too, and no one can understand your sadness as much as I do," Asaad was saying as he walked next to me and my mother after we were almost kicked out of Andrea's house. I was crying hard while my mother was harshly reprimanding me. Crying, like madness, was an established ritual in my family.

I had to go back to Suez to change Asaad's fate before it was too late and my most outrageous prophecy came true. Avoidance was no longer possible, and, no matter what, I still had to confront Asaad with my knowledge that he was behind what happened to Andrea. To me, he was as merciless as the cargo train that crushed innocent victims under its wheels and mixed their fresh blood with pure oil. What gave him the right to be my guardian?

I packed my suitcases after my first year of teaching came to an end with some measure of success. Because I emulated my professors in the few lectures I gave, I had great success among the first-year students, who were more like children exploring friendship in the co-ed university system.

No one reminded me of who I was except the quiet students. To some extent, my relationship improved with some of my former colleagues. I was able to resume my friendship with Amin, Baligh, and Siham (who was not appointed for political reasons) the first time I ran into them at the faculty office. Mahasin married a relative who had a job in Canada and only spent his few vacations with her. Amin's mother adamantly opposed his marriage to Siham and asked him to move out. They stood their ground and rented a small place. Baligh was buying everyone tea on the occasion of his wife being pregnant.

"Congratulations. What will the baby's name be?"

"Shuhdi if it's a boy and Latifa if it's a girl."

"Wonderful! Give your wife my best regards. I will visit her when I come back from vacation."

Baligh still kept his head down, smiling, but quietly watching everything around him. I was leaving at noon in the high heat, the sun washing the bruises off my skin as if it were finally time to be free. I left my uncle's house, this time loving each corner and having a hard time deciding on what I needed to take with me on my vacation, which turned into a family obligation. The first summer vacation I had as a teaching assistant at the Arabic department, the School of Liberal Arts, started off with a romantic scene that I joyfully played in my head over and over, day and night.

When joy dies inside you, Suzy, you become like a rock island. Ships may try to find shelter on your shore, but you would be the first to destroy them. Why do you become so remote? I remembered the woman I used to be. For just a minute, I came closer before I moved away. You always seemed like a woman heading toward the future with as much determination as fear. I walked among the political prisoners who were taking their final exams. I glanced over the exam books spread in front of their eyes. They quickly read the questions and started writing down the answers neatly and steadily. They had temporarily survived violence and degradation. They tasted their own salt as they lay down huddled on the floor trying to protect their fragile bodies from the blows of the big sticks or the kicks of the heavy shoes. They tapped into their innermost reserves to keep the promises that deprived them of their freedom and reduced them to nothing more than typos that a little rephrasing could obliterate.

I watch Essam as he carefully writes down the answers on a page already covered with black ink, a sign of how hard he had studied for the sake of the old challenge. I whisper into his ears, "You will pass with honors."

"I know."

"Are you still in prison?"

"You know that I am. Are you supervising test-takers, Professor?"

"Is this how you reward me for waiting? Are you jealous because I'm ahead of you in making our dream come true?"

I do not apologize, but for a while my mind wanders away from the scene whose silence is only broken by the sound of pens scratching paper. I do not want to distract him, so I come back with my first offering: a strong cup of tea with three sugars mixed with the passion in my voice as I whisper an idiom in classical Arabic literary criticism into his ear. The old flame glows in his low voice as he attacks me.

"I spent two years in jail. Otherwise, I would be in your place or at least next to you."

I feel the stabbing pain of a lost love, one that has nothing to offer except an overwhelming sense of guilt.

He writes dark ink words full of longing and hurriedly, surrealistically, draws my eyes into an autumn sun. The few words our eyes exchange in blue and black streaks stir the old anguish in my heart.

"My imaginary woman, you broke my heart and left me hopelessly alone."

"I'm here now and will banish your loneliness for many years." I did not think to say 'forever.'

"I'm sorry I was unfair and misjudged you. . . . I promise you, no more pain."

"I will wait for you because I love you, comrade, without reservations."

"Lying is what we do in prison to make up for love. So discard my rage. My problem is loving you."

New tendrils of hope sprout through my entire being and blossom into great happiness as I accompany him to the prison car and promise him that everything will be all right and that I will wait for him.

Nothing remained the same in the city to make me miss it. Yet I crossed the desert eagerly looking forward to seeing my father, my mother, my brother, and my grandmother—as well as Asaad whose crime I was forced to forgive by some overwhelming power. His crime was committed in the name of love and as his sister argued, "a lover's sin was a sort of prayer."

Asaad was quite taken aback by the open-door policy and the speed with which everything was moving. Why did he seem so disheartened? Nothing could break his spirit before—not even saving his sister, half-naked, from a sure scandal. He happened to be walking by some contractor's shack when he heard his sister screaming and thought she was being raped. After punching the big, dark man several times in the face and almost burying him in the soft cement powder, he had to keep quiet because no one would have believed that he did save her. He made sure that Hamida was able to leave without being noticed, then he spent some time trying to calm down and clean up, thinking about more violence, before he finally left the shack, surrounded by sand and cement bags and moist wooden debris. When he questioned his sister, she admitted that she was in love with the out-of-town contractor and used to meet him in the shack to make plans for their marriage. Asaad was certain that her life with him was going to be nothing but constant screaming because they were completely different species and would give birth to hybrid creatures with no specific identity. Indeed, al-Husseini became a big contractor known for the screams of girls coming out of his car, usually parked on the edge of the city at night, and the screams of his employees fighting for their rights during the day. As for Hamida, who used to be full of joy and love for everyone, she only screamed at her husband for the way he ate, shoving balls of food in his mouth when he was drunk until his stomach was about to explode, as if he was eating for the first and last time in his life.

I was working on my master's thesis entitled, "The Text's Ability to Write Itself." It was a comparative study, using two famous examples from Arabic and western literatures. I was trying to argue that the literary text corresponded to the historical context. Amin found the topic obscure and advised me to take it easy and find a more traditional one free of contrived theories. But my study in sociology confirmed that the text usually became independent from the author's intentions and sided with the implied narrator who usually clamored for a more developed language, organized according to social classes stratified in fixed levels, one on top of the other.

In actuality, my motives were practically tied to my study of the people around me, starting with Asaad, Rebecca, my father, my mother, my younger brother, and ending with my uncle, who was secretly trying to get over his heroin addiction after political stagnation in the south blunted his sharp skills. Their fates were the hidden motive for my research. As for the relationship between creativity and psychosis, I did not find Freud as useful as my mother was in claiming to have witnessed extremely bizarre incidents in the neighbors' houses when she spied on them at night. For example, she was sure that our neighbor, the butcher, used to leave every day at dawn with a bag stuffed with the meat of a slaughtered child, which he sold by the kilogram.

Asaad had big eyes, red in a way that seemed to spread from the pupils like the rays of a burning sun. But this was not how they used to look before. The call for prayer was vying with the church bells. Symbols turned into conflict zones illustrated in the competing heights of the minaret and the church tower, rivaling each other as they stood side by side. Things used to be different. Even while houses were under attack, families tried to overcome their fear by making the sign of the cross or reciting Quranic verses in the same low murmurs. Asaad wanted to be buried in the darkness. He hated the reconstruction efforts because they replaced the devastation with structures of forced authority.

Umm Kulthum's Café, which turned into a shady spot for drug users, almost disappeared except for the few callers who gave Asaad their greetings as he sat by the door lost in visions and fantasies. The café remained the same as it was before the war; it was not included in the reconstruction and retained the old graffiti written in blood on its front walls making threats to the Zionists. Asaad was smoking heavily into a cloudy, narrow sky surrounded by foggy swirls, which my presence disrupted, as if I were trying to ruin his evening. He did not rise to greet me. I had to clean my ears and rub my eyes to believe that this was Asaad turning his face away from me. His eyes had lost their color. I missed his joyful spirit, which loved life and believed in humanity. Everything vanished into the hashish smoke, which dispersed when he turned his face to stare at me scornfully, "You cut your hair short, you're wearing jeans, and you look amazing. You must be living an easy life."

"Why are you trying to insult me? What's wrong?"

"A lot. Why are you here?"

"I was worried about you. What's going on with Rebecca?"

"What's wrong with Rebecca? This was what you had in mind when you were planning your humble servant's fate."

"You were never my servant. You have always been my friend. You're the one who ruined everything."

"I didn't mean to hurt him."

"I have already forgotten it."

"I haven't and it doesn't help me to know that you have. . . . You should remember everything I did for you, Professor."

As usual, I assumed a defensive stance as if some strong will were depriving me of the right to fight and causing me to lose the battle in the end. We were like two strangers exchanging meaningless words that quickly dissipated into mutual disdain and lack of understanding. I went home discouraged, feeling even more unsettled about this new mistake. Would being with Asaad change his mind? Would it be possible to win him back? Had I not gone over, things would have remained at a standstill. My visit gave voice to an unspoken hatred, which made the imaginary distance between us grow wider and wider—much like the steam rising out of the kettle where hibiscus flowers were boiling. Their scent dissolved in the humid air. The stove burner hung over a circle of fire in the shape of a pyramid with yellow edges that swayed back and forth in the air between the two opposite doors, simultaneously entering and exiting, like the Japanese proverb, "If your house has two opposite doors, you should leave it because life will exit along with misery."

What luck! I try to close one door, but instead I anxiously keep moving between them, my heart turning cold, my mind numb, and my tongue heavy. I try to fall asleep so as either to shorten my time to live or to greet a bright morning that may unexpectedly cut the chains that tie me to Asaad and Andrea, who were both foolishly absent. Asaad begrudges me my freedom and my troubled resignation back in his drug-ruled world of prepackaged ideas. I try hard to make him see that I have an inner pain that screams with anger, weakness, and insecurity. I need to aim at the ghost that keeps haunting me. Then I will go beyond Asaad's expectations, his judgment of me through my breakdowns and his view of me as a silent Mona Lisa wearing jeans, fixing her hair, and staying in shape to look better in others' eyes. What injustice! From Asaad's door to that of Andrea, who visits my dreams standing in the garden of a house in hell, watering a strange flower with flames until it is transformed, lit day and night, a post in the ground underneath it reading "My Visitor Suzy" in Andrea's horrible Arabic handwriting. No one should ever be allowed to leave behind this much mess.

The vacation months pass quickly while I switch between two lives, one stolen and the other I do not belong to. I live in a fantasy shaped by the distance between two doors. I'm confined to one place where time feels like an assassin that has lost its skills in useless, aborted stories about love wasted in brief wars and relative victories. I await a sure death on the second floor of the house of a crazy family. I wake up to autumn. I close the door that lets in cold breezes. I watch the air, heavy with the smell of burned gas and coffee rising from the south. I spread my arms to take in the air that breaks through the rough, dim buildings and crashes into my lungs. The summer recedes and the spring fabrics my father promised to sew for me in styles befitting a college professor are lying softly in the tri-angular wooden box next to the manual sewing machine. Its small flowers look scorched by the heat of a long, hot summer, blowing its last fiery breaths over the beginning of winter. My father cannot work the machine because he is accustomed to using both his feet to press on the iron pad. He cannot make the needle move fast enough by shaking his thighs over the cotton cushion that covers his seat. For the thousandth time, I realize that he has lost one leg and that the other is fragile.

The decision to hire Essam did not come as a surprise to me because I had secretly influenced my uncle, who became completely mellow after his release from Dr. Shawki Abdel Hamid's mental hospital. The doctor's relationship with the family had grown very strong and we were in the habit of referring to him regarding everything, including the low voices that ran like static electricity through our fragile heads. Each one of us had a small plastic bag for the different drugs and medications that had specific instructions for when they should be taken throughout the day.

My father's main pastime was watching sports and televised plays. To buy him a TV, my mother established a savings club, which was the only thing she allowed herself to have in common with the neighbors. They would come over to ask about their turn to receive cash, trying to stay a bit longer to talk about why they urgently needed the money. But my mother liked no one, including me and my father, so how could she tolerate strangers who disrupted our lives every month? She would cut the conversation short by rising up, opening the door, and telling the visitor, "Your turn is on such and such date; may God help you and help us." This scene happened repeatedly until the twenty cycles of the club were over. The club forced her out of her isolation for some time in order to solve the bigger problem of dealing with my father's demands that never ended, even at nighttime, and his constant talking about their love story and Laila Murad's movies, which they watched together. She idolized Laila Murad. With a lighthearted sense of triumph, he would laugh until he had tears in his eyes about the only time she approached him with desire—when he slipped opium into her tea. He was advised to do so after her shyness and aloofness forced him to give up on her. Since then, she did not trust anyone to get her a drink, even if it was a glass of water served by me.

His behavior deeply upset her, in addition to his sudden calls, which drained her mentally and caused her to drop to the floor exhausted. So she bought a TV to distract him.

For twenty-one months, the outside world invaded her privacy and contaminated the air she breathed. My father was not a great fan of any particular soccer team, so he would wake up when a goal was scored, clap his fragile hands, and shout out, "Goal!"

The final years of my twenties led to one option, which then seemed quite convenient. Paving the way for Essam was not difficult, especially because although he was at the other end of the world, he managed to work very hard as a young liberal and graduate with only a few honors less than me. He was forced to miss final exams in the junior year but he and other prisoners were permitted to take them the following year. I was, therefore, one year ahead of him in joining the faculty. Now he was my colleague and whether we had a successful or a typical romantic relationship, it did not matter. What mattered was that his most ingenious move was taking my mind away during the student riots over the killing of Suleiman Khatir to a place where I could no longer think. The rioters were becoming wild, destroying the facade of the Ministry of Interior and setting the governor's house, along with important public facilities, on fire. Once tear gas grenades were fired, Essam grabbed me by the sleeve, and in less than a minute we were at the entrance of an old building carried away by our first kiss. Only I thought I was hearing rock 'n roll music, which Essam, unlike Andrea, never liked. Instead, he used to fondly sing Sheikh Imam's songs to move my heart:

Young woman
You with the hair dark like night and the forehead white like daybreak
And eyes, like two oceans of desire
And cheeks, like honey and fire. . . .

Essam's eyes had a certain look I recognized when he was plotting against somebody, which was not all in good spirit, as he claimed. While preying on his opponent's weaknesses, he managed to appear disinterested. Sometimes I saw evil lurking in his eyes and thought twice about being with him. At other times my soul rebelled against the deception I was seeing around me. Nothing could stand between him and what he wanted, not even how adamant I was about refusing to take off the masks I wore to hide my secret mourning over the death of myself, the self I was with Andrea, someone above the rest Why? I could not remember. But I was someone else, different from the one referred to in the party documents, more decisive, more absolute, with no boundaries or home, no roots, no rigid instructions for participating in riots and escalating violence to the highest Trotskian levels, a child standing on her tiptoes to receive Essam's kisses, which spread through my body like clusters of fire, casting their light on the crises of the Third, the Fourth, and even the Tenth World and making them seem instantly resolvable.

Sometimes Essam appeared selfish, cocky, and cunning, like Asaad and like my uncle. My mind then turned to Andrea, who was not just a boy with European features and mannerisms. Despite being only partly Egyptian of Greek descent, he took part in leading a political party and organizing student marches calling for war. On the train ride to my hometown with Essam sitting next to me, I started to slowly go over Andrea's ideas, which were more moderate than they were communist. The darkness of the night enveloped the windows of the third car, open to let in the cold winter rain in 1986. The coldness of the leather seat was giving me chills and Andrea's voice was making me shudder.

"Suzy, my beloved, Cinderella needs shoes to find justice before love can bring her happiness because you can't know happiness until you give of yourself. Everyone should have the right to live regardless of their beliefs. Nothing is more important in this world than freedom, which is our inalienable right. . . . It is also our nature to suffer from and fight oppression. We are all equal despite our differences. No powerful nation should advertise freedom like a commodity, 'If you want it, come and have it here.' If we all enjoyed freedom, civilizations would not be devastated by wars and individuals would not experience the pain of trying to remember the name of someone who was killed in a bomb attack or under the weight of oppression. If something were to happen and we never reached the other side, I would tell you that I love you as I die mad at this world that forces lovers to part. I cannot live one more day without justice. Aren't we going to inherit the earth? Everything has a purpose and our souls will never vanish. There is still so much you and I don't know about each other. We are forced to secure a rich super-power and to bury our heads in the sand when its fleets proceed loaded with historical transgressions. How can we sail through these dead seas? How can we believe promises whose grand rhetoric could not beguile even children? Time is running out while the treasures of the east are lavished on foreign agencies as bribes for expensive weapons. We fire at each other instead of aiming at the throats of those with fast cultures and freshly made take-out histories. We should not let them rule us and run our affairs."

"I'm a pacifist," I responded to Andrea, "and I like living here. So why should we have to leave? It makes more sense to try to develop our country and make justice prevail everywhere. This has been my choice since I left my mother's womb. All my life I've been closely following the way its past glories are recorded in the archives of another country that toys with fate and obstructs people's destinies, a country that profits from trading weapons to paint its face and nourish its body at the expense of the downtrodden."

This was what I told Andrea when he was tormented by his wild thoughts and torn between me and his freedom. I understood his dilemma, wondering which would win and who would be hit by a bullet. Through the balcony, I saw the colors of the rainbow dispersed through rain and sunshine as he tried his best to convince me to leave with him.

"Suzy, I need you by my side to support me and not just to watch me. Our difference in opinion should not cause conflict. I have spent all my adult years searching for justice, freedom, and equality—not just for me, but for everyone and in a way that is safe and effective because life is beautiful, and you, Suzy, you are as enchanting as paradise. Being away from you is hell. I need you, beautiful. Without you, I would be lost even if I had everything else. Stay with me and I will take care of you. You are facing an easy target: aim and your dreams will come true. If you leave me, I will perish. I will never leave you behind again."

While Essam was working hard to win me over, I was trying to somehow communicate to him that my uncle was behind his university appointment rather than lawsuits and court dates. I wanted the people who accused me of putting him in prison to know that the office of campus security approved his appointment due to a vague recommendation from my uncle. Whether it was a coincidence, it still worked and his paperwork was signed. The codes were finally deciphered as we stood in front of the elegant Cairene secretary at the dean's office. Fate arranged our first encounter, which was shrouded in silence. As if having an out-of-body experience, we floated through crowded cities and vast distances until we faced each other. His smile was a love letter that had traveled so far before it finally greeted my face with its familiar glow. We sat on the nearest two chairs under Ms. Shahira's approving eyes. Essam was wearing a striped linen shirt and a matching pair of pants. He looked young and free, the way I saw him when I met him on my first day at school. I doubted that years had passed, years I spent licking stamps and placing them on white envelopes addressed to him in prison: Essam Ismail, with the words 'Political Prisoner' in parentheses.

"Have you been receiving my letters? They had answers for questions you never asked and information you never requested. No, no progress has been made. . . . The working classes have lost their power."

"You're the one who was sending the letters?"

"Naturally, I could not sign my name. . . . You know the rules."

"But your uncle is Atef Bey, no one could hurt you."

"Do you still have those letters?"

"Of course I do. They are my most treasured possessions."

"You sound like you're going to turn me in."

He smiled absent-mindedly out of the large wall-to-wall window in the dean's office. He did not try to relieve my fear over breaking one of the security measures I was taught during my training at the organizational camp regarding handwritten information as a threat to everyone. But my information had lost its importance over time, and Essam never wrote back to me although I begged him in my short letters. I was now thinking about how to get them back in order to shred them. Sometimes I knew certain things and saw through the walls.

Here was my mother's paranoia again, taking me from one obsession to another, ruthlessly haunting the secret chambers of my brain like a specter.

The stairs were narrow, their jaggedness threatening my foot. With no hesitation, I started to climb up, holding on to imaginary ropes to stop me from falling back. All the past memories quietly went through my head in complete numbness until I was caught between the memories and the door. An unspoken absence shrouded the vague details with an endless sunset.

This time was like no other time. Andrea was not here. I was not paying him or his sister a visit. I was here to see Asaad, Rebecca's husband, who was "just as crazy as she is," as Hamida told me when I asked about him.

Why did I have the feeling even before I hit thirty that I had somehow ruined my life was already ruined? Going to Andrea's house made me feel worse by reminding me of the good life I could have had with him. At least he was sure as I remembered him standing in his Santa Claus outfit decorating the Christmas tree with a white ribbon around green bells and gold stars.

"Who is it?"

Rebecca said it in the way small hotel owners used to speak in Farid al-Atrash's movies. She asked again while I wondered if my name would make her remember me without much resentment. I was the reason given by the local newspapers for what had happened to her brother. They suggested that the attack was an act of retribution for the foreign young man's multiple relationships with Muslim girls. Rebecca knew there was only one girl. How grateful she seemed when she agreed with her mother that my presence in Andrea's life turned his melancholy into the same happiness she saw on his face when he left her womb, smiling, bringing joy to her otherwise pale face after giving birth.

"Suzy . . . it's Suzy, Madame."

She pulled the door slightly open, exactly the way her mother used to when we rang the doorbell and waited with great anticipation a few minutes before our French lesson. Punctuality was one of her most important teachings outside the curriculum.

I smiled while she looked carefully at me before she parted her lips to welcome me.

"Suzy . . . yeah . . . it's you. . . . *Entrez!*"

She opens the door to a dream that takes me to Andrea's room where the only light comes from the movie screen. His head hides part of the captions so he can tell the story of the movie he has seen tens of times, "This is how movies should be made in Egypt; they should be taken more seriously. We'll make a lot of money in Hollywood. I will use this money to make more great movies about people and the nation and love. The first movie is going to be about the siege of a coastal city, mixing fact with fiction."

When I open my eyes, I'm surprised to see Rebecca still there. She was the one who regarded this country as her home. Unlike her brother, she had no illusions about a world with no borders. She seemed as elegant as always, but her clothes were slightly out of fashion, her makeup colors ones I had not seen in years. She was smoking her Boston cigarettes so furiously that the room quickly filled with smoke. It was the same way her mother smoked when she warned her against marrying Monsieur Adel because he was nothing like her father, who sailed across the world and came home to his family unchanged. Her mother did not only verbally warn her, she slapped the groom on his face when neither she nor Rebecca's grandmother could stop this unbalanced marriage. Andrea was watching passively. Perhaps he somewhat supported his sister's decision because Monsieur Adel paid him great attention and seemed to hold him in high regard. However, this incident did not change Monsieur Adel's feelings for Rebecca, as he told her on his way out, feeling his red cheek with his fingers. They were married in a small ceremony and he ended up moving in with her family. This deeply upset her grandmother, who, until she died, would make sharp comments and turn her face away from the intruder who ate with his fingers and ordered Rebecca to remove the beer from the table. Rebecca, the stylish, charming daughter of a shipmaster who deftly sailed the canal after nationalization, loved her husband so much that she only confronted him after a long period of quiet suffering and crying. She heard that he had taken a second wife and was frequently spending time with her. She still accepted his lies and apologized for her suspicions even though she knew deep down that they were well founded.

I wanted to run away at the speed of light from the memories hanging over the furniture, the photo frames, and the small antiques. Everything was so immaculately arranged according to age and degree of sadness that my body was shivering when I finally left. The slightest breeze made the blood freeze in my veins and turned my fingers blue.

I try to remember why I am here in the first place. To inform Asaad of my decision to get married or to find an excuse to change my mind? I wish I could ask Andrea for his opinion. I see his shadow moving behind Madame Rebecca's chair, tacitly inviting me to have some hot lemon with him, which he used to drink throughout the winter to fight the colds he constantly had. He used to stay in bed for days, avoiding human contact, to prevent his colds from turning into bronchitis. His thin lips curved brilliantly when he smiled, which infused his narrow eyes with an infinite glow. Strands of his bronze-colored hair fell over his face, making him look like a playful child running around mischievously but with a man's perfect figure. Perhaps he looked like Zorba in his youth. Since I was a princess, he had to frequently remind me that princesses did not carry burdens on their shoulders and ask me to straighten up and make my breasts stick out more.

Now I stick my chest out as he used to tell me, imagining him sitting in front of me, looking at what had become of his first love. Then he gently draws me closer and rests my head over his shoulder. He puts his arms around me as we sit alone for a while staring at the screen where I see trains heading toward me, and tears fill my eyes as I watch some lover fading out, like an extinguished fire, in a dark hole where nothing exists except a slow death. From this death Rebecca saves me as she offers me a cigarette and an embroidered handkerchief. I wipe away my tears and give it back to her.

"No, no, you keep it. It's new. Handkerchiefs should not be shared. But why are you crying?"

I smiled and decided to leave before entering upon a story I would not know how to start or finish, and before I foolishly asked if I could see Andrea's room. I knew it was kept, as if for eternity, in the same way it looked the last time he and I were there together. Neither one of us had returned to it since Andrea took me home that night and said he was going first for a walk by the coast, then to the church to light two candles, then to al-Gharib Mosque to recite the Fatiha, where he was also going to make a vow; finally, he was going to stop by the café to see Asaad. But he never even made it through the gate of the church because he was attacked and bled all the way to the copper door handle of his house. His mother did not realize that the gentle knock she heard was the beating of his weak heart. I retraced his route a thousand times, hearing this knock in my head until I was deaf.

I was now the one lighting the candles and reciting the Fatiha and praying to Mar Girgis and al-Gharib, who protected the city. I stopped at the café to look for Asaad. The cold air made me shiver and tremble, but it proved kinder than Asaad's reception.

"I would love a cup of tea."

"Go inside, Professor. You shouldn't sit here."

"I'm going to get married."

"Why not? You have every right, but I don't want to have anything to do with you. Do you understand? Goodbye."

"You know what, I was wrong to come to you and you are rude."

He said nothing.

"But if you ever see my face again. . . . Goodbye!"

Why did the world seem so empty and confining when Essam assured me that we were going to make a brave new world? Was it going to be similar to my world now packed into suitcases and cardboard boxes? My grandmother had saved clothes and pots and pans for my wedding without letting either my uncle or my mother know. Did love have to end in marriage? Did I even love Essam? Long before the wedding, I had time to change my mind, which I could do even now while packing my suitcases. My mother was staring at me scornfully as she sat in front of the mirror by my brother's bedroom where he was sleeping. She had the phone in her lap so that she could tell anyone who called Selim that he was gone and she had no idea when he'd return. Hoda, who was madly in love with him, received the same answer in addition to a long lecture on the low morals of calling a single man, and a religious one at that. My father looked as if he had been quietly crying for a while. When I walked by him, he grabbed my hand, so I leaned over to hear his complaints as he shook his body on the wheelchair that once belonged to a now-dead handicapped person.

"Are you going to leave me, Suzy? I'm tired, dear, and I'm ready to die."

No one handed him a bedpan so he had to use a soup bowl until urine flowed over his hands and the sleeves of his gallabiya.

"Who else would help me out and comfort me, Suzy?"

I prepared his bath and helped him put on clean clothes. His arms had grown weak and he could no longer use the manual sewing machine that was now buried under my brother Selim's records. Selim was frail despite the hair of his beard and mustache, and his thick, disheveled hair was soaking wet after hours devoted to horribly beating on the old rug in his room as he listened to loud music and danced furiously to its shrieking beats. He left his room only to ask if the bathroom was free.

That was how I said goodbye to my family. Some sort of gravity kept pulling me down. I tried to resist it by looking for a smile that was not worn out. But we were trying to avoid even eye contact in a suffocating space void of compassion or sympathy. We were defeated soldiers unable to complete the most mundane tasks—in need of support and understanding to continue our sluggish progress, paranoid, going along with anyone who promised to sort out our mess and to take us on a new journey through dazzling lights. But we inevitably returned to our comas. Our dreams turned into nightmares where we floated in cold smoke and drowned blood blurring the edges of memory.

Act 3

Schizophrenia:
Plausible and Predictable

My lucky charms were usually silver coins. I would replace them with other coins whenever I thought they were no longer effective, or never were, but only as long as I found the new ones by accident.

Everything seemed to be happening by accident during the time I lived with Essam, which I swear that I cannot clearly remember except for a few happy incidents that pass through my mind like terrifying ghosts. My witness is the bright silver moon I see through the branches of the palm tree outside my mother's window that has now grown taller than our building. I cannot recognize the woman I was at that time. I must have wholeheartedly accepted everything he said as true. If he were to say that the sun rose in the west, I would have believed him. But while he never said that, he was simply able to make me believe that the sun set in the east. This was not the hallucinating effect of hashish, but it controlled every conscious and unconscious moment of my life. I used to sleep all day and wake up at the beginning of the night. As soon as I washed up and had my coffee, darkness would spread through every corner outside and inside my soul until ghosts started roaming in my home. So I would stay up all night unable to see or feel, daring to open my eyes when I heard the ghosts laughing, but only to see their distorted faces, a sight that drove me mad. I could not remember anything about what I had received from my father and my mother, or about all the journeys I had been through before I entered my thirties as a bride in a white gown on the morning after her wedding, walking around lightly and smiling happily and repeating, "This is my home, this is my home. Everything is new and sparkly and will stay so forever, new and sparkly."

The black dress I'm now wearing to mourn my mother would have seemed white if I had put it on during one of those early days—when the whole world seemed delightful and exciting.

There was one lucky charm I quickly got rid of. I did not lose it on the street or leave it on a public seat, as I used to do, to bring someone else good luck. This one I dropped down the toilet drain and poured a bucket of hot water over it so that I might never find it again, but it remained at the bottom of the drain for a period of time I can only recall in random flashes that burn my heart with anger and blind my eyes with rage until I lose my mind. I quickly control myself, however, especially if I am in public.

But now I'm completely alone, going over what I can remember of that life to learn how to confront it and reduce its impact.

So it happened that I married at the age of thirty a colleague only a few months older than myself. I was in love with him despite being repulsed by the way he always curled his fingers as if they were claws ready to tear through a furry hide.

Essam's cruelty deflated my dreams like a balloon. My grandmother had paved the way for my powerlessness through the world of fairytales whose common theme was wistfully waiting for a man who could decipher the symbols of the fable, a man who would save me from all the curses that obstructed my way with the talisman he had stolen from the monster's lair.

Water was for donkeys and beer was for Essam because he was not a donkey. At the beginning it seemed fine. We would share three bottles to be distracted from the void in our lives, which we faced every night until all nights, whether we were happy, frustrated, or bored with holidays, became the same. Beer cases would leave empty and come back refilled in complete secrecy so that the neighbors would not find out that the two professors were holding drink sessions every night. Everybody could come. People half-wasted occupied my world until the locked room turned into a murky tub, reeking of cigarettes and burps that smelled like the foods rotting in their bellies. Revulsion would force me to lock myself up in the bathroom to take a break from the noise and the chatter. I would choke on the stink they left in my bathroom, the room most taken care of in the house. They would start unzipping their pants before they reached its door, smiling like zombies, carelessly staining the rugs with the black mud on their shoes.

A quick escape from those horrible circumstances was the route I should have taken, but I was not ready—perhaps because I always liked to wait for the trash cans to be so overfilled that small yellow worms started to crawl around in them, treating myself to the full experience of revulsion. For Essam, I became a source of nagging when I would say in a low, angry voice, "You may not care about wasting your own time, but don't waste my life too. You are a loser."

I did not know if I had shouted these words out before or after an unexpected slap in the face that stung me severely as I stood there ready to pounce. Before I ran out of time and evil infected my thoughts, I should have left without further complications—but it was laziness again—after I received the first signs from Essam. I had only a set of dishonorable options to choose from, any one of them would have robbed me of my innocence. I entered the world of Essam's tedious games where he spoke nonstop about his ego, always with the singular pronoun: no "we" as in "she and I," for example. Same stories. Same details. He included no one else in these stories. My eyes would beg him to stop talking because none of the drunks to whom he was explaining the constant revolution was listening—because he could no longer turn the people in his life into parts of his windmills.

Pills and cigarettes to stay intoxicated; drunk fits of crying; "one hit after another"; no solution to the problem of having to pee constantly because of the beer, which cost so much that it deepened our inability to pay our bills at the beginning of each month.

My heart, please don't bleed when I lock the bathroom door, all sense of peace and safety lost. The gate of hell opens at the sound of seeds cracking when Essam rolls one last cigarette after everyone is gone. He never liked to waste any drug, no matter how poor its quality. Since I was not wasteful either, I used to eat so much that no leftovers were thrown away. I also used to double my hours of sleep to escape the daylight and its irritations. Fat started to accumulate on prominent parts of my body and I grew several sizes larger. I no longer had work clothes that fit, so I let Essam take over my classes. I became frail with no energy to do either good or evil. My time was taken up in lethargy and the pursuit of petty intrigues. Sometimes I would hear old laughter and music, Andrea's voice singing, "Hey woman, you are the definition of beauty."

I breathe in the stale air and hear the sound of rain falling heavily as I shower with my eyes wide open in panic: this is not a surreal play; this is my life, which has no life because I'm living with the dead; their clatter is as suffocating as the smell of burning human flesh, filling my lungs with fumes. But I know deep down that I am no different from the rest.

When you turn thirty, you cry like you've never cried before. You try things that never occurred to you, and they may change your life, but you will never be the same again. As you go through these things, you will probably be taking the last drag of your cigarette at eleven o'clock in a small nondescript city. You will never take care of any unfinished business. You will use the deprivation that crushes travelers on long roads as an excuse. You will always be slowly losing something and becoming someone else.

I'm powerless, staring constantly at the feet and shoes that stubbornly surround me, spreading through the house and crushing my defenses. In my silence I cry out, "Leave me alone." I'm more and more certain, but I still cannot make up my mind. Without any resistance I let Essam lock me up in a world of nonexistence.

In this city, which turns muddy in the winter, to be noticed all you have to do is smash a cup in your kitchen and everyone will hear it. Essam especially likes to throw my grandmother's glassware and clay pots against the wall. I curl into a ball as I usually do to relax my muscles. I know beforehand that I'm bullet-resistant and that the worst that can happen to me is being scorched by the fading fire, which still leaves horrible marks on my skin. He, of course, does not care because he is so wasted.

He unleashes my hallucinations over Khairiya's rape, my father's amputated leg, my mother's madness, my grandmother's blindness, my own confused ravings, which are no less than my brother's delirium, and the merciless lashing of my uncle's whip over my body. His drinking bouts reveal a deep-seated hatred beyond human capacity. It only takes beer and cheap alcohol followed by a few last hits from every joint shared with buddies, comrades, and the lowest of the nouveau riche, the "interim class," as referred to by Suzy Muhammad Galal, who sounds like a big speaker mounted to the wall that leaks for half the winter and is covered with mold in the summer. She shivers in her see-through, sleeveless shirt and tries to firmly place her feet on legal and common-law grounds, but nothing protects her.

Strangely, we keep playing the same game on automatic pilot without recognizing each other's skill at taking it to a level beyond everyday routine. Neither one expects the other to win. Such is war: you either win or lose. There is no chance for Defersoir gaps or negotiations. He wishes he could banish me to the desert to burn under the scorching sun, and I wish the cold mud beneath his feet could leak scorpions and snakes before he runs from seeing me die under the influence of drugs. My own experience supports the fact that drugs quickly destroy brain cells as I begin to recognize apathy in my saggy face. Toward the end of each evening, we have only to start playing the same hating game for others to take pleasure in watching our drama from their front-row seats, clapping hard, then quieting down for the final scene.

Not even Tahia Carioca's charisma or Samia Gamal's playful dancing could have been more riveting than the surreal drama played by the contestants Essam and Suzy for the summer and winter seasons, in addition to a special nomination for Mr. Essam, Secretary of the Secret Party, who preferred to be called "the Hero Professor." In the end, the outcome was a victory only for hatred and disagreement and a paid-for amusement for the audience who added in their own sins to the mix of exposed vulnerabilities in a drama surrounded by yellow lights. . . .

"Do you know what it means to be a political prisoner? My entire family had to undergo persecution and humiliation. Your uncle crushed my spirits. I didn't aspire to much. He put me in prison and moved on with his life without an apology or a thank-you note for his promotion, which came at the bloody cost of locking me up in solitary confinement. The only visitors I had were his polished shoes kicking me. In the raw cold, I lost my dignity; I could no longer recognize myself. Why did your uncle do all that? For your sake, to take me away from you because I'm a nobody from the lower orders that live on poverty and empty words.

But you are from Selim Bey's family. To whom does victory belong today? To me, because I have your same academic degrees and I'm now family, in addition to the honor I received when he threw me in jail."

This was how much Essam hated me, which I recorded as if with a small camera in my head for moments that seemed to last as long as death. At the end of the night, I saw in my sleep that the Marxism we had adopted did not explain why he had targeted me so. I tried to relax with a cup of boiled caraway seeds but I woke up feeling sick. I saw Essam walk in and toy with his wedding band, originally a gold one he had exchanged for silver to afford a pack of Marlboros and several kilograms of meat; it was crusted with the salt of his summer sweat as he turned it around on his finger. I was shaking violently and I almost passed out, feeling the cold rising from the river and the fields around it.

"Essam, I'm freezing cold."

"Would you like some more quilts?"

"Yes, and please take me in your arms. I think I'm dying."

"You're not going to die. You're going to live for a hundred years."

My grandmother lived for over ninety years without losing any of her teeth and with the same eyes, pure blue but blind. When she died, she had a smile on her face. I try to imitate that smile before I fall asleep so that I may die like her, smiling while shivering with cold. I try to concentrate on Andrea, who is never older than twenty-two in my dreams and in my fantasies of mixed pain and pleasure as Essam's quick thrusts tear through my body, feeling like reptiles crawling over me while I silently pray that this may be the last time.

Andrea was excellent at picking movies, but he never liked their endings. Neither did I.

Before deep sleep completely wipes away the influence of drugs, I see my grandmother rising from the dead. I'm trying to smash skittering cockroaches with my yellow flip-flops while Pink Floyd is playing "The Wall," which sounds like hammers beating down on my heart. By mistake, I turn the volume up so that the screaming is everywhere while I run around scared by the bugs. My grandmother arrives unexpectedly in a black dress, her pure white face beaming with the same kindness as she smiles. She sits next to me on her couch and she reaches under the pillow to hand me a secret she has guarded for a long time. When I open my hand, I see a blinding light. She rests her head on the cushion that she used her entire life and continues to smile without seeing that I have become completely blind. I lean against the headboard of the bed and smile.

Does anyone know what happens when the door closes for the last time on someone facing death? I do, because that night, when I woke up from my uneasy sleep neither out of breath nor terrified by my nightmare, knowing that absolutes were essentially flawed, I quietly left my bed. I found Essam fondling the maid whom he used to hold in his arms when she was a baby. She was not exactly a maid. She was a distant relative of his. Her name was Aisha. Her father kicked her out to appease his new wife and she had no one to turn to but her uncle, the 'Hero Professor,' who went to jail for the sake of the poor peasants. She was a small, nine-year-old child from the village, who worked so hard for Essam's family. I needed her help with hosting the parties and with cleaning the mess afterward.

That night she was exhausted and it was late, although 'late' had no bearing for this girl who was only given food—and lots of flip-flops because she wore them out running errands. What mattered in this scene was that Essam was crouching next to her, his hands going through her private parts, staring at her face as if to see her reaction. While she seemed asleep, her face was twisted with pain the same way Khairiya's face was behind the shutters of the dim-lit shed. In this dim light and perhaps for the thousandth time, Essam was molesting this child, who kept quiet and pretended to be asleep—perhaps because she did not understand if this was part of her job description or because, as one of the family, she deserved this special treatment. Those were my thoughts as I quietly walked back to my bedroom, climbed into bed, and curled up as if nothing had happened. I buried my head under the covers terrified by what I saw, feeling as if sharp teeth were tearing at my body. In the morning, daylight pounced on the room, sneaked beneath the soft red covers, pulled them off, and left me exposed to the cold air that freely traveled between me and Essam. He was finally sleeping next to me after he had just finished exploring some part of human nature. Was it worth the tyranny that crushed me and penetrated the mind of the child who dreamed of something more than being a servant at the house of a couple pretending to be progressive?

How mediocre were the mourning rituals! That woman in yesterday's mirror, where did she go? I could not find an answer to this question as I tried to shield my eyes from the mirror's allure. By simply covering my hair and neck, a completely different woman emerged. Essam's sarcastic voice irritated me: "Are you wearing a hijab? Congratulations. You look better."

"I have to go with the flow. The age of ideas is over, as you said."

"Of course. Nowadays no one stays the same. That's why we have to change. Wasn't this one of your brilliant political ideas?"

"I did not mean change on the outside; I meant a change of heart to eradicate the terrible misconceptions about us as young people who wanted everybody to sleep with everybody."

"Are you upset because I requested that we look like everyone else and live the way we want?"

"I never asked for anything except that we lead by example. My fear of my uncle once made me wear a burqa; it was only a disguise. The problem was feeling that I was disappearing in the same way I'm now being co-opted into everything you want."

"You just reminded me of your uncle."

"Of course, I did. You're good friends now."

Essam told me, smiling and shaking his head, that my uncle had returned with a promotion to campus security. My uncle was relatively cured from his drug addiction except for a few bango joints and hashish cubes his buddies at the Office of Drug Control continued to give him. He and Essam started to see each other quite often and a strange peace that resembled familiarity existed between them.

"I stopped by at his office yesterday. We took a walk over the bridge and stopped by the Nile to smoke two fat joints. They made the Nile turn south and made his car shake in my eyes while I was trying to stop laughing so hard at his jokes, which poured out of his mouth like a farce."

Essam does a stiff imitation of my uncle: "'I only do what I'm told, which is my job, and I know it won't make any difference to anybody; violence against violence while we all burn in the same hell, unable to grant each other peace. I'm only a bystander watching the mutual fighting where all sides are losing. Today, it is the Muslim Brothers' turn, yesterday it was the communists', and others like them. In my spare time I divide them by color like fish in a small tank and pull them out of the water when told while the others keep swimming and eating at each other. My favorite thing is watching the air bubbles rising up and bursting near the surface. I watch the game and have my club ready to hit so ferociously that everyone falls down helplessly. Nowadays, the game is subdued and uninteresting, which is making me feel old.'

"Keep your hijab on until we figure out what's going on."

Essam adds this quietly, so I tell him sarcastically, "There is not much difference between the two of you." At first he does not say a word because he is so shocked at my bold attack on his integrity, and then he reprimands me for my insolence. I was no longer an inferior believer in the arguments he plagiarized from the pages of textbooks and from others' opinions.

I try to calm my angry thoughts down. I pick up my pocketbook and drink the last few sips of my strong coffee diluted with milk. I speak quickly with my eyes following Aisha as she picks up the dirty glasses, ashtrays, and empty plates, "I'm late and time flies. You can never make up for what you miss, right Aisha?"

"Pardon me, ma'am?"

She smiles shyly while Essam mockingly raises his hands with the smile of someone who has just realized what was going on. This was his general attitude. He had to have the final word every time.

Codes and signs redolent of ideology, as if we were the only two people who understood the universe, as if he were telling me, "I know you very well and I know the meaning of your mind-boggling messages and your stories that take me to your world of nostalgia. Ok, how do you like *this* language? Does it touch your heart in the same way my last poem, which I dedicated to you secretly as my sole audience, did? I knew that your uncle was the chief of campus security. He was the one who insulted my mother, asking me if she wore underpants all the time or saved them only for holidays and trips. Then he asked the guard to imitate her as she sat by the stream. His mother could not be better than mine."

I close the door, leaving behind Essam and Aisha and the promise carved over the side of the wardrobe and over the headboard of the semi-circular bed: "We'll make a brave new world." The statement now smoldered with the fumes and smoke of our mutual ignorance, repeating surreptitiously, "Everything will be fine. There are virtues we still see in each other; there's no way we will give in to this nonsense—could the tablecloth be yanked from under glasses without knocking them over, without a river of pain flooding feelings cruelty has dried up?"

My uncle had desperately opposed my marriage to Essam because my decision reflected his powerlessness at a time when his official duties were suspended. He believed that Essam had nothing to offer but a magic hat full of maxims and slogans.

"When he was the organization's technical director," he said about Essam, "he admitted that it was a ploy to seduce desperate girls and you are not that desperate."

For long nights, Essam questioned me about my uncle. For long hot days, my uncle did the same after he suddenly regained his authority. I was completely unknown to both of them. They did not view me as an individual, but as a faded image of someone whose job was to deliver important messages. I was a messenger likely to be killed as she faced for the most part violent eruptions, sometimes unexpectedly, because the interrogations usually led to information that was intentionally kept from her so as not to distract her from her job. I became the rope in a tug of war: my uncle's contempt for Essam on one side and Essam's hatred for my uncle on the other.

Whether they lose or win, they are all gods. Suzy can go to hell.

Winter passes through the sky, causing thunder and lightning on its way out. It has rained abundantly, filling the roads with sticky, fresh-smelling mud and with fertility. I try to estimate the number of times I have walked through this city, which has stuck to me like my own skin for several years. I hear the large, noisy crowd in front of the cinema cheering Andrea, who has just planned a moonlight trip to the beach at Ain Sukhna. Our feet plunge into the sand for miles along the beach. It soaks up our soft encounter under the light that streams through the windows of the moon. My holding on to Andrea is unsure and frenetic like the waves of the high tide. Is it I who is enjoying such great happiness, such deep laughter?

I'm completely alone here except for my angry breathing; I don't know what to do. My voice is lost in the cacophony of other voices. I used to be someone else—someone planning to use her gifts creatively, but it's all been an effort that leads to nothing more than replacing the worn-out soles of my shoes. Despite my striving, I am constantly ground down by the impersonal harshness of the roads. I scream at a city as cold as death; no one here is like me and no one accepts me. I wander alone in the hallways. Female colleagues pretend they do not know me. They do not wish to be associated with me and prefer to adapt to standard molds because "innovation is heresy." My existence equals my nonexistence: a haunting, valueless, unintelligible ghost. Nothing is true in this world except my nightmares. In my sleep I return to my boats and swim through the undercurrents of my subconscious. I become a naked flower shredded by the noises that toy with objects at night. When others stifle my breathing with the hate-filled covers they throw over my head, I feel I am breathing my last, I feel I am suffocating as I try to untangle the curly knots from my hair. I live in a world that recognizes neither constitutions nor civil rights. I walk up steps in dim-lit auditoriums and go up and down with my head uncovered in the pale light of the university campus.

How could I have refused a crowned king's offer to make me a queen of a village that ferociously eats up days, weeks, and years? Continuing my voluntary captivity in constant darkness, I keep switching visions, looking for a dream that matches a mind dragging itself along behind time's winged chariot. My time is consumed on useless projects, searching for a number or a quote in hundreds of cases and boxes packed with books, perfumes, pens, summer clothes, cooking pots, canned foods, and bedrooms wide open like public restrooms. Besides, meeting the professors for tea and cake is especially annoying since I am not really there, but here, chasing after time as it gallops away in its shiny saddle, hoping to jump on top of it and ride it back to them.

Nightmares. Nightmares. They make me sit up in bed, aimlessly looking between pillows and sheets for the source of the terror during the years I spend addicted to waiting every day for a better life, heartily praying, "Dear God, where are the laws of your mercy? When will you grant justice?" How can I escape from this space surveilled by the eyes of Essam, the self-appointed king who keeps telling me how much he had to do for his people to accept me? In return, he manages the details of my life and makes them public; he robs me of any chance for peace and gags me with drugs so that I don't remember my old dreams. According to the traditions of his sacred tribe and their great demands, I'm chained to his legendary shrine until both of us discover in the end that we've made a mistake and that what ties us to each other is an addiction.

I'm one of those people who get quickly excited about something, then suddenly and oddly lose interest. This happens over matters of the smallest and the highest import. It applies to my powers of resistance as well. My crying usually turns into laughter and vice versa. If someone were to understand this about me, I would hold that person in the highest esteem as someone strong and practically beyond human error. I cannot deny that I have too often attributed these qualities to the wrong people and usually during the first encounters of relationships that ended in hatred. How awful when they were women! But Dr. Sayyid Diab has never veered from how he seemed when I first met him. Despite his easy tendency toward methodological errors, he can shock me quickly out of ignorant, conformist routines.

I had to reanimate all those dead brain cells of mine so as not to miss a single facial expression of his when he carefully listened to me saying, "What I have seen, Doctor, was so much but nothing new. I lived here for two years as an emigrant, mourning my childhood every day, and for four years as an adolescent and a young woman trying to rebel against her fears on the university campus and in the family house where I was under the care of my uncle. I'm now approaching forty and have not accomplished anything. Even the child for whose sake I married Essam, I still don't have. Back then, we agreed that we would go our separate ways so that I could keep the child and he could keep my friendship. But we never became friends or even a married couple and I still don't have a child. . . . By the way, this seems to be a common phenomenon in my generation."

"There is no such phenomenon. Humanity is aging, and that takes the form of unnatural phenomena. Your generation willingly subscribes to this infertility conspiracy. How could you raise a child when you don't even know yourself?"

Baligh said, face half-tilted, looking directly into my eyes, "I'm from the same generation, Doctor, but at a young age I started a family and I have a son and a daughter. You're talking about exceptional cases."

I slowly replied, "But none of our friends have kids."

"Who are your friends?" asked Baligh. "Name a specific group within a consistent framework. You are individual cases drawn together to a broken-down and lethargic environment, which we cannot call a phenomenon. And, if you don't mind, Dr. Sayyid, this is God's will, 'He who makes whomever He wishes barren.'"

This was Dr. Diab's response to Baligh's uncharacteristically sarcastic attack, "You forgot to add 'God Most Almighty has told the truth' to your Quranic citation, Sheikh Baligh. Of course, my son, there are many things that are hard to explain, one of which is your very presence at this university. Weren't you a communist?"

"I was the first in my class and I graduated with high honors. In a few days, I will receive my doctorate."

"With all due respect."

"Thank you, Doctor; you are the one who should be held in high esteem."

"And no one is going to undo me except all of you. Why don't you order is something to drink and fix your Works Cited list? You should not spell the same name in two different ways; it's either Shelomith or Shalomit. We can discuss the rest of the dissertation when you fix the language. You should know how to spell."

"You know, Suzy," Dr. Sayyid remarked to me, "one should worry about you and this young man. You can achieve great things; your energy is endless and astounding. Essam is different."

"How so?"

"Despite all his problems, he knows what he wants and he can accomplish it, but he has no sense of time."

I wanted to tell him all about my pain, but I was stopped by his silent smile and the look in his watery eyes that observed all the ignorance and passivity that filled the vast, cold hallways.

He seemed to be listening carefully to the echoes which dominated the lecture halls packed with men sporting shaved heads and women wearing long dresses, people clutching crosses, people turning away from this world. The university seemed to us like a paradise in the guise of an inevitable hell. I would gratefully end my life here, surmounting attempts by the herds—stunned and horrified by the knowledge they were receiving—to alienate me and censor my thoughts. Dr. Diab came back from his quick listening spell subdued . . . anguished.

"Those poor kids cannot take another change of direction; it would be a big shock to their systems."

"Pain is the quickest way to learn. They need to know how to use fire without being burned," I say.

"Dr. Hasan and his group are tired of you. I don't want you to be hurt."

"I'm learning, Doctor, and my hopes rest on you."

"Your hopes should rest on you, dear. We're done. Our role has come to an end."

There was no real reason for not having children but since Essam wanted a child after six years of our living together, we went to see a doctor who was a friend of his. Essam's impersonal approach to the problem made the doctor act too seriously for the situation. His practice consisted, under typical circumstances, of nothing but abortions and hymen reconstructions, but he decided to take my case.

"Everyone," he said, "has male and female hormones in varying degrees which determine gender. It appears that your testosterone level is higher than usual. Therefore, we will start a medical treatment program. Please be extremely careful because I will treat your case as a research project."

We laughed a good deal at the words of the doctor/friend, but Essam insisted that I take the prescriptions on time. I could not get away with pretending to forget or arguing that they were useless. Then all of a sudden I stopped throwing the medications into the sink as often as I'd been taking them. I started to wish I could have a child who would look like Andrea.

One foolish mistake after another turns me into a bank account to deposit damages I did not cause but suffered from. My good-life account is at its lowest owing to a deal I made to compensate for the bitterness of the others' private sadness. I go back to watching the lowest of the low through clouds of pure smoke. . . . Those who enjoy home and holidays, who wear thick wool and starched cotton, who sport big bellies stretched over their cold bitterness and recover from illness at an amazing speed allowing them to fornicate on their recovery beds.

I part from my tranquil self to blend with evil and violence. I'm lost in the smoke that hides the monotonous waste of life inside dirty walls stained with cheap paint—where shadows are an indispensable commodity for every woman. In my head I open the windows wide and scream into the narrow, dark street, "Help, take me out of here!"

I'm pretty much resigned to a chaos that painfully numbs my brain and slows the flow of blood to my head, which weakly succumbs to a cup sealed with the wrapper of a cigarette pack. Essam gives me the cup filled with the smoke of the marijuana leaf held up by my hairpin.

I hold the cold glass between my lips. I feel pain in my throat as I inhale. I start to panic, feeling lonely and completely estranged, simultaneously pathetic and hilarious, as if I consisted of wavelets enclosed in a gulf. I refuse to participate in the blabbering around me because it stems from a tainted space of hallucinations. I focus on my refusal to take part in them to avoid thinking about time passing while I'm wasting my powers and gifts until I'm worthless, watching from my hiding place while rubbing my eyes so that my eyelashes stick to my fingers and my eyelids burn.

The burning only stops when sharp words sting a conscious cell in my wiped-out brain and I retort, "Personally, I believe in individuality and I'm against ignoring it, not through resignation but through analysis to define the danger in bad dreams. Do you know what these brains are made of and what they are stuffed with?"

"Fried rice?"

"Even better with mallow-leaf soup or any vegetable with tomato sauce," Essam responds to Yusif, sniffing in his head the imaginary meal I will have to cook the next day.

But I stubbornly go on, "If you stop thinking with your bellies, you will understand the consequences of ignoring the other's power and will."

"Stop talking about food, potheads, and pay attention," Sahar says as she exhales a thick cloud of smoke, watching it float over her head before humorously adding, "Suzy's words are useful and make sense. You only talk theoretically, not even knowing what you want or where you are going, and, of course, we have to close our eyes to avoid seeing the monsters. Don't talk to them—okay, Mama—or else you may become like them. But there is real danger, and step by step we are going to be huddled together like chickens in a coop until our heads are cut off."

"Watch out, Joe, the women are taking over."

"It's okay, buddy; we've already sold them our brains and we act according to their whims, so why should this matter?"

Essam slowly drops a few peanuts in a sweetened cup of tea coated with melted butter. Fat blocks my arteries. I resist with sharp pain in my head while Essam's words fall upon the numbness that isolates me and undermines the few reasons I have to survive.

"What's up with Ali?"

"Don't you know? He and Mina were arrested. They are in for a serious fraud case," Yusif says, smiling, his eyes glowing like two big white circles surrounding a white and black space.

"You're kidding?"

"I swear to God. They swindled fifty thousand pounds out of an entire village by promising to help them immigrate to Italy."

"Did they help anybody?"

"Not a single one out of fifteen people who paid the fees; fifteen morons from the same family, farmers with mud sticking to their fingers. What would they have done in Italy?"

"Do you know any of them?"

"Of course I do. Can you believe it? They gave them an enormous banquet!"

"Were you there?"

"Yes. Roasted turkey, stuffed pigeons, ducks, and meats steeped in butter, in addition to beer and booze. We partied all night and in the end, they drove us home like celebrities."

"Did you know they were swindlers?"

"Even if I did, it's none of my business. I only like to watch. I can't get involved in a scam on this scale. They offered, but when I turned them down, they told me that a friend of ours in Italy was really going to send employment contracts. I pretended to believe them and I kept quiet."

"Why can't we do something like that?"

In my childhood, I used to wonder what boys did with their extra body parts, which did not resemble what girls had. Now, I'm wondering what males do with their extra heads, which don't resemble ours. "Are you out of your mind, Essam?" Sahar yells out. "Leave my husband alone and do what you want on your own."

"I meant travel abroad, not go to jail. We all move to Italy and never come back to this hell of a place."

"What about our jobs at the university and our doctoral degrees?"

"What jobs, Doctor? Do you call that work? The education system is in shambles and even if we receive doctoral degrees, how much are we going to make? Unless we sell lecture notes and textbooks for profit. Can you make students buy them, Doctor?"

"Doctor" was an accusation that made me feel defenseless whenever Essam used it. The extent of its ugliness showed when he introduced me to someone as "Dr." Suzy Galal, Colonel Atef Salem's niece. He bites his lip now before he adds, "I have a question, but it's inappropriate."

"So what's new?"

"No, seriously, just listen. A man would take off his pants anywhere to do one thing; what is it?"

After entertaining an array of wrong answers, Essam proudly solves the riddle, "To pee. Ha ha . . . ha ha."

"Of course, that has to be the reason."

"Well, not really. Have you tried the pleasure of peeing your pants? It is an exceptional release."

"What release? How disgusting! Change this subject."

"Why?"

"But this is not a bad idea. Let's share those private moments with each other. What do you think, Doctor?"

"As you like, Doctor. You're holding the mike."

One time we were on our way back after watching fireworks marking the anniversary of the beginning of the siege and the local Resistance. We were drunk without drinking alcohol. The magic of the end of fall softened our hearts. Only Asaad's heart remained hard. He watched my love for Andrea with stony eyes. I ignored him, proud to be the center of attention of two completely different young men. Andrea was two steps ahead of us with the fireworks in the background creating a magic carnival of lights; he spread his feet and arms after taking his penis out of his pants. He raised his face to the sky and a soft sound rose from the grass—the sound of him peeing. I was drawn to the seductive line that divided the muscles of his back. Was my infatuation with him so powerful that Asaad had to attack him when he came back to sit next to me with a smile? Asaad started angrily yelling at him, "That was obscene. How dare you? Right in front of her?"

"Don't worry about her. I know how to take care of her."

"I'm her man in spite of you."

"Asaad, I'm in love with Andrea."

Sometimes winter suddenly leaves only to return with a vengeance after we have started putting on light clothes so that our bodies shiver with the unexpected cold. Winter gives our hearts a nostalgic pang. Where will I be next winter? I wonder. . . .

I feel the old shiver. I shake and cough with laughter as I tell Essam, "You swindler, how did you fool me and leave me shivering in this cold?" I laugh and cry until they say, "You're high, Suzy."

I was not high. But I always laughed and cried at my odd choices without moralizing or pretending to be forced. I cannot deny that I belonged to the world of "rats," as we called ourselves and our friends, and that my guilt was slightly eased when I took part in the outworn chatter and worthless conversations always interrupted with the pivotal question, "Hey, what are we talking about?"

"You're the one who was talking."

"Are they going to start arguing?"

"It would be better than messing with our heads and making fun of us all the time."

"All right, Suzy. You always have to sound rational and pretend that you understand."

I could not stop eating out of the plates lined up on the floor in no particular order, as opposed to the way my mother taught me or as I used to see on Andrea's table, where everything was so elegant and amazing, even the way tea was served.

"Everything you see and like," I remember Andrea saying in response to my compliment, "we learned from the pharaohs: bed-making, the value of sitting at a table, fabulous makeup. If you saw their drawings on the walls, you would know that what you like comes from your own history and from no one else."

I remove the dishes that are completely empty of food. Sahar follows me. I try to ignore her while she chats nervously and incoherently about issues that make me bristle with anger and insult.

"The men sit like princes while the harem serves them," she says.

"That's okay, it's one way to pass the time."

"Your willingness to serve others is remarkable. I can never be like you."

"Well, this is my house after all."

"It's not for me. I like to be served everywhere I go."

The whistle from the tap and the sound of the thin stream of water surround me as I become more engrossed in washing the dishes. There are leftovers, wine glasses smeared with fingertips and dry lipstick, and the cheap spring flowers Hasan the janitor gave me when he was serving me a cup of coffee in the faculty lounge, formally whispering to me,

"Happy New Year, Professor. There is no better gift than flowers and I have been meaning to give you something for a while because you're the best one around here. Take care of yourself, my dear."

How and why was I a good person and the best one around here? I decided to give him a big tip but he refused to take money even for the tea and coffee I ordered that morning while I waited to meet with my supervisor. The meeting with him concluded by quenching my great enthusiasm for the dissertation topic I proposed. Smiling in an encouraging and energetic way, he said, "Study hard, then choose the topic, and avoid methodological mystification."

By indulging in fantasy, I try to overcome the voices that invade my head and threaten my mental stability. My own mind takes me to the lowest pits of anger or indifference; I look for ways to make the night go by so that I may rise in the morning like the princess in *Swan Lake* when she comes back to life. I have to do something with my life and, disguised in darkness and silence, take advantage of the passing of time and of Essam's and the others' involuntary sleep. They are an inseparable part of my everyday life and, even with good intentions, they can deprive me of my existence and force me to be on their side like a servile shadow waiting on them. One should never give for nothing; this one is evasive but I will now demand payback.

I re-enter the room and rush toward Essam. He is smiling at a cigarette he is stuffing with tobacco and crushed bango as he tells Yusif, "You are rude."

I forget what I am about to say and look at Yusif, who says cunningly, "The shipment is too big. I don't know where to store it. You should keep it here and we will split it, but make sure you have enough room for it."

"Sure. Suzy, would you like to spend a couple of days with your father? Your uncle told me that he was sick."

I nod in agreement and compliance. This is an old trick Essam uses whenever he plans to seduce some woman, maybe he shares her with Yusif. Now Yusif comes up with another idea to kill whatever time we have left.

"Who can keep a cigarette standing upright after it burns into ashes?" asks Yusif.

"Potheads," I respond, so he gives me a mean look.

"If this is a challenge, I'll take it," Essam interrupts.

"Oh, yeah, you're the man for a challenge," I say.

"Would you like to see?" asks Yusif.

"Why? I know I can't but I will give it a try for your sake," I reply.

Sahar laughs as she looks at Yusif. Oddly enough, we are all able to keep the ashes of our cigarettes standing up a few seconds after we inhale them. Sahar drops the ashes on her clothes and brushes them off on the chair and the rug, coughing hoarsely and holding her neck with her hands as if painfully choking.

"Son of a bitch, you ruined my chest. I mean Essam, not you, Yusif."

Yusif turns to me, "Just so that you know, I can keep it like that for half an hour with my super power."

"At any rate," I respond with the same confidence as I turn to face Essam, "our ability to keep the ashes standing up indicates not only that we are potheads but that we are sick as well."

Essam is able to place his cigarette on the table for a short while before it falls apart. Then he takes a deep breath.

"What's up, Essam? Control your wife, dude. She is going to make us feel bad."

"Don't get upset, Joe, the Doctor has been reading Freud for a couple of days."

"You must be out of your mind, Sue! Are you going to psychoanalyze us?"

Sahar's laughter dies softly this time. Her usual nervous laughter somehow affects me, making me laugh hard and nonstop until tears fall out of my eyes.

"God damn the circumstances that put me together with you, rats."

"Rats" was not a curse as much as it was a description of all of us. We arrived at it without prior agreement one time when we were sitting in a circle around plates and containers as cold as my small fridge, which was making strange noises. To find the source of the noise, I dragged the short white fridge away to peer through the darkness at the small pipes and the motor covered with moist dust. They started laughing at me, so many of them, all of them.

Turning my palms up in self-defense, I said, "There is nothing here, you rats. No mouse or cat."

"We are not rats. Your apartment is haunted!"

Since that night, we became "rats." I couldn't remember who said it first, but the fact that the house was haunted stayed on my mind. It reminded me of what the milk-woman said about Ms. Inayat, the woman who spent two-thirds of her life in this apartment until she died as alone as she lived. "She never talked to anyone. She died in the winter and a long time had passed before I could smell the stench when I brought the milk." That was what Umm Shehata told me, the elderly woman from the countryside, who liked to bring me milk and dairy products because I reminded her of her daughter who lived abroad to serve her husband and his family.

On the night we invented that title, Ms. Inayat's presence made me feel that there was something of hers here, something no one else had found. Maybe that was why my amulets did not work and why I had to constantly replace them until I started to frantically search everywhere. My life hinged on a coin shining in the moonlight. As soon as I found it, I had to throw it away because it was bringing me more bad luck. My main preoccupation then became looking for her belongings in the house until I had an intuition—my intuitions were usually right—to search behind the drain pipe that was corroded where it connected with the back wall (through that wall the sun lit up and warmed my kitchen all day). I found there, inside many plastic bags, a bundle wrapped in the torn leg of an old pair of pants. It was so old that it fell to pieces when I was taking it out of one last black plastic bag, through which I could feel the roughness of its contents. When I touched it, I heard the same crackling noise. My heart sank and I shoved the mysterious bundle behind one of the bookshelves. I never told anyone about it and I indefinitely postponed exploring it and resolving its mystery.

Yusif and Sahar leave and Essam and I are alone, staring at each other, grinning, and thinking how we are going to kill the time until we fall asleep. Essam's preferred way was to spray his semen inside me. He knew that because of my mental confusion, I had no desire for him. I did not even want him to touch me, not now at least. I see his ugliness magnified when he forcibly hammers at my damaged nerves. I feel something strange taking place inside of me when I close my eyes and silently scream, feeling as if I am Khairiya or Aisha, as if I am anyone but me.

He is finally overcome with exhaustion and falls asleep. I gather the scattered pieces of my heart and try to mend them in the darkness of my usual loneliness. Sad looks and dead smiles live in my old wounds. I'm here suffering inexplicable pains from psychological states that neither

Freud nor anyone else has ever cared to analyze. My insanity is imminent like rain even if it waits until winter's end. Thunder hits nobody else in this world but me and my locked windows. What is the point of living given my bewilderment among nebulous wars and conquests? The wind outside blows at my door and declares the end of the world. I join the cannibals who leave behind squeezed cigarette packs and hundreds of bloated cigarette butts in a big ashtray filled with water. I do not like to squeeze anything, not even cigarettes. The trashcan is filled with scraps of paper cut into equal pieces along with interrupted words. Smoke from smoldering fires makes everyone cough. Empty food plates are spread like a violated woman who never has the right to choose who ravishes her.

All women claim that they are average except in two situations: making love and fighting. Only then do they speak with superiority and distinction and refer to some exalted family tree whose branches extend to God. I'm of course one of them, but I have lost this tendency. My sense of self is gone at the beginning of any meeting; silence is my last resort in dealing with any issue. I feel special in my subconscious as I walk confidently and calmly. I sport a poker face but on the inside I'm seething with anger and contempt.

Run, sheep; trample each other. Do you expect to find paradise there? Well, I'll meet you there, if there is a 'there.' Now, there is here. You will never catch a glimpse of a woman obsessed with looking for a young man called Andrea, recording her thoughts on the glass windows of closed shops. She stops to look for yesterday's newspapers but will have to miss them as she hangs out waiting for the tellers' windows to open at the bank. My father taught me to show up early in order to view the whole scene. Although I am usually late, stressing about my father's feelings made me jump out of bed early despite having had no sleep all night. I washed my face and brushed my teeth in a hurry and put on clothes appropriate for my unusual mission and for the people I would have to deal with. I rushed down the stairs after chewing on half a stick of gum to fill my mouth with the taste of sugar, a taste that would quickly vanish and turn into the taste of tears.

My mission now was to pick up my father's pension, his handicap pension. On the marble steps in front of the bank with its heavy locked doors and iron-barred windows, several people were standing in the cold, trying to blow some warmth into the palms of their hands. Their faces were roughly etched by poverty, handicaps, helplessness, and neglect. How proudly stood before them that wise country that tortured its servants and froze all their accounts! The reward for self-sacrifice was hardly enough money for my father to afford a week's supply of cheap alcohol—after which he would always go begging to my brother, but in vain. My brother would yell at him and curse him with my mother's approval because no decent man should ask his own son to buy him alcohol, let alone ask a daughter, who sneaked alcohol under the heavily waxed legs of her father's stationary chair. I tried to lie to my mother about the true amount of my father's pension while the suspicious smile on her face indicated that she knew I was lying.

"You will never change, Suzy."

"What do you mean?"

"Your problem is your father."

She uttered this remark quite often. Some sort of pride made me not want to ask her about what she meant; I would just sit quietly and stare blankly ahead. I had many opportunities to visit my family, and at the thought of how barren my life was with Essam, each visit brought to mind my decision to pack my bags and leave him forever. Every time a woman waited in the wings, he would suggest that I go take care of my father. The pair of them always left the same things behind: fast food containers and an open wine bottle one quarter full; matches arranged in crisscross patterns over the pages of old school books; a huge amount of lemon halves, dried up and brown (I still do not know what they were for). Since the details were always the same, I could never figure out the nature or the age of Essam's lover during my marital vacations. My father did indeed need my help, and since I had no place to go, I always headed toward that house, which had not been touched by the war. I left to give Essam the opportunity to live out his psychological problems. That was the quick excuse I gave myself whenever a friend hinted in jest at what took place in my absence, and all the more so when the women were more adamant. Despite their female heritage, some of them still felt some love for me, perhaps because I was a woman who kept what she heard to herself in addition to my "willingness to serve others." For me, it was simply that I liked to listen as well as to forget, so they poured their stories into my ears with no omissions or embellishments. Siham was the one who liked to tell her story the most.

"After I was arrested in a big to-do and cursed all the way to police headquarters, I had no one to turn to. Even Amin completely ignored me. Although he was released right away, he still did not try to contact me or send me a letter—maybe he was under pressure from his mother—but what we had was not insignificant. My days were very sad. I needed all the support I could get to face the insults directed at my academic integrity and my honor. Everyone knew what an excellent student I was, what an active member of the party, and what a revolutionary public speaker. My relationship with Amin was not secret. Isn't marriage about publicity? We did not hide our relationship from anyone. Even my family and my uncles, the butchers, accepted the situation because they knew how different and distinguished I was from every other woman in the family. Things may have been different for Amin because he was not cautious by nature; he always had his mother to fix his crazy mistakes; at the same time, he thought of me as more affluent, more committed, more energetic, and so on, while we slept next to each other in his bed with the window open. He could forget, but I always looked forward to being completely free from the taboos imposed by others to obstruct progress. Only when I was being interrogated did I feel that I was wasting my voice, did I feel naked before the prosecutor, who was experienced in dealing with people from my social class. He tried out all of his techniques: he defiled my dead father's honor, then he defiled my own honor while pointing his stick toward my body and staring at parts of it that no one should see. In my mind it was as if he became the eyes that always looked in through Amin's window. I became open to all sorts of humiliations regarding my social errors, and not only mine but everyone else's I knew, beginning with Amin, who was known for stealing small things, including books, using their unreasonable prices as an excuse if someone found out. Amin tormented me for a whole year before he admitted that he loved me, costing me tremendous amounts of sandwiches and gifts and putting up with his mother, who tolerated me only for his sake. When they finally let me go, your uncle gave me a verbal release order: 'Next time use some mallow stalks; you don't have to go all the way to Cairo for an abortion.' An overwhelming disappointment made me decide to accomplish two goals regardless of what they would cost me: to marry Amin and to have an important job in a field like foreign relations."

Were Essam and Amin alike? Were they the same man with two faces? I was shaking as I listened to her frankly describing exactly what I suffered from in my marriage to a man only seemingly different from the one she married. He married her after great concessions from her family. To cover up the scandal, they made the down payment on the house and paid for the furniture from the money her father had left her. Amin had to pay for the rest so as to show his appreciation of their precious daughter, who had already set her eyes on the next goal, which became even more unattainable, not due to her incompetence, but because she was overwhelmed by Amin's affairs and wanted to show him that she could do the same. This was according to an agreement they had made even before they were married.

Amin was not good at covering up the traces and always left behind concrete evidence, which Siham tried to ignore until his victims started to share their stories with her. He was the villain in all the stories, but he dodged them like rubber bullets, sometimes by lying and denying and sometimes by accusing her of being insane and ordering her to see a psychiatrist. She believed him and was put on so many medications that when one time she saw him kissing a colleague who ostensibly needed his help with her master's thesis, she simply went back to her room, locked the door, and fell into a deep sleep. When she woke up, what she saw seemed like a dream—even when she cleaned the faded spots on the sofa he had in his office for relaxing. It became his regular bed except when he was sick; he would then move to the bedroom where she could take care of him all the time while his mother lay next to him, reciting verses from the Quran or passing the time in reading the information on his multiple prescription drugs. Siham would move as if in a dream unable to comprehend what took place around her, her numb mind turning everything into a delusion.

"Even if my mind was conscious, what could I do and where would I go? I do really love him. . . . For the sake of a love only I care about. I'm completely lost without him. I have no father or mother or even child to give my love to. Amin has become my child and I'm comfortable with fixing everything he ruins, even when I act like a nurse during abortions and listen to the confessions induced by cheap anesthesia. They would use my bed to recover from every operation paid for by Amin, who would dicker over the fees so that money would be left to buy drugs from the big pharmacy on the first floor of the doctor's office building, and to buy the chicken I would cook, stripping its meat to make noodle soup that I myself would feed these women. I myself would pick up the bloody pads from the bathroom floor and shove them into black plastic bags to hide them from the old garbage collector's eyes before I went back to washing the sheets for the thousandth time.

"What can you say except that I must be crazy, absolutely crazy. Everything would be over like a dream, but it kept coming back. He would tell me that nothing happened and I would tell him that it was a dream. Dreams are free. So be it and welcome to madness!"

My father really needed my help and I thought it might be better to stay for another week with him. My brother was unbearable, and so was my mother; the rest of the world seemed void of family and friends. Maybe I would pay Rebecca a visit to see Asaad, her husband, who was as crazy as she was according to Hamida. I was privy to how much Hamida hated her husband and constantly wished that he would die. My brother completely lost his mind after Hoda slapped him in the face. He had told her that he could not marry her because he should look for a girl from a good family—someone whose skin was white, who could cook and do only what he told her—and that this decision had nothing to do with her but was a question of principles since he could not take the risk of marrying someone who easily gave in to him outside wedlock. He was now still unmarried and still a prisoner in his room.

"There is nothing you can't do, hero," my father was saying, lowering his voice so that my mother and my brother could not hear him. "This will be the last time, Suzy, and I won't do it again. I'm your own loving father. You don't believe me, do you? I will swear on the Quran; where is it? Come on, sweetheart. Dad is in a bad mood."

"Things are tough now, Dad, not like the old times. I have to go a long way and you know how people would look at me."

"Then how come you buy your husband bango? Asaad told me."

"Dad, that was quite a while ago and he would not dare ask me to do it again."

"Okay, okay, that's unrelated. Come on, sweetheart, you know your way."

First left, second right, perhaps? Nothing here was like what it used to be; the city was strange and closed off to me. The streets, some of them ruined, were paved with old memories. According to the security guard, I was not permitted to stand any longer even at the shoreline at the tip of the gulf. "It is illegal to stand here," he said, startling me.

Large cargo ships covered the narrow, calm canal until they reached the gulf filled with soldiers and heavy artillery. Was there any goodness in others? I placed my hand over my stomach, which was tightly squeezed into my jeans. I tried to calm down the baby, which began to take shape a few days ago. It resisted the common methods for abortion. I tried them because I did not want to have a baby shoved by force into my womb, which had been closed for so long over bitterness turned sour through time and rejection. Amm Ishac no longer sold liquor and switched to selling appliances. But my father kept chasing me off with his imploring looks so I went to see Asaad, whom I knew would do what I wanted despite his hurtful show of disrespect. "You must want something," he said, meeting me with a stern face.

"Asaad, I came to see you."

"Do you think I'm your mother? A saint? A holy sheikh? Your private trashcan? You take off and come back to tell me one story after another; they are all exactly the same. First it was your uncle, now it's your husband."

"Asaad, please not you."

"Why? Why not me? Because my skin is burned with smoke or because in your honored opinion I'm a defeatist? Or are you afraid to fall in love with me, your honor, because I'm lazy and have nothing to offer but the joint I give you every time you stop by to see me? Pay attention, Professor. Have a cup of tea and a cigarette and wake up, but don't mess with me. This is a silly game."

"I'm tired, Asaad, at war with the whole world."

"Oh, stop, you're going to make me laugh until I fall over. What war and what conflict? Your father's bullet is no longer effective. And you seem fine being a loser. Everyone is holding your keys, like handcuffs."

"If Andrea were here . . ."

"Don't try. With or without Andrea, you are going to be the same."

Even if I were insane, he would not have been appeased. I could not place my helplessness into his hands because he used them to lash out at me with the horrifying truths I used to think did not apply to me. But life did not have to be right all the time. I walked away feeling ashamed. This was how everything came to an end. In order to find a way out, I had to prepare for my last chance to be free from daily demoralization and to reassign roles ruthlessly. Andrea was no longer relevant. My marriage to Essam was a failure on all accounts. Asaad continued to be like a bet I was losing all the time. The tears I shed over the cold tiles of the concrete landing in front of his door no longer had any value for him. He left me shrouded in loneliness. I tried to resist giving in to his attacks, which were grounded in misunderstanding. Feelings of loss were more powerful than any judgment. Those feelings put an end to the trust I had in someone whose friendship I thought would last forever even if I continued to live in this dim light. I had been waiting for something indefinable to happen, then I ran away to forget about it. I'd been fighting oppression for a period of time I could not determine—a month, a year, or four full decades? During all that time I had been accidentally acting like an ambassador, forced to take generous gifts to the enemy with a smile that stretched up my cheeks.

In the end, I lived in exile under constant threat from a lover or a friend whom I could not trust. I expected harm in the absence of caution. I was ruled by hysteria, where there were no windows or doors to escape through, no phone calls, no mail. I took refuge in silence and obesity until I became a sponge floating over a sea of madness before drowning forever, pulled down by heaviness and gravity. I could not feel anything except my defeated retreat, shedding blood over every inch of the life I surrendered to those who used my weakness to take full control over me. Asaad was no longer the same person who seemed to stand outside time; he was not the one I came to know during my short, occasional visits; he was not the same person who used to sit on a wooden sofa covered with quilts made from different worn-out patches. They reminded me of the blankets given by the Red Cross, along with bright-colored, large-sized clothes, and canned goods during the siege. I forgot how I used to walk next to Asaad feeling that he was five thousand years old. Now he sat as if handicapped on a sofa of cold stones instead of quilts. I was so shocked at him that the recklessness that governed me throughout my entire life now took the shape of my mother's face distorted with grief over losing her daughter. Wondering whether my mother could forgive me haunted my sleep like a nightmare. Perhaps I should ask her; she might at least say that she forgave me, even if she didn't mean it.

The darkness of the long hallway on the first floor greets me. The first floor in our house is divided into three distant rooms. The main door is still wood despite my mother's constant wish to replace it with an iron one. A large foyer, then two steps, then the room my grandmother occupied, which I have not entered since her death. On the opposite side after five steps, there is another empty room. Then the stairway to the second floor to the right; it winds around an old lavatory, which Fatma Rushdi once used when she was old and still beautiful despite her heavy makeup. She was in the company of a friend whose name I cannot remember although I can still see his broad, composed features surrounded by wrinkles that were not related to his age and did not make him any less attractive.

At the end of the hallway, facing the main door and the street, there is another room used as a storage space for my father's old machines, small piles of clothes, fabrics, rags waiting to be sewn, and thread spools, some colorful, some black and white. A thick layer of dust covers everything although the room is completely locked up. It has one shut window right next to the wall of a new apartment building owned by the Atwan family, all of whom had gorgeous dark skin. One of them was a good friend of mine, although I cannot remember her name either, I can well remember how she closely resembled a famous movie star with the same skin color and hairdo. With heavy feet I climb up a few steps, smiling at those times. Where did they go and how did they come to an end? What has happened to my memory? Are drugs, supposed to cause memory loss, to blame? Only names are lost, but I can clearly see faces and details.

The second floor is not much different from the first one except that the bathroom right next to the main door has been renovated. The floor plan is identical on each floor except for two new rooms built on top of the sewing shop. My mother rented out the shop to Amm Samir, who used it to sell herbs and spices. The two rooms had big windows overlooking the narrow alley and letting in its loud noises and the pungent smells of spices and incense.

Although the first few days were tough, I quickly got used to all of this. The smells no longer woke me up coughing or made my nose run.

Initially, I thought they would diffuse the fumes of the few cigarettes I secretly smoked so that my mother would not find out although she was no longer able to distinguish smells or noises. Loud noises had become too commonplace to urge her to find out their sources.

The house on the opposite side was also undamaged by war. The balcony on the second floor still faced our windows. Although the faces of the people who occupied that house were much changed, they maintained the gloominess they acquired after the scandal of their daughter, Thanaa. She fell in love with Kamel, the black driver of a Peugeot. He used to drive by day and night, hoping that she might be able to sneak out and meet up with him at the corner where he used to park. On the morning of a certain day, a few days before Andrea left, the men of the family ganged up on Kamel and beat him up with heavy sticks until Thanaa started screaming at them from the balcony, "Let him go. Let him go." Only then did they stop, at their leader's command, as he shouted, "She loves him and she wants to be with him, so leave him alone and let her marry him; she will have to face the consequences."

Kamel already had two wives, one a belly dancer and the other the daughter of some overweight waiter at a coffee shop. Thanaa used to be beautiful and sexy. That was before her jaw was broken and permanently disfigured when later on she asked him for a divorce. Despite the desperate attempts of Amm Rashed, her mother, her siblings, and the entire neighborhood to dissuade her from marrying him, she was adamant. After she married him, she completely lost touch with her family. No one knew much about her; she had children; she was in the Women's Orthopedics Department at the hospital with broken bones. In spite of all this, she continued to love him and to passionately defend him.

The phone rings incessantly for long periods of time. It must be Essam. I decide not to answer because I know that his mission is over and he now wants me back. The weight of this prospect makes me take to my bed. Should I go or stay? I don't think I should go back. This is the first time in decades in which I feel that I belong in this house more than anywhere else. I can also start working on choosing a topic for my doctoral dissertation, especially since the room overlooking the street and conveniently secluded from the rest of the house has become mine. My clothes are lined up on the shelves of the small metal chest for the first time. Here I belong to a world that has deep roots in my memory, which seems to be reviving after almost two weeks. Avoiding words that invoke my feelings of shame, I spread my papers out and scribble crossed lines and squares and triangles. Then I write my name in Arabic and in English in the soft light coming from behind me that makes everything seem enchanted. I trust nothing more than I trust coincidence and possibly epiphany. Sadness and happiness should have nothing to do with work. Far from being mutually exclusive, hovering between pleasure and pain, they are ridiculous feelings and one should not hold on to them because they are slippery and dangerous. Andrea's name remains the best option for my fast-moving pen, which runs out of ink, forcing the name to withdraw from the blank page. A history of foolishly thinking that I made others' lives better now comes back to haunt me.

"You have to learn to assimilate. If you were in England, which language would you speak?"

"English, of course."

"And if you were in the world of men?"

"That's a tough question."

"Here is your free answer: be a woman, a strong woman. Don't ever become a daughter or a mother or a follower. Let me teach you some English; your French will not serve you well these days."

"Teach me about love in English."

"Love, my beloved, is like a true winter; it cannot be described. I have my own winter, its coldness and its severity are not like yours. For you, love has several stages—the first is to be touched by the sword of a knight riding a horse. He frees your heart and departs, raising his sword for you and never against you regardless of how your feelings change. When he comes back for another touch, everything will change and you can take the lead if you know how to react and receive his touch as you move forward. Be careful not to fall in love looking back. You will have nothing but regret then. Don't chase ghosts. Forget about them and move on; there are boundaries even they cannot go beyond."

You were right, dear Andrea. You were never a ghost. You are a winter that will never come back no matter how much I expose myself to the cold in the evenings I spend exiled on the rooftop.

My mother outside makes the same disruptive noises over and over: she opens the door and closes it tens of times so it squeaks loudly. Her slippers make a cracking sound against the floor as she walks back and forth for hundreds of times; she alternates turning on the faucet and closing the fridge door; she stirs the spoon in her half-filled teacup. These noises fall on my brain like sharp razors, swelling my heart with anger. As I'm trying to connect with Andrea, my mother comes in smiling as if trying to probe the depths of my boredom. I feel compassion stirring in the remote places where I used to hide in the besieged city. But a sudden rage makes my face burn. My screams, which I have to suppress, are barely audible through my chattering teeth. My words are incoherent, "You are doing this on purpose."

"I thought you were sleeping."

"How can I sleep in this cacophony of noises?"

"I'm just going to the bathroom."

"Give me a break!"

"What's wrong, Suzy? Is something bothering you?"

Is this my mother asking me what is wrong and what is bothering me? When was the last time she did that? Why now when I am lost? She did not do it when she forced me out of this house at the time it was bombarded daily to send me to hell, my uncle's hell, and the hell of Khairiya's shed and her silver coins, which I now turn into amulets and feel pressing against a rupture in my right shoulder. She did not do it when we both went to say goodbye to Andrea and were kicked out. What a curse! Whose fault is it, hers or mine? It does not matter how long or short the moments we stand facing each other are. What matters is that she is giving me the chance to cry, feel the pain, and see the injustice as I look back over the decades that have passed with me stuck in the same place, my body bearing the weight of the waves heaving against the rock wall of the bay before the sun descends into the night. This woman who is now hugging me and softly patting my right shoulder with her hands is the one who brought me into this world as an idiot and the one who made my brother a monk and a recluse. Why is she doing this now? Is she planning something and trying to lighten her burdens first?

Then she splits my heart open and shoves in the same old charge, "Your problem is your father, Suzy. Take care of yourself, love."

Although I am a good judge of character, I am always taken aback by others' skill at dissimulation. Time and again, my own insecurity causes me to place all the blame on my sorry self. I wish for a death more absolute than unconsciousness. Andrea's voice caresses me. . . .

"Life is so beautiful, Suzy. But in order to live well, we have to take advantage of whatever we have. Greece is a mountain civilization and Egypt is a riverine civilization; if we were to build and cultivate in the same spirit, the whole world would be fine. We would integrate and invent."

"Does inventiveness apply only to filmmaking? Do you know what everyone says about you, even your own family?"

"I know, Suzy. Take it easy. A punk and a loser and a hopeless case. Don't believe them."

"What would happen if you tried to find a job? You speak several languages and you speak Arabic like a native speaker. Many places would love to have you."

"Or I can start my own business in maritime imports, or I can open a hotel instead of the one we lost. Suzy, don't talk like them. What I love most about you is the language you use to speak for yourself, not your mediocre imitation of others. You really are different. How could you forget that?"

"I love you but it is difficult for me to get away from here. I could go with you but come back without you. I don't want to lose you," I tell him.

He turns his back to me to go over his videos while I ponder the prospect of my life without him.

"Do you know when movies based on novels are successful, Suzy? When there is a scene where only the voices of the hero and the heroine read passages from the literary text because language is more suggestive and immediate to the viewer than just watching. For example, in Greek and Egyptian literature there are countless themes related to resistance. Old memories stored in my consciousness now inspire me."

Is that my voice talking to myself or is it Andrea's ghost, which I kiss a thousand times as I spin around excited and elated over what I've discovered? Blood loaded with adrenaline rushes through my veins. The glow takes me to the hallway, where I pace back and forth with a trembling heart as I go over the details of my inspiration, over and over until I fall asleep as I have never done before.

In the early morning, I pack one suitcase and decide to leave. My father asks me, "Are you leaving, Suzy? Did anything bother you?"

"Not at all, dear Dad. I'm just very happy. It won't be too long before I come back. Goodbye, Mama. Take good care of yourself. . . . Please."

I shyly kiss her and pick up my suitcase. I knock on my brother's door as if I'm playing a drum and say, "Bye, Selim. When I come back next time, we'll spend a lot of time together."

I no longer remember my mother, but I still see her kissing my little shoe after she took it off when I was seven years old.

The road proceeds with difficulty as it leaves the desert behind. My mind is racing ahead toward the green I am now seeing as beautiful for the first time. People have cultivated it, wishing to make it fertile. My life is perfectly ripe for a change. I should push Essam to work as well. He is not an assistant professor yet and it would not be right if I receive a PhD before he even gets his master's. I jokingly tell him that, "We should be one step ahead of the masses."

The small town seems peaceful and calm now that Khairiya's screams are gone. But as usual in beginners' books, sometimes the wind blows in directions sailors do not wish for. The house is packed with friends and filled with smoke. Debauchery stretches out in the armchairs of the living room where they are preparing for the arrival of their partner in crime, Suzy. They look like mourners at a crowded funeral. The herbal drug blanches their faces, making them look half-paralyzed.

Why should kicking the habit be so impossibly hard, forcing us to back off into imaginary walls that protect only our futility and worthlessness—traits here fully evident? But this is not an excuse. My formal attire, the pain in my face, and my fake repetitive yawns are not enough to interrupt their laughter and chatter. I snatch the joint from Essam's lips and completely finish it off so that they finally notice me with surprise, "Are you crazy?"

"You smoke like a chimney."

"You finished the whole joint in two puffs."

"Without even dropping ashes."

"I could have died when my car almost rolled into the river and you are giving me a hard time over a joint. . . . Rats."

"Now you're adding insult to injury."

"Is this how you show your friendship and your concern? You're not even welcoming me back to my own home."

I peel my eyes away from Essam's and throw myself in a chair. Apologies and reluctant greetings are forced as if at a funeral. Can't they have any new, innovative phrases suitable for the occasion? Hatred never parts from Essam's eyes as he lashes out at me, "What's the matter, sweetheart? Is this the first time you've been away?

His tone encourages them to echo his sentiment.

"Looks like we are being insulted in your own home, dude."

"What's the matter, Suzy? Get real."

"What death and what car? You look perfectly fine."

"Okay, everybody, let's go to Osama's. Or we could just go home."

The situation has completely changed and now I feel that I have to give in to Essam's reproachful looks demanding that they stay.

"Look, I'm sorry, everyone. I think being exhausted combined with a strong joint must have made me lose my mind."

I huddle in my chair. All I want now is to fall asleep. It does not matter if I'm rejected by everyone. What matters is that I should have some privacy to enable me to find my lost voice. Now, to everyone who wants me to serve them, to bring something over with a dutiful smile, I say, "Go to hell; I want to be waited on tonight."

"Why tonight?"

"I have arrived at a topic for my doctoral dissertation."

"Wow! This fast?"

"Well, listen: Greece and Egypt are two civilizations, a mountain and a river. They were both under the Ottoman occupation almost during the same time, right?"

"Keep going."

"Greek literature deals with this period."

"Kazantzakis. Death, freedom, and . . . I can't remember."

"And in Egypt?"

"Well, a lot. Fathi Imbabi's *River in Heaven* and Saad Mekkawi's *Sleep Walkers*."

"Great. If I do a comparative analysis of the Resistance hero's character, we see how the two civilizations complement each other."

"Like you and Andrea, of course."

He drags me behind him to the kitchen where I stand in a fog trying to defend myself.

"Why do you have to ruin everything good?" I say.

"Look for a different topic and stop being shallow."

One breath after another. I'm stuck in the same spot. I stretch my leg over the marble tabletop. Nothing will make me change my mind. I look toward my female friends with an understanding, encouraging smile inspired by an inner power I know they share despite how tough their lives are. Siham and Sahar belong to a world where fathers are absent, love affairs are stupid, marriages are forced, and friends stab each other in the back. Sahar dreams of getting rid of Yusif, but she is closely tied to him, not only through marriage, but because she has nowhere else to go. She cannot go back to her former life, which was caught between two homes, one at the top of the street with her father and his vicious wife, the other at the end of the same street with her stepfather's contempt. The mother deeply hates men and everything that is male, even if it is a rooster, and the daughter keeps shuttling between the two houses. Even when she is able to find a job with her English degree, she works at Dr. Rafiq's translation center. Two pounds per page. Sometimes she gets a bonus: an item of clothing, a bottle of perfume, or spending the night at the office until she figures things out. Her only cost: drenching her hair in sweat against the black leather sofa so that she has to go to the hairdresser whom she must pay in advance for the hot shower and the straightening of her disheveled hair. Marriage to Yusif becomes her only way out. He bites her white flesh with a violence that hurts her; in the morning he enjoys looking at the bruises spread over her skinny softness.

We dash toward the gateway of annihilation with our petty tricks. We burn, running and crawling, weeping and laughing, loving and hating. We tear down the ramparts of eternity fueled by an unquenched yearning for tragedy. We stop to catch our breath under an old acacia until our time is up; the shade of its branches falls on emptiness, wreckage, and dust. I take a look at Siham behind the thick smoke. She is covering her face in agony as if constantly drinking from an endless cup of bitterness. That she does regularly, regardless of what her psychiatrist says. He prefers her to regurgitate the shameful details of her life instead. She takes me aside to give me a sedative. I take it to forget who I am and what I want. As if I never had a clue, I become someone other than the person I was yesterday. Siham holds me as her captive audience, telling me whatever comes to her mind.

"We are a generation destined for wretchedness. There is no way out, Suzy. Try to adapt. Believe me, you will only end up with loneliness, insomnia, and fear if you fight back. Still, it would make no difference.

Perhaps if we had children, our lot would have been different. Why should I live with someone like Amin, talking to myself, laughing at unintended jokes, throwing up my memories each day in the bathroom? Every time I run into Amin, I ask myself, how does he see me? I see him as a scoundrel and I keep on taking pills to bolster his image, and I make up excuses for him."

Her advice wakes me up like a slap in the face. I turn the other cheek and I walk past her as if possessed by the black magic of a stupid, silly ghost. There it is: something both extraordinary and commonplace, something I did not create or wish for. Love and hatred force me to stand on my feet among perpetually dim walls that close in on me. There is only a white sink. I vomit smoke and red wine. Purple spots splatter every which way over the sink. I cry out in agony hoping that Essam will hear me; perhaps if he asks me what is wrong, my decision will be different.

I found last evening somewhat dramatic. I sat through it like a wall with two ears—and a tongue in between to moisten my lips and my mouth. No one knew anything about how broken my heart was by the aftermath of war, a war without spoils. We were all martyrs under siege, victims of historical amnesia. Every house was emptied and surrounded with filth. But there were also normal homes filled with the voices of children. Mine would not be one of them. Therefore, in the morning I decided to see Dr. Kamal and take his first offer, shoving an extra ten pounds into his assistant's hand after the doctor negotiated the fees with me in a way that implied I should change my mind. He knew that I was married and pregnancy was not a disgrace to be effaced by abortion. I did not have to tell him that I had decided to leave Essam and that I no longer wished to have a child that looked like Andrea. I wanted to run away, to flee, leaving everything behind me and have no roots to pull me back. I suffered at every step. Although the assistant prepared everything for the procedure, he still could not make the anesthesia work through my blood. I heard the doctor scolding me as I lay down between this world and the other.

"Drugs. . . . That's why the likes of you don't have children."

After an additional shot of anesthesia, I went into a blank state of non-being; nothing had color or taste or distinction. Only a lifeless odor. I came back climbing a spiral of throbbing pain in my head. I placed my hand on my stomach as the light from the window suddenly forced my eyes open. I saw the recovery room empty of everything except the white bed where I lay. In the first few moments of waking up, I could only see a white space as if I had left this world. Then a nurse entered the room, uncovered my arm to give me a shot, and I felt a great pain in my ear.

"This shot is an antibiotic. I'm sorry I had to pinch your ear hard to wake you up. You were saying some terrible things; everyone was laughing in the office. Dr. Kamal even wrote down what you were saying."

What could I have said that made me the center of this surreal play? Did I say, for example, that I never told Essam about my pregnancy? That, therefore, I was having an abortion without his consent? What would he do if he knew? He did. Someone must have seen me wobbling outside the doctor's office and everyone knew what Dr. Kamal was up to.

"I could put you in jail. You have committed a crime, Professor."

He attacked me with two punches to my stomach and insulted me by cursing my mother's name.

"You must be out of your mind. We have been trying to have a child for years."

"You are the reason. . . . Our life is a mess. . . . We can't have children to share our failure."

"Speak for yourself. I was hoping for a child to change my life for. What's the point of fighting for the future of others' children? I have nothing to live for except a child bearing my name."

"What about me?"

"You . . . you're a curse . . . a lunatic . . . a beast."

He kicked me until the neighbors interfered and he told them about my crime.

"She had an abortion without my consent. She killed an innocent life. . . . This infidel, this bitch."

Usually, our fights ended quietly and we each went our separate ways—except this one. Its details were delivered to my uncle by some do-gooder, perhaps, who volunteered this information to kiss up to the colonel for some future favor. After all, these were the times when the law did not prevail and my uncle had devoted himself to studying the applications of emergency laws to serve the interests of the people who hired him.

He quietly had Essam pulled from a party at Osama's engineering and construction office. Osama used to invite Essam and other important people over whenever he had a new client as a way to advertise the fact without calling attention to the nature of the new contract or its legitimacy. The evening proceeded and everyone was smoking dope but Essam alone out of the entire group was arrested. The rest remained in shock for a few moments before silently resuming their evening.

When one goes to bed at night and wakes up in the morning, a whole day should be over. Not for me, though, not since the first night Essam failed to come home until the following day, and my losing count of the days lasted indefinitely because I had locked myself up at home after I found out what happened and understood that it was my uncle's doing. Had Essam been someone else, he would have been arrested at home since our parties had almost gone public due to the loud laughter and talk and smoke clouds floating out of the windows. My uncle wanted to protect me again from Essam—at the wrong moment and in a way that implicated me. Everyone knew that I wanted Essam to divorce me. No words could express my feelings of utter frustration with him, a monstrous hatred visible to the naked eye.

"Love can be born in an instant, and turn into hatred. I can't go on."

When I told him that, he left two cigarettes on the bedside table right next to the two remaining anti-depressant pills and kissed me on my hot forehead. I spent the night in a peaceful tranquility interrupted by the smiles we exchanged all night, since neither of us was getting any sleep. I stayed in the bedroom trying to be strong, trying not to waver. Either love or we go our separate ways. I repeated my decision to the sound of my footsteps over the rough rug and the polished floors. Was he going to come in now after walking past the kitchen on his way to the bathroom? The low sound of running tap water made me nervous and expectant. What would his decision be? I would tell him that I didn't expect an answer now, to give it some more thought, but even this was wavering. I asked him for a decision now. Now. I tried to read and jot down notes or at least look as if I were doing so when in fact I was staring at the rectangular electric plugs and imagining they were a deck of cards. The noise increased in the bathroom. When it stopped, his face appeared at the door. I could pretend to be sleeping, but it wouldn't work. I was drawn to his silence until he incomprehensibly said, "Good night now." He resumed making noises outside. I resisted getting up to make a cup of tea as an excuse to smoke the two cigarettes. I had decided to quit smoking, but yearned for some distraction in this burdened, anxious life which I continued to live under the illusion of needing a refuge—a man different from all others. But what difference and what others?

I lit the stove and the sight of fire rekindled filled me with hunger and sleepiness, but I continued talking to myself. Work hard, Suzy, and own your strength in the battle—before you are completely consumed by smoke and violence and turned into an insignificant detail in Essam's grand story. He saw me as a woman he made and owned.

"You owe me everything," he said.

"Even my breasts, my hair, the color of my eyes, my ability to speak, my control over going to the bathroom?!"

"You are ungrateful, a bitch like all women."

"Since you are so capable, why don't you make something of yourself?"

"Feel free to pontificate. I gave you your chance and made you a professor."

"One of us has to go, otherwise, we will kill each other."

"I will go."

Silence has become our second nature, his and mine. Except for Radio London and Al Jazeera, we would have lost our relationship to language. He eats while he checks his e-mail and enters chat-rooms filled with flirtatious women. He drinks half his cup of tea and puts out his cigarettes in the remainder, then takes a nap and gets up at nighttime . . . to wait for the rats while I swallow the tears of my bleeding heart.

"I'm tired today; I need some fun." Essam issues a "fun" time for everyone and casually declares halfway through the party, "Suzy and I have decided to separate; this is our last party together unless she and I stay friends after divorce. The Professor does not like our lifestyle. She says she feels that I'm being bogged down in a mire of some sort."

"I never said that. Why are you lying? To get away with saying whatever you want?"

There were so many things I wanted to explain, but his declaration took me by surprise. This shock made me blind and insane. My eyes were hurting me as if I were wearing someone else's glasses. I felt like bursting into tears. I could not tell from which direction danger was coming at me. I saw the falling star of all my hopes and wished to die. I was still hoping Essam would fight for me.

Siham tries to calm me down, "He can't live without you. He's just high, silly girl. Essam loves you more than any of these men love their wives."

"He just stabbed me. He made his decision public without even informing me. But I have more to lose than he does."

"It's all the same; let's go back to the shit we were doing and try to forget it."

She holds my hand and seats me next to him. "If true love existed, it would never end or die." Everyone claps and yells, making Siham blush as she sits down, proud of evoking laughter over a statement she meant as a joke.

Andrea's ghost materializes. His smile fills up the room. A cloud of smoke gathers in the blue of his eyes and in the glow of his cheeks. He is wearing an off-white shirt and looking at me, the words coming out through his white teeth, "Suzy, love of my life."

"Thank you very much," I said to Essam on his way out with the rest of the men to continue the party at Osama's for which they were already late. But he never came back. Whether it was his choice or my uncle's choice for me, it did not matter. What mattered was that in the end I was confined to a space where only the wretched and half-talented were allowed, powerless in the face of hurtling violence. What was he thinking now and what would others think? Would I be misunderstood for the thousandth time?

How could life go on while I'm losing faith in justice? My uncle kicks the air with the tip of his shoe as he sits cross-legged and points his finger at my head.

"What kind of justice would you like to see, daughter of the Resistance hero? Look with your own eyes and then make up your mind: Here are letters in his own handwriting in which he turns you in along with some other insignificant people. Your name is at the top of all the reports he writes about the university: Suzy Muhammad Galal . . . Suzy Galal . . . Suzy, Suzy, Suzy. . . . Here is another one. He is ratting you out: anti-communist forces, anti-terrorism, and drug control. Is this fair? Should I let him hit my niece in front of all sorts of people? He needs to be taught a lesson."

An apology! I should apologize because before my uncle puts away his folder, he shows me the letters I wrote to Essam almost two decades ago while he was in jail.

"Isn't this your handwriting, Professor? If it wasn't for me, you would have disappeared without a trace."

Was I shocked? Or did my constant wish to play the leading role in this drama finally come true? When I used to visit my uncle as a peacemaker, fighting for freedom, with the world as my witness to defending Essam's rights, my uncle would appear half-human, egging me on to carry out his scheme. Each succeeded in humiliating me through the other. I was torn like a blank canvas pulled from two different sides until I could no longer recognize myself.

How did I look now? Now that I was eating and sleeping for the sake of eating and sleeping? With difficulty I tried to hover in my imagination. The ringing of the phone and the knocking on the door did not merit a response. Time descended like an infinite black fog.

I tried to face my uncle's accusation and face up to its consequences before I reached the age of forty. It did not matter whether or not I had enough strength because I believed in chance.

Silence and a hundred hours of isolation enabled me to confront myself, but only after I could burn away the surrounding, degrading humiliation, such as that caused by friends acting true only as long as I didn't need them, then disappearing when war was in the offing and I found myself in a disadvantageous position on the battlefield. Either suddenly or gradually I lost the spirit to fight and the ability to know what was right. It did not matter. The antidepressants poor Suzy took made her even poorer, especially since she had to educate those demons who did not value reason, "You should not use your head, it's heresy." She had to let them wander, rummaging through the dumpsters, shamelessly exposing their private parts. Now we were all stuck in the same situation, burdened with fear and indecisiveness, eating what we could find and drinking our chlorine-spiked urine. We became creatures of the lowest order. I fought very hard, my voice getting so much louder and clearer that a pin dropped would have been disruptive. I used to believe in my words then, viewing them as brilliant and prophetic, seeing their light reflected in the beautiful eyes of my students, male and female, Christian and Muslim, rich and poor alike. Their eyes would shine with rebellion, which gave me the energy to press on since not much time was left. In these lecture halls and in the rare opportunities I had when I volunteered to sub for one of the teaching faculty, I was able to outgrow the training ground, which seemed like a revolutionary stronghold, to prepare for the revolution itself, declaring that dreams did not accomplish deeds, only force would, a force acquired in our new world, which would have no bars to hold back hands and dreams. How could I have known that there was a spy among my own people, secretly taking notes? But his notes were important to a certain someone who controlled campus administration. Therefore, I was barred from public speaking and was politely told I could visit the campus only to meet with my dissertation supervisor or to receive my paycheck. I had to respond with the same politeness, asking my supervisor to meet with me at his home, and Muhyi, the payroll clerk, to please drop off my check at my home at the beginning of each month. If I happened to not be at home on that day, I had to go to the campus myself to collect my paycheck despite feeling practically unemployed. I would slip Muhyi ten pounds under the rosters because I valued his usefulness above my own.

If I died now, no one would notice my absence. Perhaps my corpse would rot like Miss Inayat's. I had not yet unpacked the keepsake she left, now hidden among the bookshelves. There was no keepsake for me yet. I didn't wish to die this way, lonely and outcast. Everyone leaves behind chaos; I planned to sort out everything before I died. The doorbell rang just as I was about to die. I got up quickly, dizzy and staggering as I tried to properly put on my slippers. As a result of lying down awake for several hours and trying to get up so quickly, I felt lightheaded. The visitor whose help I needed turned out to be Siham. As soon as I saw her, I threw myself at her and started crying over my situation since Essam had been arrested.

"What's wrong, love? What's the matter? I thought you were gone. Don't worry. I'm used to this; people like to throw themselves at me and cry."

"Do you know what happened, Siham?"

"Just be thankful. This was a nightmare. I wish they had taken Amin with him and we would have gotten rid of the two axes of evil. This is your only chance: file for divorce quickly and take care of yourself and your future plans. No one would blame you. Essam was never for you. You don't have to say anything, just run away, go back to your family. There is nothing to wait for here. These men are bad luck."

We laughed and I started packing. Siham's company stirred a secret pleasure in my feelings of guilt toward Essam.

141

"What should I take and what should I leave?"

"Take only what is important."

Of course, take only what is important, like what my mother told me when she took me away many years ago. I could hear her voice now as I was about to die at the beginning of my forties. I was about to enter a new life, knowing neither who I would be nor the face I would present to the world—not this fat, sad face.

"Stop thinking about yourself and listen to me. . . . I'm in love."

"You're in love every day. What is new about that?"

"No, this is for real—and has been for a long time. This is the love of my life, but it has no chance."

"Keep hallucinating."

"Honestly, I was in love with him before I met you, which is why I'm friends with a fun-sucker like yourself. Of course, later I began to really care about you. Do you remember when your uncle beat the shit out of you and barred you from taking the junior year finals? I used to go ask him about you every day to cover up the fact that you were actually taking the exams. This was the first time I was close enough to see the torment in his face. Maybe then I fell in love with him."

"What? My uncle Atef? This is the first time I can even imagine that someone could actually fall in love with my uncle Atef."

"It was like the thrill you get from watching *Frankenstein*. You cover your eyes with your hands but watch the scary scene through your fingers. I used to feel weak at the knees every time I walked toward him. He would stand watching everything as if he owned the universe, with one hand in his pocket and the other one stroking his hair. How I wished it was my own hand! I thought he was misunderstood, as if he were wearing someone else's clothes."

"You kept all this to yourself?"

"Everything was a mess and I was in a relationship with Amin. But your uncle was just as strongly in my heart. Maybe I should have known that my relationship with Amin was irreparably damaged when he avoided me after I was released from jail. But a few months afterward, Amin started to be very gentle as if he was trying to make it up to me. I couldn't leave him but I should have when I knew he would never be there for me. I helped him in every way I could, but in the end he was an imposter who should have been hanged on the gates of civilization. I took the risk and decided to stick with him, dreaming of one day wearing maternity clothes. I still cannot get pregnant. All the doctors say that we are fine and that our infertility is psychological and can easily be overcome. But how, when I take drugs to get over feeling sick every time he touches me? My head scarf makes me look like someone's mother. But I've only been his mother.

"'Dearest, you would not mind if my studies take me away from you, right?' I would tell him.

"He would respond, 'Of course, darling, I'm jealous but I can't be in the way of your career.' At the same time, as if that would not distract me and waste the little time I had as he kept pestering me like a difficult, stupid child, he would say, 'Sweetheart, are you working hard? Good job! Would you like a cup of tea?'

"'Thank you. I've had one too many.'

"'What's for dinner tonight? I'm already hungry.'

"'There are some leftovers in the fridge.'

"'I really would love to have stuffed grape leaves.'

"'Right away!'

"'Well, but I don't want to keep you from your work.'

"'No problem; I can finish later.'

"I always quietly gave in and quickly got up."

Siham decided to take a break and leave the room on the pretext of making tea. I realized that she was in deep pain and did not have the courage to show it. She left the room. What a mass of pain she and I would make if combined into one!

My attention quickly shifted to Andrea at hearing the sound of the German movie machine that changed the world. A horror film was playing, making our hearts pound at the explosion of the huge machine on the screen. But our shadows were falling on its black and gray colors as we danced the Syrtaki, which resembled a Nubian dance in the way shoulders and arms stretched next to each other like a tight circle. It was the only dance I knew how to do, just as a pendulum knew how to swing. I moved methodically to the right, then to the left, never losing sight of Andrea. His smile mirrored mine as we danced, pining for each other, until our souls were united. Was socialism for the sake of justice and equality then being carved into my consciousness? So that each could feel for the other as if all were one? So that a united world would emerge with no secret factions? So that we could witness the dazzling materialization of superior civilizations?

When the secret of survival became clear to me, however, the dream almost vanished. I suddenly discovered how we completed each other—through my being a woman and Andrea's being a man. A simple dance with no revealing outfits uncovered the secret to me, making everything seem clear. It exposed the curse of my unstable relationships with everyone. It turned my juvenile running away into a compendium of all my mistakes during the years of Andrea's absence—and perhaps even before then, before I saw him wrapped in bandages, his eyes turning away every time I tried to make them look into mine as he was being lifted up to the massive white ship that was taking him back to his country of origin. The ship was split in half with a thick blue line, like the one we would use to draw different sections on cardboard sheets to make wall magazines at school. We would post them on the wall together, Asaad, Andrea, Ijith, and I, all of us a symbol of the union of ancient civilizations.

Siham's voice woke me up before she entered the room, carrying tea and some sandwiches on a tray. "I was hoping to be exactly like Magda al-Sabahi in the movie *Naked Truth*: work, study, and marry an open-minded man who would take the risk of marrying a comrade. But, I swear to God, thanks to Amin I have become insane. The son of a bitch humiliated me and forced me cover up for him as he went after other women. I became ashamed of my own dreams. So one day I decided to have a fresh start and to pay your uncle a visit in his office. Do you know that I saved that date in my diary? Listen to how it went:

Fall, September, 1992
My strong resistance to Amin needs to be solidified. I told him to forget about 'love' and to let us be friends, seeking each other out in times of need. The demands of life were more pressing than his eagerness and I was tired of giving without receiving (except the minimum). This could not be resolved with empty words about 'love' and psychological battles in bed.

I feel that this nightmare jeopardizes my future and I want it over. I feel that he is shallow; nothing of what he promised me will ever come true because his conscience is dead and his mind is incapable of comprehending.

Remember to overstate everything you do even if it means nothing to you; don't sell yourself short.

Take advantage of everything to accomplish your lofty goals in life.

Never beg. Order, reproach, and be angry; your natural gifts grant you these rights.

Give yourself enough time to build your glory so that your name outlives you, since, as a woman, your children will not take your name. . . . A perfect recipe; I would repeat it to myself as I kept looking for a way out.

"I had to start a new, safe life, find a stable job, and establish some measure of acceptance with everyone. I decided to visit your uncle, Atef Bey, in his office to ask him to help me with my university appointment. The driver went a few meters past the building; I handed him two pounds. I walked toward the soldiers and intelligence agents rigidly posted in front of the building like the army of a deferred war. The details of the old torture made my body tremble. I was deeply frightened as if I was not the same woman who had been tortured there. I tried to calm myself down. 'He is only human like the rest of us,' I kept telling myself. 'I know. . . . God help me.' They were randomly arresting people at that time, but at any rate, listen to what followed. I started to walk confidently as I raised my voice, 'I have an appointment with Atef Bey.'

"The soldier at the gate turned me over to another one inside. The building was in better condition than when I was in jail. Today, my hands were free, but the prisoner inside of me was whispering, 'I have nothing to lose.' When I felt guilty, I thought that whether the comrades forgave me or not did not matter because everyone completely abandoned me when I was alone in jail and no one visited me."

"At that time my situation was very bad," I interrupted, "I was too afraid to even leave the house. Everyone hated me." I wanted to defend myself fiercely. Siham's eyes showed understanding, but she continued with her story.

"I was on a sinking ship, quietly abandoned by my friends who left me tied to two rough oars, fighting overwhelming undercurrents all by myself. I withdrew convinced that there was no other choice and that I was pre-destined, like a violated Magdalene virgin, to receive one condolence after another for every wound to my body until that body became an empty shell. I directed my anguish toward your uncle Atef's locked door until the security guard opened it and I quickly walked in. He rose from the chair that was surrounded by the huge desk, extending a slightly fat hand, not the same hand that slapped my face and left its mark when I was defending my relationship with Amin and saying that I was free.

"When I reminded him of this incident, he said, smilingly, 'Well, back then things were different and you did not cooperate. There was no reason to be stubborn. Everything would have been over quickly if you had cooperated. I calmly asked you for just a few names and details, which I already knew so well that I even tried to refresh your memory with some of the evidence I already had. You only had to go through the motions to have the forms filled out with names, places, dates, statements, manifestos. You only had to speak up to put an end to your suffering and go home.'

"Oh, how sweet he was, and naughty, as he licked me with his eyes as if I were a sugar cube he dared not touch. I looked strong, pretty, and smart, and it made him so proud of me."

"Is that why he is always asking about you and Amin? I thought he was cross-examining me. You really did shake him up, didn't you?"

"Oh, Suzy, does he really ask about me? Oh, what a sweetheart. Well, then, keep listening. I was not feeling any fear despite having had no food or sleep all night and half of the day. I was forgetting everything I had suffered as I went over the painful details of my jail time when I used to carve shorthand messages on the cement wall—'With my own blood, I water the seeds of freedom,' and stuff like that. These slogans were no match to his inner fire when he said, 'Okay, would you like to start. . . . Or would you like me to start?'

"Oh, Suzy, your uncle is a real gentleman, calm, kind, disinterested. He was turning into someone else, someone who understood everything as he tapped the papers with his pen and carelessly leafed through the files.

"I became more like myself. When I talked, his silence was only interrupted with smiling nods as if he was my therapist. Then a coworker of his suddenly barged into the room and dispelled the softness that had permeated my meeting with him. The fellow greeted him, gave him a hug, and left. Then, without even looking at me, he became exactly the way he was years ago. He loudly banged the desk with his fists, his voice ringing through the walls and over my head as he spoke on the phone, 'How could someone just walk into my office like that? Prepare to sleep in jail tonight.'

"White mixed with black and blue in the paintings over the wall. Pens and pencils seemed to shiver over the desk. I was rattled. I began to melt like a sugar cube shoved under rotten teeth. After a forced promise from him to help me, I left feeling as if I had committed a crime.

"That's what happened with your uncle that day, which I have never told anyone. It was Amin who betrayed me and told everyone. When I reproached him and reminded him of his multiple scandals, he told me he was a man, entitled to do whatever he wanted; a bunch of lies and fabrications—he makes one mistake after another and calls us women with frail minds. That's why I'm a feminist now."

I had heard about this incident from Amin but something inside me sympathized with Siham. I understood her crisis and her loss and ascribed her decision to turn to my uncle to her right to be appointed at the university. She graduated at the top of her class, yet some of her classmates with lower GPAs were appointed. I knew that she was helping Amin with his doctoral dissertation after he mysteriously finished his master's thesis. He could not refer to its topic without turning to her, which she presented with passion and deep knowledge. He systematically crushed her, completely subjecting her to his will. Precious and beautiful years, days and nights, were wasted in such obscure dealings that we started to think they were facilitating certain things for each other.

Siham started gathering her stuff, promising before she left to visit me in Suez after she divorced Amin, so that we could have our fresh beginning.

"You know what, this could be the season for divorces: you and Essam, Sahar and Yusif, me and Amin. . . . God willing."

Amin was the root of evil, my uncle ruled in a way that provided protection only to the powerful, and Essam was a gang leader. And we were their cronies. We finished their demonic artwork with our innocent touches in this perpetual epic of fear. Evil—the evil lurking inside of us—crushed any attempt for a fresh start.

I was in a battle with myself. I had to honor the decisions I would make after phrasing them in a way that enabled me to define my world and recognize my enemy—regardless of how difficult this might be. The essence of the game was lurking around the enemy. Agatha Christie's words, but they might make sense in these tough times. While we all seemed victims, we had raised the banners of violence, destruction, and waste of resources when we let the world be ruled by arrogant bastards. We took note of their victories over our unnamed remains as they ascended on their dreadful way to overarch bright stars, declaring, in their melodic voices, the end of the world and the beginning of the age of peaceful negotiations. We should scream at them demanding that they do not sign sales agreements and concessions before we give them a detailed account of their historical betrayals, their purchase of the cancers that devoured both the children and those great people who face massacres with paralyzed, dark-skinned smiles. Someone has to be there to diminish the brightness of their smiles as they prepare their heirs after escaping punishment for running people over on sidewalks, accepting human sacrifices like false gods disguised in the drugged minds of the wretched.

I hold Ms. Inayat's bundle in my hands. I think about opening it and throwing it in the river after I burn it, but I'm too afraid. If Siham had waited a bit longer, we would have opened it together. I fearfully shove it into my suitcase while thinking, What could have been slipped into Christ's plate at the Last Supper? Was I a good supper for Andrea the night he was slaughtered like a wild pig? Did it make any sense for me to install Essam in Andrea's place and enable him to finish off what Andrea had left untouched on his plate? Did it make sense that I let him destroy me while he was only pretending to be celebrating—others, meanwhile, enjoying the show as if devouring a royal dish seasoned with conspiracy and secret ingredients? Andrea arose as I smiled at my vision of him. I saw them lapping up drops of wine that had fallen to the round wooden tabletop and regretting each drop that dried up.

What would I do with myself? How could I recognize what was real? These questions went through my mind day and night, making me delay leaving for hours and for days. I was trying to clear my head. I recalled details, sorted them out, tried to have an objective understanding of the Other, any Other; it was important to determine my exact relation to this Other so that I didn't hold on to fantasies.

A sudden impulse strengthened my resolve and I decided to answer the phone if it rang and open the door to the first caller, who turned out to be my uncle telling me about my mother's death.

Act 4

Feminist:
Forty in One

From which ending should I begin? This is the question to which I had devoted myself before I decided to emerge from the blank space of my self-imposed isolation.

When I began to arrange for reconnecting to the world and looking for true friends, Siham was the first one I thought of. She was the one who found me first and paid me a surprise visit at my father's house.

I was living by myself on the third floor before it was even finished. I moved my mother's mirror and my father's manual sewing machine in, thinking I might need the machine to adjust the clothes that no longer fit me now. I went to see Amm Munir, the old Marxist, who used to lend Asaad books. We used to visit him whenever we needed closure to one of those long irresolvable debates we would have. His face was the color of antiques and his body was as delicate as the wooden artworks precariously stacked up all the way back into the dark recesses of his storage room. Heavy steam cut the darkness as it gushed from a teakettle on top of an old stove in the middle of the room. I had planned to furnish the third floor with old pieces of furniture to match the French style of my mother's mirror, and he was still selling pieces left over from the old palaces.

"A little bit of paint and glue and it would look exactly as it used to," he said as I followed him over the dirt-encrusted cement floor of the cellar. Assuming he knew what I still believed in and regarded as relevant, he kept talking about his old friends who embraced socialism as a valid idea, three generations fighting oppression, poverty, and a class system that was devouring the world from within.

"We were Christians and Muslims, rich and poor, men and women, all looking forward to the masses, dreaming that justice would invigorate their faces, that their weakness and their poverty would be erased, hoping to defuse the hatred that made them spit in the face of life all the time. Your generation wasted everything and desecrated our struggle. You took nothing seriously, as if this was merely an opportunity for the rich to show off in their spare time, for women to find husbands, and for the poor to get even and make the rich pay back. . . . All alike, everyone looking for a way out without any faith or ethics. Now 'communist' is an insult we evade by using the word 'Marxist.' But you're also victims. You're a college professor, how much money do you make? You're buying used furniture and your eyes are filled with sadness. In any case, look at this. This was the desk of the chief of Abdeen's court; he and his clerk used to sit next to each other. That was the time when socialism and a will to fight still existed. Now, we are yelling in the middle of nowhere. Notice how wide it is. Have you ever seen anything big enough for a chief of justice from the upper class and a poor clerk on the lowest step of the ladder? Take what you want, Suzy. I'm tired. I want to get rid of everything. Don't worry about the price tag. I just want someone to appreciate and take care of this stuff. I'm moving to Canada to live with my kids. There is nothing for me here."

I picked up a few pieces that seemed to match. As a gift, Amm Munir gave me a frame identical to my mother's mirror but it contained a beautiful painting of the Virgin Mary. He also gave me two chairs finished with ebony that I planned to put on each side of the mirror, facing the frame, to make the place look more in order. He invited me to stay for tea with him and his friend the archaeologist whose career boiled down to fitting together loose pieces of arabesque. After the time he spent working in museums in Genoa, Italy, he decided that restoration was not done correctly in Egypt and mentioned in passing some petty thefts. He was not trying to implicate anyone in particular. But as a result, he was the one who was punished. After that, he turned to silence and to long debates with himself. These debates led to a conclusion he often declared in a loud, tremulous voice, "Anyone who spends huge amounts of money on monuments and takes the risk is bound to treat them with extra care. It is one way to protect our human heritage from those who don't even know its value. Do you know how they invented the train in the west? Do you know how clean their streets are? Why people there walk fast? Because they respect their heritage and know how to build on it. People who know history, dear lady, avoid repeating the same errors. People who don't care about it never find peace or sustenance. But the problem is that when our entire heritage is stolen or lost, what will we have left?"

He placed his cup of tea, two-thirds full, on the table and got up. He became absorbed in gluing one piece of arabesque to a wooden screen. Through the spaces in the wood, he looked so admirable. Whenever a piece of arabesque fit, he would say, "Many thanks, many thanks."

This was a lover grateful for the idea of reunion with the beloved. He looked skinny in his oversized woolen sweater.

I also bought such a fantastic chest largely because of its small, secret drawers. I saved Ms. Inayat's coal-colored bundle in one of them. I no longer felt as thrilled about it as I used to feel when drifting away in clouds of smoke from tobacco mixed with those ever-present illegal substances. Had I lost the ability to feel surprise, fear, or love? A new outlook was making me lose the desire for everything, as if I were a faded old scrap of paper left over from a distant death. I hired a pushcart to move my new treasures and gave the driver the address for him to go on ahead of me. I thanked Amm Munir and asked him to give my regards to his friend. I left feeling deflated and no longer excited about the independent new home I was about to have. I was wondering why the appearance of good people in our lives only indicated frightful futures. Regardless of whether they were consciously doing so or not, all the wretched people I met were engaged in the process of fitting together pieces of arabesque infested with termites. Termites were already tearing through the pieces of furniture I bought from Amm Munir. I asked him to come over. He kept walking in circles around the furniture distraught by the fine dust that surrounded each piece.

"Termites! Termites in my wood! That has never happened to me before."

Then he looked up and calmly said, "I was taught by Italians in Alexandria. They taught me everything. But no one expected termites. At any rate, it doesn't matter. Stop by anytime to pick out other pieces."

He left me bewildered, trying to figure out ways to defeat the fine dust I was finding every day until I decided that the termites were so slow in devouring wood that I could live with them for a long time. In fact, these termites inspired me to act quickly, as if I were fighting a mysterious force and had no time to spare.

Wasn't it fitting then that I preferred to drink the cup to the last drop? That I knew the sky could clear up after being darkened by airstrikes? These were the thoughts I entertained as I lay down on the big metal bed that replaced Amm Munir's Marie Antoinette-style bed. I was watching the mosquitoes, which somehow knew that I had pots of plastic flowers lined up from the main door of the apartment to my bedroom. I was watching them through the green mosquito net my father had sewn with a long needle like a small blade that seemed to grow larger in his hands as it went through the large holes in the fabric. The mosquitoes seemed now to be falling like black-shadowed rockets whenever they surrounded one of the bright yellow holes in each sunflower pot.

How can I find a way out? Long days here or short days there. . . . Either way is a waste of life.

At this moment Siham was knocking at my door. To stand up, I lifted one corner of the net and squished a hungry mosquito, leaving a dark stain on my tent for a long time. The rest of the mosquitoes swarmed upon the green surface among the sunflowers and their dried dead comrades until I had to take the net down and wash it to avoid being completely crushed under its weight.

I felt that God had deprived me of my mother's embrace to feel permanently cold. I could not turn to my father. Men do not embrace except in the times of sadness that leave indelible marks on their souls. During the siege, we used to rummage through Red Cross donations, looking for stuff we could use. We saw signs of wealth and luxury. Even the dress I found wrapped in paper the color of sunset sand was huge and embroidered with flowers that looked as if pressed against rotten grapes. I kept it, thinking that I was going to put it on one day to show off my long neck and shoulders. I would sit cross-legged to show off my knees through the slit in the skirt. I would put it on and take it off and put it on again, switching my legs, until I finally took off to hide it deep in my closet.

Now I was brushing against the flowerpots that lined the hallway connecting my room to the main door exactly at the top of the stairway. Siham, relieved to see me, stood on the wood landing.

"I didn't think you were home and I didn't know where to go!"

"Oh, my God! How did you get here?"

She was trying to put down her suitcase while I was hugging her with deep affection, longing for someone who connected me to another world, outside this house, someone that knew everything about me.

For the first time, I felt that I needed a witness to my failure. I explained myself to her and she listened with understanding. We talked about everything that related to our marriages, but of the marriages themselves we did not speak. Perhaps because what went wrong with these marriages was not only the result of relationships that did not work out, but was the basis of all the losses incurred once we lost our faith in everything we were taught. We went over everything and everyone and came up with as many amusing comments as we could. We ate a lot and had many cups of Nescafé with condensed milk. Asaad had sent me a big box of Nescafé and a few imported red apples as a gift.

"Why don't you introduce me to this Asaad? He sounds like an amazing character."

"If you want character, I'll show you, but not Asaad. He will make fun of both of us."

To show my gratitude to the friend who brought me back to life with her sense of humor, I took her for a walk along the main road that split the city all the way to the tip of the canal. On the way back, we took one of the back roads by the shore. I showed her the secret route I used to take, the Gharib Mosque, Asaad's café, the Coptic Orthodox Church, and, finally, we went to Andrea's house after my decision to introduce Siham to Andrea's sister. That was the highlight of my efforts to welcome her. She did not try to hide how impressed she was as she passed her fingers over the small pieces of furniture that decorated the house or how fascinating she found Rebecca and everything she did, even the way she sat down keeping her thighs straight with a slight space for air between her knees. When Rebecca got up to look for plates, I whispered to Siham, "What would you have done if you had seen Andrea?"

Before she could answer, Rebecca came back with a tray of small pastries and placed them by the teacups on the small, low side-table. She sat down and began to talk. How wonderful it was to have someone who knew the same stories; now everything was coming back to life.

"Do you remember Monsieur Adel? He sent me a letter threatening that if I didn't stay out of his way, he was going to hurt me. What else has he ever done to me? I fell in love with him and I married him. He stole my money, kidnapped my daughter, and divorced me. Then I married Asaad who drove me crazy, locked me up, and confiscated whatever I had left. All I care about is my daughter. The purpose of my life is to get her back. I tried the police, the consulate, and now I'm turning to bullying. I only have one demand, my daughter, and I don't care how I get it done. I asked the consul to help me. 'If you look for him, you will find him. Kidnap her like he kidnapped her before. I will do anything to get her back.' He smiled, gave me money, and personally walked me to the door. He thought I was crazy. Am I crazy, Suzy? Ask your friend. What's her name?"

"Siham. My name is Siham."

"Do I look crazy to you? I can feel my daughter close to me. I see her looking for me in the photos of mothers with children safe in their arms. I can't leave this place without her. I have no one to turn to. I did all I could. I asked everyone for help, but these are the days of complete detachment."

I walked up to her and took her in my arms. She must have forgotten how wonderful it feels to be in someone's arms. She held on to me and cried quietly, her soul and her body reconciled like a child finding her way back home after being lost among streets that all looked alike.

"My daughter, Suzy. . . . You know a lot of people. . . . Tell them my daughter needs to be in my arms. I'm tired of holding on to air. I need to touch her, show her how to play piano, read poetry to her, and teach her different languages so that she can talk to the world in whichever language she likes most. Help me, Suzy. Asaad always said that you were important and well-connected. My little girl never liked her father. He used to scare her. She would never have left with him of her own free will. He kidnapped her and took her away from me."

Mariam, Rebecca's child, must be over thirty years old now. The last time I saw her was more than twenty years ago. She was jumping up the

154

steps of the ship ahead of Andrea who, covered in bandages, was being carried on a chair. His mother's face was hidden behind a black lace scarf. The family was heading north of the Mediterranean to one of its small islands, leaving Rebecca behind by herself. She caused havoc whenever she went, unable to hold onto anything, even the ability to have a second child.

"Just forget it." That was what the doctor told her, which she mimicked with such conviction that we had to laugh as she dropped her cigarette in the water that filled a marble ashtray. Like me, she could not even crush a cigarette butt.

"'Not even a cat,' he said. 'Your acids kill embryos. . . . Being honest is the only way I can help you. Don't expect to be pregnant again.' Would you like some red orange juice? Do you remember how much Andrea loved it?"

"Of course she does," Siham said, looking curiously at me. We kept smoking, drinking, and laughing until a foggy state enveloped us along with the intertwined clouds of our cigarette smoke, three losers putting up a last fight against their fates whose endings were looming—to hell with marriage, and with work, and with family. We were huddled against each other like three barren trees. Our eyes had a frantic, empty, broken look. The three of us were divorced and over forty. Siham was trying to make up for her elimination by writing master's theses and sometimes doctoral dissertations.

"For the low price of three hundred pounds for a master's and four hundred for a PhD. I don't even care if I'm not invited to the defense. I already know the outcome and get no less than honors. As for high honors, I'm saving those for myself when I finally finish my own master's thesis, which has now been postponed and revised for so many times. It is an excellent piece of research."

Rebecca no longer dared step into the hotel, which Asaad took over and was using to commit atrocities, according to what she said.

"He slaughters people and stuffs them into big bags. He drinks their blood when he is thirsty. I wanted to run a five-star hotel. I wanted to handpick its guests and teach them how to be classy. Oh, mon Dieu!"

We were three women in a daze, consumed with sorrow over what we had lost, going through our old debts to write down what others owed us whether in the form of years or free gifts, pretending that we still had a reason to stand on firm ground. I was almost incapable of sustaining any effort except missing Andrea, which I pursued as a way to help me figure out my life. This was similar to what research meant to Siham— a way to show her superiority—and to what the hotel meant to Rebecca— a symbol of the status of her family whose roots were cut off by bigoted, ethnically motivated upheavals. Like dear little girls, we exchanged stories about our sad interactions with others, but with an insanity fit for gods devoted to taking care of the children we never had. Rebecca tried to banish silence with memories.

"I used to trust Asaad. I thought he was going to help me and show me a way out. I found myself living under the same roof with a stranger who stared at the layers of fat in my body and filled me with nervous despair. He was so revoltingly methodical. He only spoke to me when he absolutely had to. He had clandestine relationships, visitors in expensive clothes and strong perfumes that spread through the house like waves drowning me in fear. I did not think he was connected to any one important or unimportant. I thought he was against everybody, an outcast like me. I could never imagine him socializing, cracking jokes, and patting shoulders. I always saw the little boy inside him, incapable of hurting anyone. I knew a lot of men, but he was the only one who taught me how to make love—as long as it was in the dark. He would turn off the lights, close his eyes, and make me feel like the brightest and prettiest concubine in the whole world. But when the lights came back on, he would again treat me like his mother—at best—or like a whore or like one of his cronies who worked for him in dealing drugs, hard currency, and weapons."

When did all that happen? Where was I? Rebecca must be talking about a different person. She ignored my questions and brought three more bottles of beer to the table, which we did not drink out of glasses as we proceeded with our women-only session.

She told us about the meetings he ran with utmost strictness, with people who had nothing in common except their dependence on him. He would entice and frighten them, controlling them with silk ropes he held in his own hands. He could either loosen or cut those ropes, depending on how loyal and humble they were.

"When he turned against his brother-in-law," she added, "whom he considered the root of all evil, hidden crimes and buried bodies floated to the surface. What could I have done when I heard with my own ears that his brother-in-law helped him get rid of my brother? Fear is palpable, my friends. When it hits—like death perhaps—nothing remains the same. I turned to rage and craziness to avoid reality."

"At your service," these were the words that frightened her whenever he used them. He would sound like a cook with secret recipes in a big kitchen. First, she had to overcome the feeling that she needed him before she could decide what her next step should be. How could he read her mind? She did not know, but he was able to make her feel awful while he assured her that he would not stand in her way and that he was there only to advise and help her. Every time she expressed her wish to sell the hotel and leave, he said that the time was not right yet.

"'You're too tired to make a decision like that, just wait a little bit.'

"'But I feel good. I feel more than good.'

"'You feel 'good' or you feel 'more than good'? You can't even talk straight.'

"'I have to go, Asaad.'

"'Where would you go, honey? You belong here with me. Take your meds and go for a short nap.'

"I would take the meds to stop him from harassing me. Convicts usually know why they are behind bars, but I had to bear burning against the cold steel of his insurmountable prison. Fear haunted my uneasy sleep, which was interrupted by Asaad's return from his mafia-like business. The pills made me confuse fear with loneliness and need for human touch. He would come home late at night with a big plastic bag held to his chest, filled with unimaginable stuff. Fear would spread like cancer through my body and sever the ties I had with him. It was never love that brought us together; I just needed him. When I saw him reloading his gun, I finally broke my silence and screamed out. He held me down and stopped my mouth with his hand until I passed out. When I woke up, he and his belongings had disappeared; I looked everywhere in the house, filling the void with my prayers. How could one reason with a senseless power? All I want is my daughter, divorce, and going back home. Could you help me? And you, what's your name?"

"Her name is Siham, Madame, and we will do our best to help you."

Her body started to go through convulsions as she sat huddled over in her chair. We bade her goodbye and walked out in silence until Siham said, "Nothing makes more sense than insanity. Why should we start from the beginning? On the contrary, we should start from the end and work our way back bit by bit until we reach the beginning; by that point, we would have figured out the problem. Right, Ms. Intellectual?"

We burst out laughing uproariously, disregarding our conservative appearance and the contemptuous looks we received from outsiders, those who took over the city and shrouded it in darkness.

Every word now has more than one meaning. Every promise is likely to be broken. Loss no longer counts and the story goes on. Is it women's fate that their stories be filled with anguish whenever their memories are invoked? Is it true that we are essentially alike regardless of how different our beliefs may be? Is this my own voice or Siham's anguished one telling her story?

Since her father passed away, her family started assigning to her the small jobs her cousins would turn their noses up at either because it was too hot or because they were too busy with schoolwork. . . .

"Thus, it was always my lot to burn under the scorching sun and to have to set my own priorities aside. Yet, a strong, persistent urge to find a way out carried me through those times when my uncles were using me. Everyone treated me like an orphan. I no longer had my father to protect me by being the head of the family whose opinion was needed for everything, even the amount of fat in meat and the difference between wrapping it with paper or plastic. There are laws for cheating among butchers. Would you believe me, Suzy, if I told you that a butcher is always intimidating to a customer regardless of whether the customer is poor or rich? Around that time, my grandfather had just returned from performing the Hajj. In the butcher's family, this ritual indicates the point at which the father turns his power over to his son, now more knowledgeable and wiser in the ways of butchery. That was the position saved for my father, who had earned it by passing several tests with remarkable success. For example, if a beautiful, seductive woman is buying meat at the shop, how would he act? That was one test and my father had to pass it regardless of how he felt about beauty, poverty, or even a hungry cat starving for a little piece of meat. He had to keep his feelings to himself with no one to confide in except me. In addition, he had to endure his brothers' animosity until one day one of them stabbed him in the heart as he was stepping into the main butcher shop. The brother claimed that he did not see him and did not mean it. A fight erupted between my uncle and my grandfather while my father stood there, squeezing his bleeding heart with his hands until he could not resist the pain anymore and fell, eyes shut, against the fresh meat hanging from the meat hook. Perhaps death relieved him from haggling with some woman over the amount of fat in half a kilogram of meat, some woman carrying fresh vegetables on her way home from work, who had to buy meat to satisfy her husband's belly. My father died and left us on the top floor in the family house. No one stopped by to see us except to give us meat they did not need. I always had to remove the pieces of blood-stained paper stuck to the cold meat. There are no theories to make up for the loss of the father.

"'It's not your turn to clean the stairway yet, but could you have Siham mop it anyway? The kids don't want to do it and they are stubborn; come on, Siham.' I hear my uncle's voice calling my name. I look at my mother reproachfully on my way to the bathroom. I fill the bucket with water gushing from the hose like the anger pouring out of my heart. I rush to do it before she does. I knew she would gladly mop the five-story stairway with running water instead of me because, although she never said it, she was worried about the young men in the family staring at my rear. Although they went to college, they worked as butchers and had to undertake the same tests. My main goal was to show them my superiority and make them look up to me. That's why I made every effort to stay at the top of my class and to be an activist able to run meetings and draw people to great ideas. But look at what I've become now."

Siham is able to walk in a straight line along the sidewalk. I like the way she walks, especially when the streetlights shine over the tips of her rose-colored walking shoes, accentuating the steadiness of her steps. I say with what has become my characteristic wisdom, "You should take pride in what you have."

"All right, Ms. Intellectual. Have you heard the news? It turns out that Judas is innocent. Not only that, but according to the internet, there is a manuscript that says it was Christ who used him to obtain glory. What a catastrophe! How are they going to fix that in all the poems and novels and therapy sessions? Can you believe that the son of a bitch compared me to Judas when I went to see your uncle about helping me with

159

my university appointment? But I graduated valedictorian and the university recognized me in the graduation ceremony with the rest of the students who graduated with honors. I put on the regalia and the cap. True they were a bit faded, but the photos my mother took of me with my uncles, my cousins, a few high-ranking people, and some professors are good enough to testify that I was valedictorian. I should have been appointed because I deserved it and I had to defend my right. But such is my luck; every time I try to stand up for myself, I fall in love and forget everything else, even myself. Why? Can you tell me why that happens?

"If there was a reason, it wouldn't be luck. It would be something completely different."

She told me about the nature of her work as an editor of dissertations, which went as far as rewriting them as long as the title and the basic, simple idea remained the same, a copying and pasting job that did not contribute to any academic research. Since her job did not end until the dissertation was successfully defended, she had to act as a mediator between several parties. She was known for having good connections with many people and was even using chat rooms to look up friends. She taught me how to use them one day before she left early one morning to continue running in her rose-colored shoes. She left me pondering the value of a glory one achieves at the cost of others. This was the first question I posted in a chat room, hoping that someone would have an answer.

Ijith's e-mail address was included in his last letter. His letters were few and far between, filled with clichés we learned at grammar school. I did not wish to write back letters that would sound as dry as his, but I typed up his e-mail and found him online. He responded immediately and we exchanged a few empty words in English before we were able to communicate with some of the old sincerity.

"Suzy, how are you? I miss you."

"I miss you, too. What's going on? Any news?"

"A fascinating story about using new technology to study an old manuscript; it reveals that Judas had an agreement with Jesus in return for the latter's glory."

"I heard about it. Do you think it's true?"

"There is nothing new about the story. The real issue is the timing. This is not a good time to bring this information to public attention. It's not good for you or even for us. Judas's exoneration will cost the world a lot.

"Suzy, where are you? Did you log out? Finding Judas innocent will not erase their crimes; they will remain the same, perhaps even more aggressive: wars, conflicts, unequal use of power. Everyone would pay the price. The map will have to undergo an ethnic makeover. Reena is on the phone, she is hiding in a hotel in Paris. I have to log out. Do you remember Andrea?"

"Andrea? I only remember him and his words and the maps drawn in his blood, the color of red wine."

"I don't understand. Goodbye."

I spend my time reading, which makes me hungry. I share my food with my uncle's cat. I take care of her whenever my uncle visits his daughters, which is not a visit in the usual sense. He waits for an hour or so in front of the apartment building where his ex-wife now lives after selling the Faisal Street condominium that cost him an arm and a leg. Their divorce papers were peacefully signed without her dragging him to court, which she had initially threatened to do, because he gave in to her demand for power of attorney over his pension payments. The money from his retirement plan went into a savings account he was able to live off in addition to what he made out of selling the family estate. Essentially, he lived like a bum in my grandmother's room downstairs out of his early retirement money, only going out when his ex-wife permitted him to see his daughters. When that happened, he would try to make it all up by buying them expensive clothes and taking them to fine restaurants and such. He had to take them home to their mother before nine o'clock in the evening, loaded with gifts. But they didn't even care enough to wave goodbye from their balcony, to which his eyes stayed glued until the mother remembered that she should let him know the girls had made it safely to the seventh floor and waved her hand, signaling that he should leave now that his mission was over.

With his daughters and his ex-wife, my uncle pretended to be extra liberal; he assumed a democratic stance that verged on the neutral. When he asked me to watch his cat while he was gone, I let her in through the small cat flap, which meant he didn't have to see me. There was no such small door for Siham to see him before she left. We had heard the chains rattling around the iron lock when he was unlocking the main gate, then heard him loudly slamming the door to his room. Perhaps if he had heard the cat meowing, he would have opened the door. But I didn't pursue this because I felt that if Siham were to see my uncle in his current state, the infatuation she had spent the whole night describing, until we were yawning and stretching in the daylight, would have ended. Her voice had a richness that made it sound deeper when she talked about how they resumed their relationship after she and Amin broke up.

"I was lost. I had no faith in myself or in anyone else. My uncles' and my cousins' eyes haunted me, prying into my failure. I happened to run into your uncle. He was gone as soon as he arrived, much like a hurricane. I could not distinguish joy from pain in the way he smiled, always leaving, always tossing me into a wild sea until I became weightless like a leaf, floating down from a blue sky to a green fragrant moss. It was a new beginning and I thought it would be the last one, descending upon me like a divine gift of youth and strength. But he was consumed with feeling sorry for himself twenty-four hours a day until the whole world revolved around his injured ego. He was like the hero of the novel *The Tartar Steppe*, who wasted his life preparing for a war that removed and sacrificed him at every political turn. The only thing he could give me was a profound fear. Important aspects of my life would upset him. Reproaching me was a daily routine as bitter as black coffee, which we had to drink every night before we went to bed to turn our angry nightmares into a destructive reality. I did love him, Suzy. I know it was wrong, a betrayal of my old Marxist ideals. When a man knows he owns you, he shows his ugly face—so imagine how ugly the face of the head of intelligence forces would be. But my willpower vanishes when I think of how much he needs me. I can't live without having people needing me. I'm thinking about posting an ad."

Before she left, I promised to help her see my uncle on her next visit. Usually after visiting his daughters, he shut his door and his ears to all pleas, no matter how persistent. He would crawl into a hole, grow his beard, and disavow anything that might bring him back to life, which of course included Siham, who was always eager to lend him a helping hand. She stood at his door like a supplicant lover for a long time, begging him to let her in, calling him the sweetest names, while I sat on the front steps in despair until she left at five o'clock in the morning. That was the day I resumed my old relationship with Ijith and revisited those old memories.

It was hard for my uncle's cat to share my food with me. She circled around it and sniffed it several times before she walked away to crouch over the monitor and watch me taking a short nap with my face pressed against the black keyboard. Everyone was rushing into my room, trying to look at me exposed. Essam was smiling, determined to hurt me. They were all there, watching and having a good time. Andrea was standing farther away behind my grandmother's shadow. Ijith, the thinker, was waving behind the siege. Asaad Gomaa, who lived for others, had half of his face disfigured as if by a bullet. My friends' heads were turned to one side. Those running for office were giving subtle signals to crush women when they stuck their demands for freedom into the ballot boxes. Unjustified anger pushed bullies to harass women at voting locations until they were forced to leave. Siham was chasing some scoundrel, drawn to the way he was contemptuous of her, even in her sleep. My father and his friends were having a side conversation before the siege was lifted, "Not every death is martyrdom, Nasr, and not every martyrdom is death."

My flesh was still eroding. Khairiya was still bleeding as she reached out to clutch a ten-piaster coin with her fingers. She held it close to my eyes, then feebly said, "Glory to the cities of eternity; shame on the cities of silence."

The cat's feet were walking over my back as I leaned forward. The keyboard buttons were now hurting my face. I pushed her off my back and wiped the corner of my mouth and my eyes. It was an awful sleep, invaded by the whole world, turning me into a mere object that screamed and called for help with no response, with no voice, torn by bloody conflicts with no blood.

Black keys will not fill you up, white-haired cat, and you won't like cigarette ashes either. If you like my flesh, go ahead and eat it instead of sticking your claws into the flesh of a fool over forty, just waking up, a woman who never sleeps soundly, whose body is regularly exposed during the carnivals held for the memorials of dust. Sloth confirms the end of my life together with my autonomy and my sanctity. Bombing is everywhere while I'm covering my own face and body with dust. I keep my eyes focused on the wood post that does not look like a cross except in its lower half. The same verse from the Quran is engraved on every tombstone, "From God and to God we return." But destruction surrounds me and I give in to loss; I call for the end of the resistance in the heart of the siege. I run in three directions: Adabiya, the Triangle, and Ismailia Road. The roads are filled with bandits ready to ferociously attack the pilgrims' caravans. In cases like this, I can only escape through the eastern harbor to Andrea's ghost.

No matter how much it will cost me, even if I have to turn to the devil himself, I have to win a scholarship to get my PhD from the University of Salonika, Greece. I will be able to save whatever is left of my life there, now being projected on an old screen in self-imposed exile day and night. Faces control my thoughts at all hours: neighbors, colleagues, friends, an ex-husband with humiliating intimate knowledge, my awkward feelings toward my family. Andrea is like decoding a message that brings memories buried deep in my estranged heart back to life. What a way to justify running away and looking for home away from home!

Neither hunger not thirst could distract me from my work. Some lukewarm water was enough to suppress my hunger. During the siege, hunger never stopped anyone from entering new battles. This time I have to set the battle's goals using my own language; with this language I have to be able to define my world, identify my enemy, and assess his ability to use violence and force.

My dissertation proposal was angrily dissected by the committee. The topic of my research, The Hero in Resistance Literature in Egypt and Greece, A Comparative Study, was rejected.

Although no one else in any other Egyptian university had researched this topic, the committee did not think it had value or potential to contribute to this field of study. Not a single member of my committee approved my subject. I kept looking helplessly toward my adviser, who remained quiet, pulling off hairs of his chin with gross focus, his eyes lost in the empty space of the bare classroom.

The worst part was the way they all stared at me: my family, pieces of furniture, and every empty space around me. Everyone was making fun of my failure, but, given its regularity, their humor was black, making me angry and hateful of everything in the world.

"Don't worry about it. It's not the first time. Let it go. You'll find something else."

That was my brother. As for Essam, the bastard, I saw him walking up through the empty rows to greet me. He was smiling, a cigarette stuck at the corner of his mouth, and an expression on his face saying, "You really are shallow."

I really am shallow and a fool for holding on to this mirror—I will smash it right now—because I only chase dreams and like a coward I shut my eyes during disturbing scenes so that I can see only what I want to see; because I insist on walking forward, dragging all my baggage with me wherever I go for people to see how innocent I am of every crime; and, as Siham told me, because I want to know only what I want to know.

"You must be so naïve to think that your uncle locked Essam up for your sake. Stop being silly and give up on romantic comedies. This is the time for drama, for tragedy. The plot starts out simple, becomes more complicated, more characters are involved, conflict arises, and evil always wins for one simple reason: there is no good; it's all evil. Take any man you knew and try to remember how he used to be at the beginning. I don't think that someone who plays Cinderella like you could remember how her last time was, but I know that it sucked, Ms. Innocent, and that it was shitty, like he had decided that you didn't deserve to live. However, that's not everything, just keep your eyes open and act like a man, exactly as our grandmothers used to say. 'For a woman to rule, she has to be a man.' This is the basic idea. This is one chapter in my ridiculous master's thesis, and as to that, I have no idea when it's going to be done. But time is not of the essence. 'I'm building my posthumous glory.' This is the opening of a poem. I swear on the soul of the son I never had that the next story is going to be one hundred percent realistic down to the names."

The girl whose name was . . . well, there is no reason to mention her real name because it might hurt our cause. Let's say that her name was Khairiya. Khairiya was sitting on the edge of the rear fence of the farmers' market, exactly behind the fishmongers who sat on the floor in front of large containers of fresh fish and canned sardines. Khairiya liked to watch the fish being carried alive from the containers to the table to be cleaned. She would follow the process with a fascination that took her breath away.

First, they slit the belly open, then cut off the fins, scraped off the scales, and threw away the leftovers in a pool of black blood. Only cats fighting over a small portion of guts would finally wake her up. Add to this the sight of salted fish after being fermented and Khairiya could

165

not possibly have the time or frame of mind to deal with customers who wanted to purchase her lemons. None of this was planned, but the same commonsense that had led Khairiya to this particular spot inspired her to tell her girlfriends, who were offended by the stinking fish and preferred to run their business on the other side of the farmers' market, "You just don't get it; anyone who eats fish is going to need lemons."

Khairiya barely finished elementary school and was not able to enrol in vocational school for the reasons commonly cited in ads promoting family planning: her father dies; her mother remarries; the number of the members of her new family exceeds the first one; and the new family head, who is not at all the breadwinner, declares, "Listen, you dumb asses, I can't keep putting food in your bellies. Each one of you should start looking for a job. I don't want to see your stupid faces until you have some money."

Khairiya did not aspire to anything like Cinderella's fate. She already knew that her greatest, yet still attainable, wish was for Muhammad al-Deeb, the cabbage seller who stood across from her in the market, to poke her, accidentally of course, below the waist or to brush against her breast with his elbow while helping her to either lift up or put down her big sack of lemons.

At the other end of the world, four awful guys were in a state of peace more dangerous than any war. After they smoked pot and started to feel hungry, they went out looking for food.

"How about some grilled fish?"

"But don't forget the lemons."

"Who exactly is going to the market?"

"We are all going, your honor!"

Their loud laughter cleared their way through the busy market crowded with sellers and buyers until they reached the lemon girl. At the end of the day she was following the dead fish in the fishmonger's duffel bag with her eyes. She must have seemed like another pothead, especially when her attention suddenly shifted to the different-sized lemons in her sack. Her eyes met with theirs time after time until a deal was struck with the owner of the most expensive lemons in the market.

"Take a shower and wash your hair with shampoo."

"Wear this nightgown; it belongs to my wife."

"Wait until I adjust the water for you."

"But hurry up and don't spend too much time in the shower."

"What else could I have done? What's the difference between them and Muhammad al-Deeb's elbow? I should be able to live my life, enjoy taking a shower and putting on a skimpy silk gown. This one is imported and it fits me perfectly."

"Please eat, Khairiya."

"These kebabs are like nothing you and your family could afford."

"Take it easy. You shouldn't talk to her this way."

"But first have a drink to loosen up."

Only a few things in Khairiya's life changed. She no longer allowed Muhammad al-Deeb to help her with her heavy sack of lemons. She continued to watch her favorite scenes with a pleasure she did not care to hide. For four days each week, she came back with some money and an empty sack. She spent the other three days resting while watching the daily killing.

When the smell of stinking fish started to really turn her stomach, the lovers argued over the identity of the father. He would be the one to take her to the doctor and pay the expenses. Since this would prove too complicated, I volunteered to take her to the doctor four different times, each time an abortion was performed, until the doctor begged us to keep the babies.

"If you keep the baby, I will follow up on your pregnancy for free. Otherwise, it's one thousand pounds for the procedure, plus the cost of medications."

"Here is the money, Doctor. I will immediately buy whatever else you need."

I ran down the stairs, admiring my wisdom; I had single-handedly resolved a conflict between my husband and three of his closest friends, and I saved the girl, who did not end up being a belly dancer or a doctor's wife, but who only knew how to sell her lemons.

"Now you know why your uncle had Essam arrested. This was something between men and had nothing to do with you, honorable granddaughter of Selim Bey. I'm not telling you these things just to share information either; I'm telling you to change your state of mind. Just remember this and if you ever feel lonely or need a friend, call me. Take care."

I had no invitation to make me feel welcome and I was not looking forward to meeting those professors or others either. Although it was my first time wearing that dress that I'd had for many years, and although its color appeared so vibrantly red against the white floor, I was simply doing what I had to do to have my research proposal approved and signed. I wanted this proposal to receive a scholarship partially funded by my university, whose file cabinets were stuffed with nonsense called academic dissertations. Even if my own nonsense was to be added to those cabinets, I still would follow a strict scholarly discipline. That was what I had planned even as early as the first few moments of that pink night where cigarette smoke conjured the image of dust stirred by my father's foot running along the canal. I did not know if I should scream out or run after him to alert him that his leg was falling off along with his blood that gushed over the sharp rocks. Or should I just remind myself of what I had read recently about how one could still run with no legs? I had also read that giving birth underwater was the most gentle for the newborn and for the mother. The source of this information was the internet. I now had an intimate relationship with my computer and with Ijith, who was much more than just a newscaster because his reading of the news was always enhanced with fitting Buddhist aphorisms.

"Believe me, Suzy, I'm just a lost soul with no particular identity. I live in constant agitation. When I'm at work, I resist becoming Americanized. At night, I either go out with coworkers or try to fall asleep to avoid having to think about anything. Long days of hard work pass by so quickly that the early part of my life seems like nothing more than a bad memory that takes me back to the port of Suez through which I left Egypt. I have no homeland. I grew up in Egypt. It was there that I tried to set my roots. These roots were cut off once and for all when they came into my shop with their dirty white clothes and their dirty long beards. But the worst was those rusted weapons that were wiped clean against my body as their bigotry lacerated my flesh. Do you think that I'm still garrulous, as you used to say in your timid way? Not anymore. Now I can abruptly get up and leave the table once the deal falls through. I can leave feeling indifferent, paying only my share of the bill, and taking my revenge right then and there. I never feel anything afterward, no pain or regret, just a cold feeling and a sense of uselessness. Today I tried to cheat on my wife, but for the thousandth time I failed. She is in India, my home country, which I only know as a headline for repeated disasters. I felt the need for a woman, for any woman, maybe just to talk or to have a different outlook on life. Carla was the director of program planning at the station. I asked her over the phone to meet me for dinner with a good bottle of wine. We sat facing each other. She let her body fall slowly into her chair in a way that exposed her dark cleavage. That woman can advertise anything in the most remarkable way. But I was feeling smothered as I sat there with a smile on my face. Anyone who works in the media is a failed actor and cannot distinguish fact from fiction. Even in the age of globalization, he has to appear superficial. Carla's conversation had nothing to do with me. I was so tired of the chase that I had to leave; I politely told her that I was feeling a pain in my chest and was afraid I might be having a stroke. I paid for everything, even the steaks cooked in wine, still sizzling in the pan, sending off a trail of white smoke that invoked the first awkward moments in the encounter of two new lovers. You must have seen something like it in a movie. I did not touch the meat or even finish my glass of wine. I left everything untouched, even the woman, who perhaps continued to wait for someone to save the night she had waited for with much anticipation before it ended in disappoint-ment and a paid dinner. I have to pack because I'm leaving. I really need to see my wife. Bye!"

"Goodbye."

My feelings of despair returned when I realized that Siham and I were not friends—at least, not tonight. She was doing her job while I was look-ing for a way to solve my problems by having my proposal approved and receiving the scholarship by the end of the night at the latest. I had no more time to waste.

I was listening to their chatter and their laughter. Their quick exchanges followed the beat of the loud music. I should have tried to imagine this world before I entered it. Maybe that would have helped me figure out where to sit and with whom to talk—or at least how to find my way to the door once I became too tired of this chitchat, which was half serious and filled with curses that sounded less vulgar when uttered in foreign languages. What was in store for me as I walked around with a fake cheerfulness fed by hopes that conflicted with the gloominess of my soul? When Siham sensed my fears, she smiled at me across the room, calming me down a bit. The fake smile plastered across my face stopped me from proposing a game of quick kissing to fight boredom in the intimate atmosphere that glowed like cheeks after the first two or three drinks of whiskey or vodka. A bottle of red wine stood upright on the low table next to the high sofa where my feet were stiffly hanging down. I was trying to think of a way to remove the cork without an opener, which must have been either lost or never even purchased by the owner of the house. I moved to the kitchen to search through old, hard-to-open drawers until I found a knife and a small hammer. I was able to get the bottle open and started pouring wine into plastic cups and a single wine glass that belonged to Dr. Sherif Helmi. He insisted that there were only three ways to drink wine: either poured out of a wood barrel, out of a hose in an old bar in one of Alexandria's ancient alleys, or in a wine glass with blind Ruby who used to stand in the middle of the coastal road and insisted on wearing black sunglasses until the meeting was over.

"Have you ever seen her without her glasses?"

"Honestly, I've never even seen her."

"Sorry, Dr. Sherif, but my friend Suzy does not know that you don't really like blind women, you only like to dream of them."

"Hi, Siham, how are you? Why don't you introduce me to this young lady?"

"Young lady? He's calling you 'young lady,' Suzy."

Was there ever a better introduction than a man telling me I looked like a twenty-eight-year-old woman? This would make my father's old wish come true, the wish that used to send me from staring at old pictures to my mother's mirror, searching for signs of aging in my face.

She left us alone so that I could pursue my goal by engaging in a long conversation with someone who seemed important. Our talk was interjected with lively smiles and meaningful nods. We scribbled down e-mail addresses and different phone numbers for private and urgent calls.

I did look like a twenty-eight year old, but not the way I was when Essam was my target. Here there was no target. This man filled me with a safe feeling that grew so fast until there was no one else in the room, only he and I standing next to each other. Whenever his shoulder brushed against mine, I was overwhelmed with a wave of heat that urged me to hold him tight as I imagined us walking back and forth along some ancient path. My eyes were desperately searching for his behind our dark glasses. I was caught between the blackness of his eyebrows and the frame of his glasses. This is the call I had been eager to hear and I responded ardently, like a small bird trying to soar as high and as far as possible from its cage. Powerful feelings lured me out of my usual silence. I had been waiting for a man to fully love me and set me free with infinite support and understanding. I had always expected him to be Andrea. But I was sidetracked from my path when I met Sherif, his loud laughter expressing his happiness and gratitude to have me next to him.

Feelings of guilt gently drew me apart from the rest of the party. I watched as it settled into small circles that filled the corners of the reception area, extending all the way to the river through the big porch covered with glass that made the floors shine with the light it reflected. I was going over the events that had started earlier with searching my phone book under S, where only Siham's number was written down. That was all I needed. Then I agreed to go to the party. She said it was "nothing special; just an opportunity for people to take care of business. So get ready and meet me there. . . ."

I took my anxiety to the closet to search for a dress. To complete the outfit, I found a shawl my grandmother had left me along with many other possessions. It worked well with the Red Cross dress, which I had crucified on a hanger for a long time before I finally decided to wear it. The red and white colors in the dimly lit closet made me look forward to being elegant and charming, as Siham demanded. She also insisted that I use humor as an additional asset to support the way I should look and act, but then she had to hang up in order to arrive first at the party.

"A pro always arrives early. But I'm really tired of this hustling and I've decided to start teaching informal Arabic to foreigners—an easy job that pays well and also a good way to meet a lot of people."

The taxi driver cut through busy traffic with compulsory patience until I felt the cold breeze of the Nile on my face and saw the lights reflected on its water. We drove by the American Embassy, which occupied a large portion of Garden City, or Garbage City, as Mary Munib, the famous actress, used to call it. The taxi drove past black-uniformed armed soldiers and roadblocks.

"Around here, please."

I stepped onto the sidewalk, trying to sort out my anxious thoughts. I inhaled deeply and fixed my eyes on the fence that extended into infinite space. The flashing of many small yellow lights made my eyes bleary. My destination on that desperate night was one of Garden City's historic buildings. Its entrance gave me a chill I rarely felt. I walked around the building several times trying to find its gate and estimate its ability to contain my fear. Siham was waiting for me at the door to introduce me to everyone. She led me from one person to another, telling them how I used to be a leftist and an exceptional student. Then she asked, "What's the title of your doctoral dissertation?"

"A Comparative Study of the Hero in Resistance Literature."

"See, Doctor, tough topic, but she can handle it."

"Of course, she can. And she should be able to. I'll do my best to help her."

Everyone was taking advantage of everyone in this crowded room, as Siham said, relieved now that the toughest part of her mission was accomplished. She left me alone to rest on the sofa while I watched her intent on her work like an artist.

Someone's voice reached my ears defending Bush's right to exact a cruel revenge upon anyone who had witnessed his failures because empires fall and winners today are losers tomorrow. I watched him place his glass of red wine on the speaker. The loud music coming from the stereo prompted one of the female colleagues to dance very skillfully in her tight work clothes.

"Clinton had good taste in women," he continued. "Other than four women, what could any man want but money, power, fame, and youth? No woman has ever been able to satisfy me."

His eyes were fixed on the dancer's breasts, which seemed to defy gravity, sticking out with the same energy that moved her waist and shook her belly and made her legs cross over her two small feet.

Was I really here or was this a hallucination caused by a coincidence and three glasses of sweet wine? I understood the implication but I played dumb until my turn to dance and I was nothing but a belly that had passed. I was here in the company of a friend who fabricated dissertations for a living. Sometimes she received thank-you gifts for her help and she knew to respond with another thank-you for learning so much from the research. That was a game with its own rules and codes so that agreements were reached with a few vague words. Such was the extent of corruption in this world. While these were my thoughts, in actuality I was careful to mention my uncle's name, without referring to his retirement, whenever I was introduced. They still feared him despite everything. "I'm Colonel Atef Salem's niece."

One single reason had brought me here among my honorable professors. It had also brought me to my uncle's house before, and to my mother's house after she died and was buried in the national cemetery among martyrs for my father's sake. Lastly, it had brought me to Essam's house, which was more of a prison cell filled with chaos and moral decay in a deep catacomb of diseases and complexes stemming from the misunderstood word 'freedom.' That was my husband; that was my uncle; and that was my mother whose family tree hung over a wall where harmful weeds proliferated.

I turned my attention to another group sitting on round chairs. I overheard their conversation but my mind was otherwise occupied.

"Ptolemy I was responsible for bringing the pharaohs' glorious age to an end."

"Historical truth can be stranger than fiction."

"Hundreds of thousands are now fighting against capitalism."

"No one here can stand up to capitalist globalization or to political Islam for that matter."

"There is no revolution without revolutionary rhetoric."

"Do we need more rhetoric?"

Sentences flew by my ears and fell on the shadow I cast outside the window where spots of soft light spangled the darkness. I remembered the crushing failures of times past: in those noisy and busy times, our socialist slogans were like silk ribbons floating over oppressed peoples. We were drawn to the center of gravity, staring at the clouds and crying even before rain started falling. We became like doves trying to let go of fear. Somewhere among the huge columns across from the balcony where I stood, Essam's face emerged. After his last detention, I was no longer the bewildered woman who passively watched what was going on, content to know just a little bit about everything. I reminded myself of that fact as I banished Essam's ghost. Perhaps its presence was a suicide wish, for it made me wish to fall dead over the low roof of this old four-story building, a structure that took up a large triangular space by the eternal river that softly flowed through my country. My eyes were gazing at the gigantic columns that reached up to the gloomy sky like a temple eroded by sunlight. I was searching for someone, someone who had learned the secrets of eternity from the stone and saved the rituals of mummification in his head, wrapped in layers to protect it from erosion. I imagined sleeping at night at his feet and in the daylight copying magic codes, walking barefoot over the mosaic floor where an old imprint of his footstep was saved. I would step on it to become one with his trace. I guarded the secrets that were forced out of the stone wall. Sherif and I were together; no explanation was needed.

"Suzy, why are you by yourself?"

"Nothing, I have to go. Bye, Siham."

"Wait, Professor, we are not done."

"I'm tired. I have to go."

Nothing compared to failure. I felt like a boxer receiving successive blows to his heart before he fell on the floor, trying to gather all his strength for one final blow. My audience was a bunch of educated drunks, drinking wine to wash down fried calamari and listening to lines of obscene love poetry recited by a colleague in tight pink pants and a short blouse, her black hair framing her Bedouin features. Her face was blushing as she read the lurid details of the parody of a famous love poem. Her name was also Suzy, which gave me the chance to practice hearing my name when I said it. I found that it sounded stupid, that it had no sound.

The mission was somewhat accomplished. The official document itself was now a formality Siham would be able to take care of and deliver to my door. Perhaps this time she would be able to see Atef and drag him out of his shell. She was thanking Dr. Sherif for giving us a ride. He dropped her off somewhere downtown and drove me all the way to Ramses Station. I said goodbye to him in the same way I said goodbye to the forlorn statue and with the same pang that accompanied many haunting dreams, weighed my soul down, and wasted my precious time.

Under the rain that poured over our heads and shoulders there was nothing but an open, peaceful space, completely empty except for the piercing cold that made us tremble, intoxicated. Sherif was opening up to me. I fell for him like a damp, rich soil. He was sharing his worries and sorrows with me.

He asked me suspiciously, as if trying to figure me out, "Are you a gift from heaven where I used to see nothing but clouds of gloom and loneliness or did someone send you to set me up?"

"Of course, I'm setting you up."

Fear spread through my soul like fire when, as I heard him describe his obsessions, he gently touched the small of my back. As I sat on the bus on my way back to my hometown, I tried to determine how reasonable his fears were and wondered for how long others' suspicions and presumptions would define me. Old love songs were playing in my head as I fell asleep, smiling, and watching the highway swallow the dark night. It became my habit now to choose the third seat, and the third floor, and the third everything. A wonderful feeling lingered in the small of my back, which I kept touching exactly as Sherif did.

I should not have put much trust in anyone's love, not even my father's—and certainly should not have arrived home at the dawn call for prayer in a slinky dress and a soft red wool wrap. Stepping into my uncle's room, as soon as I took off my leather coat I could smell cigarette smoke and wine on my breath as I kissed his cheeks. I was exalted by the magic of the first touch from a man I stumbled upon as I searched for my place in the universe, finally arriving at the sacred temple where I knelt and confessed my sorrows before the highest-ranking monk.

"Were you ever taught," Sherif was asking me, "that admitting your mistakes rather than blaming them on others was a step toward self-evaluation?"

"Am I on trial?"

"The right to self-government should only be granted those who possess leadership skills. You did not take us seriously."

"What leadership? Where is your kingdom, leader?"

"Well, it's gone. We lost it because of the way you trivialized our ideas. You directed the struggle to non-fundamental issues we had no time for."

"I had my own beliefs. I wasn't one of them."

"I'm happy for you! On whose side are you?"

Sherif and I walked by the complex of government offices which stood in the heart of Garden City like a gangster in one of Naguib Mahfouz's novels. When we went down to the subway station where I would take the train, I was feeling myself splitting again and becoming more like the person I was bound to become, especially if I were to join all those other modest and pious occupants of the women's-only car. Sherif's eyes were taking me in as he felt the ground shaking. Men and women were looking at us with hatred and mockery. But we only wanted our moment of surrender, our euphoria, to pass uninterrupted. We were randomly talking, but everything we said seemed so vital, shouting at each other like children.

My father's great anger, verging on tears, finally brought me back to reality. I saw that I was replacing one set of chains with two sets: from forty years of misery to Sherif and Andrea fighting over me. I was tempted to give in completely even if it tore me apart every day. Conflicted, I reverted to my broken mirror if only to stop my father's screams from reaching my brother's ears. My brother would have summoned my uncle and their verbal abuse would have likely escalated into a slap in the face from my uncle or a volley of punches from my brother, who was in the habit of being physically aggressive toward me.

"Just kidding," he would say.

"Well, I don't like it."

"And do you think I like it when you're kidding?"

"But I have never laid a finger on you."

"Just try and I will break your arm."

"I never laid a finger on you because I love you and I can't bear to hurt you."

He would remain quiet for a while. Then he would lock himself up in his room to listen to a musical collection that included the likes of Shakira, Pink Floyd, Sami Yusuf, Mohamed Mounir, Michael Jackson, and ended with Ruby or Britney Spears, and finally Abdel Basset Abdel Samad.

He would stomp his feet on the floor, trying not to make a lot of noise, or he would sway back and forth like a Sufi trying to calm down his agitated soul. This ritual would conclude with demonic screaming and hysterical pounding on the roof. But he wasn't stupid as I always thought. He knew so much about religions and people's belief systems, and longed to travel to America, which, hard as he tried to trace it, had no rich heritage despite its power. What was the difference between beauty and madness? This boy, who was both mad and beautiful, to what extent did he suffer from what he knew? To what extent was he lost in the fine line between creator and imitator, between the laws of age and gender and his own superego?

I closed the door to my room as my father wretchedly, hopelessly gulped down a drink. "What have I done for you to treat me like this? I always thought I could rely on you, but now for the first time I see that I lost the one leg I had left. Alcohol, Suzy? And coming home at dawn like a whore? You should have at least waited until the morning. What would people say?"

I keep reminding myself that I cannot be like Hercules or even Hitler. I'm not ready. Not yet. Because my mind is so cluttered, I should have everything sorted out first before I braid my disheveled thoughts with Sherif's silk ribbon, which I can feel gently tapping my back. Meanwhile, I burn with the desire for an embrace and wait for news from him.

"Sherif is abroad at a conference."

"Sherif is back."

"Dr. Sherif has a defense scheduled tomorrow at seven o'clock at the School of Liberal Arts; you should go."

I couldn't go. I climbed the marble staircase several times and every time I turned back to be lost in the crowds. I could not bear the silence anymore. Finally, he called.

"How are you and where are you? I need to see you."

"I wish I could, but. . . ."

"No 'but.' Meet me tomorrow at the National Union of Journalists office at seven o'clock in the evening."

"Make it eight o'clock."

"I will wait for you until eight in the morning and until eight a hundred years from now."

Everything becomes a memory at the NUJ archives. Natural disasters become matter of fact after a few days. Lies spread in less than five issues. No one pays attention because in the end everyone backs down to protect their personal interests. Did Christ back down to protect his personal interest? Did he really form a liaison with Judas?

That was the search topic I pursued through several international newspapers and periodicals. But I didn't find a conclusive answer. No one knew anything for sure except that a manuscript that dated back to two hundred years after Christ's Ascension was found in some cave in the Egyptian desert in 1970. Also, literary and theological books were based on Judas's betrayal.

177

"Do you think you can fall in love with me?"

"Of course I can and for the rest of my life."

"You must be lying."

Why do people complicate love? This was a line from a popular song. Well, I had an idea why. My own incompetence made me drop everything and head toward the NUJ office before sic o'clock instead of eight o'clock. I spent most of my time at the Information Center looking up names, dates, and random information. The prospect of love seemed more like a joke as I painfully tried to suppress the smile that quivered on my lips and hide the dancing of my heart under a heavy winter coat.

The flame that burned through me reminded me of Andrea, which took me away from Sherif. I don't remember at what particular moment I began to warm up and feel my nose and hands again. I felt dejected, recognizing pain at every threshold.

A deep pain as sharp as the first kiss—an infatuation that I can barely remember now after I said goodbye to Sherif once and for all. I set my target and I shot at it unequivocally. To act slowly would have been a sin I had no time to forgive. I buried my feelings in a dark tunnel where Sherif's light loomed so far away. In my dreams and in my waking hours, I joined him as he danced bravely, defiantly under the lights of Tahrir Square while the crowds were shouting out the names of the martyrs who died on the borders. Loud screaming, images splattered with blood, everything boiling and overflowing. My pupils, taking in everything and nothing at all, dilated to meet his anger and his mockery. I gave him the key to enter the inner chambers of my soul where a cancerous hysteria wildly spread. Still, he did not reside in me. Brief visits made short for security reasons. In such a short while, I became nothing for him but an entry in his schedule book, a voiceprint recorded on tapes for national security, too insignificant to make the novice officers laugh. It was inevitable that the dream end this way.

"I'm sure that you were sent by someone to spy on me."

"Are you serious?"

"Why didn't you tell me that your uncle worked for national security?"

"It never came up. No, this has to be a curse. After everything I've been through, you're still mentioning my uncle?"

"I'm sorry, but you're not straightforward. A few things don't sound right."

"That's true, but not where I'm concerned."

And so on and so forth: an accusation, followed by self-defense, followed by an apology. Complete madness. Love should not be this way.

"But from the get-go, we knew it was our incompetence," said Siham. "Just look out for yourself. Go on your scholarship, finish your PhD, and look for Andrea. He may now be a butcher with a beer belly, a fat neck, and six kids."

"No way, not Andrea. . . . He will never change."

"I don't care if he's the president, just finish your dissertation."

"I will, God willing."

"Ok, Ms. Religious. I'm going to try to see the honorable Mr. Atef now. Maybe this time he'll let me in. I'm not going to stop until I am his wife. The Butcher Shop meets National Intelligence. How do you like that?"

"Congratulations on your future incompetence!"

We laughed until nothing but her shadow stayed in view as she went to see my uncle.

The elegant terrace, decorated with statues of historical significance, overlooked a green park where two lovers were taking a stroll at the far end by the water. I watched them as, for a few stolen moments, they tried to embrace. A stocky policeman stopped them, inspected their IDs, and was gone after the boy stuffed some banknotes into his pocket. In the meantime, the clerk at the airlines office was handing me a ticket, stressing that it was only valid for forty-five days. If I needed an extension, I would have to contact the airlines at least one week ahead of time. I was thinking it would have been better to travel by water because I needed some time alone before I arrived at Andrea's island. In fact, the sight of the two lovers walking side by side made me go back to the airlines counter to change my trip date from two weeks to a whole month later. I still had too many unresolved issues.

There seemed to be a heavy weight tied to my feet and dragging me to face a dilemma I had had to grapple with for the last forty-one years—and now for an additional forty-five days—before I headed into the unknown that had haunted me for all of those years. First, my life had to amount to something great, as my father wanted. Second, I had to finish what Andrea and I had started. If I had to describe what was on my mind at that moment, I would have honestly said, "everything except him." I was forcing my mind to imagine his face without the features that no mortal could possibly have: copper hair, blue eyes, a smile that infused his face with an angelic light that guided my way through dark clouds like a dream. In this way, my desire to feel whole had to always be deferred. "I will go to the ends of the earth for you."

"If you keep staring at the mirror, you will go insane—even more insane than what you already are." That was my uncle's warning. But it never worked because I always went back to the mirror to stare at my face torn in pieces, which confirmed what my uncle must have seen in it. Deep down, I knew that I inherited my mother's insanity, but I ignored this knowledge and at times even relished it. My mother never entertained the idea that she could be insane; she was convinced that she simply knew and saw more than other people. I, on the other hand, was grateful for at least having identified the sources of my madness, which was now enabling me to compare what I had ahead of me with what I left behind me: I had forty-five days to make sure everything was under control.

The maid who would clean and cook was to come every day and stay for several hours. She was also to bring her beautiful young daughter with her so that my brother might be reminded that life still had something to offer.

I had to meet with Dr. Diab several times to explain everything.

I said to him, "I admit that my generation has done you and your compatriots a great disservice and that the corruption that we unveiled hurt you as much as it hurt us. Perhaps your loss is even greater because your career is coming to an end without much being accomplished. We still have a chance to make up for everything, which is exactly my goal: to have the opportunity to gain knowledge and to transfer it to others."

There were also several linguistic and grammatical issues I wanted to raise with Dr. Diab. For example, I believed that colloquial Arabic had to be part of formal discourse because it was the language people actually spoke. Standard Arabic reeked of conference halls and media control. He would nod his head in agreement, his face surrounded by his hands like a lotus flower between two branches. He would say, "You do have a point there, dear."

He would then start reviewing all the compelling theories grounded in the history of language that indicated a correspondence between language use and developments in the class system. To be fair, my long meetings with Dr. Diab, during which he revealed secrets about himself or about people either still living or at least living in others' memory, always left me feeling free and optimistic. Yet, my fear that I could lose him along with others like him felt like a tight grip on my chest. Amm Munir was getting ready to shut down his shop and leave his collection of antique furniture and paintings on the street. He was leaving the country for good to spend his last days with his sons and his loyal wife, who had always lovingly said, "Our marriage saved my life and the life of my children. No better man could ever exist." The wives of these two great men had the same to say about their husbands. Both men loved saying that they were true communists with traditional belief systems. "The only woman I ever loved was my wife. No one else before or after her."

I could not tell how Asaad was able to withdraw from my life with such ease when he was the only man who always said he loved me ever since he was a boy. "I love you, Suzy; you're the only woman I have ever loved."

He was the one who changed my mind about taking revenge by hiring thugs to beat up the young men who did what they did to Andrea. In truth, was I trying to overcome the haunting guilt that increased whenever I saw coins that reminded me of Khairiya, whenever I saw running legs that reminded me of my father, and whenever I saw an invalid about to take a compulsory trip that reminded me of Andrea. I could not tell where Asaad found his simultaneously compelling and terrifying responses. For example, when he told me, as we were walking by the canal with the foam of the waves as cold as steel on my face, "Justice, Suzy, can only be achieved when you restore your energy and your humanity. Justice is the gift of the powerful, not of the weak who waste their time in hatred. Resignation is the only comfort you have. Try not to fill your heart with hatred. You will only have loneliness and rage."

I imagine his face at the end of the fight he is bound to lose, according to what Hamida told me between her sobs, "All the tests indicate that the tumor is malignant; cancer is spreading through his throat, nose, and ears. I don't even know how to ask him to go through chemotherapy without telling him that he has cancer. I'm so overwhelmed and I can't handle this by myself. You're the only one who can help him. Please, Suzy, be by his side."

Not a sad tragedy, a terrible turn of events that sharply separated the bulk of the previous years from the few days ahead.

I could not even remember whether it was Asaad or I who initially spoke of hatred. This had always been my problem, something I had to learn from dealing with my uncle. I had no qualms about being civil even toward Essam whenever we met on campus or at dissertation defenses. To others it seemed as if we had unresolved issues. He married the daughter of an influential professor. Everyone knew that she received her faculty position due to nepotism since her father had connections with several members of the faculty. Her father had a distinct way of drawling his words, almost like a prostitute displaying her body, especially when he talked to the dean. He would speak with a coquettish tone that contrasted with the large size of his body, "I love you, Doctor, I swear to God that I do, and I will do anything to be with you." Whenever my eyes met Essam's, he tried to hide his embarrassment with a vague smile or else he would move his lips as if saying, "I love you," which forced me to look away to avoid him.

I looked into Asaad's eyes. I saw in them the thick walls he had built around himself, their long cry for help, and the wild look they had when opium coursed through his bloodstream. Hamida, my friend through better times, now took me to Asaad's world. This world was as insidious as cancer itself, a country within a country, one link within a tight chain of gangs surrounding cities and securing their borders with petty sentinels— unfortunate fellows who had missed their turn to receive free education or free anything, and others like them, now letting us in with a smile, as if instinctively resigned to their insignificant roles in history.

I was finally in Asaad's presence. He had no idea that he was going to die and that when I left, to return in two years, I might not see him again. If I did, he would be emaciated, having no hair or self-confidence left. Once his money could no longer keep him alive, he would lose his mind and die preferring to sacrifice "the man who clothed him" to live in pain. If Andrea was Christ, which one of us was Judas Iscariot? Was it me? Was it Asaad? Judas must be innocent. Why else did he return the silver coins and kill himself? He was the one who revealed that Christ walked over the Sea of Tiberias after its water had iced over, but it did not matter. He was a devout Christian and not a dishonest Jew. In the end, he returned the money and joined his Savior.

Asaad owned the hotel, the rosary, and the marijuana joint. Hamida was convinced that the latter had been the cause of his disease. I whispered in her ear that cancer was an epidemic and did not have any known causes.

In one corner of the room, there was a wooden box older than Asaad himself. It was filled with small weapons and hard currency spread out like a whore, forever young, forever protected by the power of dollars, forever green like the color of leaves in the spring.

When he opened the box, it seemed as if he had a whole arsenal of weapons under his control. But he was no longer Asaad, my friend, who used to offer me guidance and solace. Now, he was sick and doomed to die. He was a small cog in a bigger wheel that crushed him along with anyone who dared to protest.

"Well, I still can't wrap my mind around it," Hamida said while we were waiting for Asaad to finish dealing with what seemed like a state of emergency. He was yelling at his cronies for pursuing their own personal interests. History was repeating itself in the reception hall, which had not changed much. Asaad, Hamida, and I seemed like an unnatural growth in that place which was so old that I was afraid it might collapse any minute over our heads.

Much of Asaad's former rhetoric now seemed disgraceful to me. When we were young and had our lives ahead of us, his way of speaking about justice and its laws always inspired me and stirred my soul. Today, he himself was breaking those laws. We used to dream about being above the law by being completely insane or super rich. Deep down, he knew that we were fallible and doomed to suffer by the very knowledge we were adamantly pursuing.

He was wearing a gallabiya so white that it was reflected in the tears in my eyes. It also illuminated the swollen side of his face. He kept dabbing at a nostril with a handkerchief of the same type my father used. I had to wash those handkerchiefs by hand and iron them for my father. I would have to remind Umm Ashraf, the maid, to make sure to hand-wash, iron, and fold them into four perfectly equal parts. Asaad now truly resembled my father. The tumor that disfigured half of his face resembled in its pure red color the way my father's amputated thigh was unevenly rounded. For the thousandth time since I ever laid my eyes on Asaad I had to note this resemblance. I wished I could just leave at that point so that everything would remain the same in my mind—the way we disagreed and the way I used to leave, knowing that he would always be here, always waiting for me.

"Asaad, my friend, thank you for everything."

"Still your 'friend'? Fine, as long as I know you're okay."

"I'm okay."

"But if you need anything, anything at all. . . ."

"I know to come to you—who else do I have?"

"Nice."

"Nice" was Asaad's way of expressing approval, admiration, or hope. It was the talisman he invoked on every occasion. Now, a terrible disease was eating his mind and face and erasing his personal history. Would his approaching death mind if I tried to escape insanity and blindness through the glass niche at the end of the corridor? The corridor led to the reception hall of the hotel he had forced Rebecca to give him before he agreed to sign the divorce papers. But she warned him, "Andrea has an equal share in the hotel; I don't know what he would do if he found out."

This statement reminded Asaad that he could not kill all birds with one stone. It meant that he had to continue planning and scheming. It undercut his remarkable success at instantaneously making business transactions—he had conducted a similar transaction to have Andrea beaten and to have me in his possession. Later, he deprived Rebecca of the hotel, which he turned into a dark den to keep his illegal business out of the reach of ineffective laws.

He paced the floor nervously, his gallabiya flapping against his legs, trying to show me that his position was indomitable and any attempt at swaying him would be viewed as a threat, to which he would respond with the utmost severity. Yet he looked at his most vulnerable. I kept trying to engage the part of his soul I knew best. But I found a dictator, about to be yanked by death from his throne. He could not see that he was about to be crucified at history's gate and that he was surrounded by devastation.

Asaad was the youngest among the Resistance heroes who fought valiantly during the siege. I was with them as they waged an imbalanced war, their sense of humor even in the face of death filling me with hope. I read the maps they drew with coal on tabletops and walls. "Either

Victory or Martyrdom." Idealists by nature with one motto: "Fight until Death." Their instincts guided them through a long struggle for liberation. There was no Judas among them.

Judas is now innocent according to the Maecenas Foundation for Ancient Art in Switzerland, which published a manuscript, dating back to 300 AD, in which Jesus tells Judas that among his followers he "will exceed all the others" by sacrificing "the man that clothes me," referring to the human form that clothed the divine spirit.

I read this part over and over until I memorized it, trying to figure out if this was a conspiracy to serve Israel's interests. I was about to tell Asaad about it, when he asked me, "What can I do for you?"

"Nothing; I just missed you and wanted to see you. Right, Hamida?"

"Of course, but I have to go. My kids won't stop calling my cell phone."

He cast an angry look at his sister, who brought me to see him. I pretended to be looking at the guns and the verses from the Quran that decorated the dim walls.

"You've never come to see me unless you wanted something, madam."

The word "madam" used in this way was insulting to me and Asaad knew how much I hated it. It reminded me of infomercials for new beauty centers, which usually opened with the phrase, "After the madam returned from her travels abroad." "Abroad" usually stood for working at the homes of oil sheikhs. He was intentionally insulting me but I had to pretend that I did not notice. My job was to tell him the truth about his tumor and to have him go through chemotherapy as soon as possible before it was too late and his chances diminished. I remembered our laughs that ended abruptly in silence, and I remembered the way we closely and passionately followed the news from Vietnam and how foolish the aggressors seemed. Now the world was heading toward a dead end, forcing everyone's history to undergo plastic surgery or liposuction.

All the men in my life, Asaad, my uncle, Essam, and my father, agreed to respect and honor Guevara but without being like him.

This type of speculation was more suited to the marijuana sessions that used to be held at my wretched home. I felt a pain in my guts whenever I thought of them. My attention was now drawn to Hamida as, with tears in her eyes, she prepared to leave.

She whispered in my ear, "I have to go. I need to find my husband before he gets drunk and makes another scene. The minute I turn my back, he starts drinking. Please don't leave him. He has to know but I can't tell him."

I told her in a shaken voice, "I can't do it by myself, Hamida. . . ."

Asaad overheard me and said, "What is it that you can't do, Professor? You can do anything."

Hamida looked down to hide her tears of sorrow over an inevitable outcome. She left without saying goodbye, so he harshly told her, "It was nice of you to stop by for such a short while. Say hello to your husband and keep in touch; you're still my sister, you know. But this is the first time you've done something good."

The last part was directed at me. Hamida left sobbing. Words hung between us in midair. I had to summon them to face Asaad's ignorance about the disease that malignantly spread through half of his face. He handed me a joint, which I held gingerly between my fingers as if I were afraid of touching it.

"You just don't know how to talk without being rude anymore. Why do you have to keep mocking me and your sister? Behave yourself. *And* I have stopped doing this sort of thing for quite a while now."

I carefully inhale the tightly wrapped cigarette. I keep looking at him, my smile getting bigger and bigger until by the time I'm done with the cigarette and half a cup of tea, it turns into hysterical, nonstop laughter.

"Do you know that I'm going to Greece? I'm going to look for Andrea. You, my friend, you're dying anyways. How did you come up with cancer, Asaad? I always thought I was going to die before you and before the people I loved. But, apparently, as Essam used to tell me, I have to watch death from the outside before my turn comes. Do you remember when we planned on committing group suicide when we turned forty? Do you know why I haven't done it? Two reasons: One, what do blind people see in their dreams? Two, when someone is dying, who do they see right before they go? How funny it would be to see oneself! Did you know that Judas was found innocent and that Christ was using him? May God rest your soul, sweetheart."

And we cried.

Finale

As if a curtain was drawn over a person I once used to be, I became someone else, someone so cruel that she could commit murder without losing her smile. I shot Asaad with several verbal bullets: my decision to travel to find Andrea, and the cancer-confirming results of his medical tests.

Feelings of guilt torment me. I blame my behavior on drugs. Drugs make people say all sorts of things. That does not alleviate my guilt as usual. In the meantime, Asaad tries to wash his hands and his conscience clean. He returns the hotel deed to the Georgianis. He gives money to the poor who need radiation or chemotherapy but do not have health insurance.

I come up with strong reasons to convince myself that I must be doing the right thing for the first time in my life. For example, in a state of exhilaration, I admire my ability to meet all the requirements of the scholarship. It will finally take me on a great journey after a series of humiliations that has lasted for almost half a century. I have lost so much of myself in trying to appease Essam and my uncle. I nearly died in their prison where I almost lost everything my father saw in me. For the forty-first time I decide to begin again and to plan where I'm going to be next summer.

I met Sherif to tell him about my new research topic: Judas in Egyptian and Greek Literature: A Comparative Study. I could not determine how cynical he looked behind his dark glasses. We wandered through al-Hussein district, where the walls of the historic buildings were as damp as autumn. The sun was caught behind the minarets, casting its light over the roads that shined as if they were jewels and pearls in the treasure known as Old Cairo.

"You could stay here and make the same comparison between poetry and fiction or between fiction and drama. This is a new topic and you can have your own students cite your work."

"That's true but it will limit my research to the characters that influenced local culture. I want my dissertation to have a global reach."

"Wow, you've changed so much."

"I will be back in a year or two."

"But do you know what a year or two can do to us?"

"What can they do? A total transformation?"

"As you wish. In the end, you always do what you want."

We ride his small car, a two-door coupe. On the back seat, I see the contents of a mobile home on wheels: fast food, books, magazines, and newspapers, a small soft pillow, a fluffy blanket, and boxes of medication with their information sheets.

When we arrive at the taxi station, we silently look for signs that read 'Suez Taxi.' He is careful not to touch me as I climb up into my seat. I look at him through the closed glass window. I mumble a few words that he cannot hear. I jump out of the car. I squeeze his shoulder against mine and surreptitiously guide his hand to the small of my back. Then I quickly press his hand against my hip. My eyes light up when I ask him, "Can you really love me? You don't have to say anything right now."

"Can I love you? Am I crazy?"

"You're definitely crazy!"

He smiles and remains quiet. I feel that he is the most important person in my life. The car starts to move once I climb in. I pay double to avoid having anyone sit next to me. I have no wish to hear as much as someone else breathing next to my ear.

The reasons that urge me to leave are the same ones that urge me to stay. First: I have to find Andrea. The large reference books I'm carrying with me do not explain why I have to take a plane at dawn to Athens.

From Athens, I am to sail to a small island, as if in a movie, but with no cameras to record the crucial divide between my life before and my life after. Second: My brother follows me as I lock the door to the third-floor apartment. I can no longer see the mess once I switch off the lights. The staircase is narrow, poorly lit, and has no railing.

"Please, don't leave, Suzy. This time I really need you. You have to help me."

I almost drop my bags and with them my resolution when I reach the small foyer. Selim stands in front of me in his shabby pajamas, disheveled in a way that accentuates his skinny face and his short beard, the miserable features of someone going through life exhausted at every stage, already an old man at twenty-six. Third: I no longer know if I should embrace my relationship with Sherif or reject it. Finally: My father is forcing me to look away from my brother's beseeching eyes. I try to make up a clever excuse, but I know ahead of time that my motives are weak.

"I have to go. I need to make something of my life."

"What life are you talking about? Everything that needs to be done can be done here."

"There are things you cannot understand."

"Like what?"

My father sits between us. I see the reflections of our heads merging on the wall, but I look away, fearing that I may have to give in to someone else's will again. A small battle fought with words as weapons one quiet autumn night among three generations each defending his or her position in what seems like an eternity.

"Please try to understand. This is my life. I have no more time to waste over being unsure. Dad, you have always said, 'Aim at your target and shoot.'"

I start walking fast as if I'm trying to run away from guilt. But I trip over the old rug, which is falling apart, drop my bags, and fall on my knees. My brother gently helps me up and my father starts to do the same but stops when he remembers his amputated leg. I feel something about to explode when I sit on my grandmother's love seat. But my father finally says, as if willing to end the battle, "At least, eat something before you leave."

My brother looks at him first with anger, then with resignation. He turns his back to us and goes back to his world, yelling at empty space,

"You don't want to change your mind, fine. But you have to learn your own geography first, or neither one of us will accept you. You will only have yourself to blame, sister."

His voice is lost in the clutter of his room, where Pink Floyd music screams and lights dance on the computer screen. He fades away in the darkness behind the door, which he slams before disappearing like a ghost into the noises.

This scene happens all the time, as my exhausted mind tries to reassure me. To face my father, I invoke his old dreams for me. I try to shake off the memory of a woman's face smiling victoriously as I plunge into a pit of shame. I remind my father of a pact we made three decades ago when he said, "You are free. Live your own life, but take care of yourself."

Why did I make the choices that deprived me of my freedom as if it were something I was eager to give away? Why did I continue to live the same way even when it was damaging to me, a woman who decided on a new beginning every day—while dousing her face with a cold trickle from a stingy faucet, and while running the electric toothbrush in a mouth tasting bitterly of ground beans till her teeth would bleed? At the end of every day, I saw clearly how bad my choices had been, but I would always have run out of time.

My father draws me closer to him, shaking his thigh and patting the part of his trousers that has nothing underneath.

"Come, sit in my lap. Don't be mad, hero. Do what you think is right."

"Right" according to my father was not the same for me. Something was always missing between us. Now I found it in the kind smile that buried his sadness in my heart. This trip is the only way out of my siege. Perhaps nothing will come out of it. Perhaps I had no choice but to change my mind in the past. But this time is destiny. I have to pursue this quest for knowledge no matter how unhappy it makes me or how much it turns me into my mother, my mother who thought that some higher power was working against her.

I bid my father goodbye after I knock at my brother's door without getting an answer. I descend the stairs slowly, holding one bag tightly under my arm, and holding the other one with frozen fingers. I walk by the room where my grandmother lived for a while before she died. Because she was blind, she stored in her memory old photos of how we looked. Whenever I ran into her, she gave me some money to buy something for

190

myself even after I had my own income. Whoever said that death had a kind face did not see my grandmother's distorted countenance, smiling hideously as she tried to lift her body up to conjure death from nowhere, demanding that her dead mother intercede, "Take me away, Mother."

Death finally claimed her.

Now my uncle was in her place. I did not know what transpired between him and Siham, but in a matter of days he went through a drastic change. He started to go out on a regular basis dressed up as fashionably as a movie star. I found out that they were planning a marketing and real-estate business involving foreign investors and organizations.

I recall the pain he has suffered in his isolation. I tap on his door with the tips of my fingers. I have not seen him for quite a while. He does not open the door although I can hear him and his cat moving inside in their solitary confinement. He tries to make it up to the cat by petting her head or rubbing her back with the tip of his shoe. I knock more, with my full hand this time, speaking through the keyhole, "I'm leaving, Uncle, and I want to say goodbye."

"Goodbye, Suzy. Take care. Essam will still try to harm you."

I leave the house. I wrap the metal chain at the gate and reset the big black lock. I can smell the cold rust on my hands. As I'm about to pick my bags up, I see Asaad waiting for me with a frail smile on his face. He leans forward as if to stick his body against mine as he tries to carry my bags for me. My body starts to burn up.

"What do you think you're doing?"

"Nothing, I swear to God. I have taken a large amount of painkillers and I can't even feel my body."

"Are you trying to commit suicide? You could have a heart attack."

His eyes had a spark of happiness I had never seen before.

"I want to take a look at the city with you. I promise I won't make you late."

"Okay, Mr. Romantic."

We walk together. A strange gloominess envelops the streets. Night is withdrawing but daylight has nothing to offer except a light shower I can feel on my face. Asaad's face is beautiful; his eyes shine with such a rare spark.

"Why are you so beautiful today?"

"Because I love you."

We cross the Arbaeen Square to the coast past Andrea's house, the church, the Gharib Mosque, and the closed coffee shop with its hookahs and tea sets. We stand with our backs to the city and its tales to face the sun climbing out of the sea. His cheeks and forehead glow like red wine, his eyes as bright as two oases at dusk. Why have I never seen him this way before?

"Before you leave, I want you to know that it was Andrea who asked me to do what I did. He said he needed to leave to pursue his career. His family was tying him down and you were in his way. He thought if what happened to Ijith happened to him, he would be expected to leave right away. When the bullies attacked him, he got carried away and forgot that he was acting. He wanted to be a hero and beat up the bad guys. At first, they did not know what was going on, but then the make-believe turned into a real fight. He was outnumbered. His bones were crushed and his blood soaked into the soil. That was what he wanted. That was his idea of realism so that he would be able to believe that he was a victim. The same role we have played all our lives."

Asaad took me in his arms and tightly embraced me. I tried to come up with questions but what purpose would they have served?

A host of celestial bodies seemed to have landed on earth to witness our sad farewell. As I wondered about where we were going to be the following year, I felt Asaad Gomaa's head fall on my shoulder, the one with the old wound. He died. I softly stroked his head. The sound of the waves alone rang loudly in my ears.

Glossary

Abdel Basset Abdel Samad (1927–88) was one of the most well-known reciters of the Quran. His mastery of the rules of recitation and his brilliant voice won him international acclaim.

Abdel Halim Hafez (1929–77) was one of the greatest male singers in Arabic music history. His music provides expression for the deepest feelings of love, especially its agony, and his name is synonymous with romance in Egyptian culture.

Amm literally means 'uncle.' In colloquial Egyptian, however, it is used to show respect when addressing someone older.

Ashura is a traditional dessert served on the tenth day of Muharram, the first month of the Islamic calendar.

Bango is a locally grown variety of marijuana.

"There is no chance for **Defersoir** gaps or negotiations. . . ." During the 1973 Arab–Israeli War, a gap between the Egyptian Third Army in Suez and the Second Army in Ismailia enabled Israeli forces to completely encircle the Third Army. This had a significant impact on the outcome of the war.

Eid is an Islamic holiday. There are two major eids on the Islamic calendar: Eid al-Fitr, which is at the end of Ramadan, and Eid al-Adha, in which Muslims remember Abraham's willingness to sacrifice his son.

Fairuz (b. 1935) is one of the greatest female vocalists in Arab music history. Together with the Rahbani Brothers, she revolutionized Arabic music by mixing Lebanese folk notes with classical Arabic and western music. She is perceived as a concept, a symbol, and a legend.

Farid al-Atrash (1910–74) was a legendary Arab musician, composer, accomplished lute player, and brilliant actor. His profound love songs left an indelible mark on Arab culture.

Fatma Rushdi (1908–96) was one of the pioneers of early Egyptian theater and cinema. Despite her rich legacy and her massive contribution to the arts, she lived in poverty and oblivion at the end of her life. She died shortly after she was offered free housing and medical care by the Egyptian government.

Gallabiya is a traditional Arab dress for men and women. For men in urban Egypt, wearing a gallabiya can be associated with being old-fashioned, unsophisticated, and poor.

al-Ghareeb is a district in Suez named after the famous al-Ghareeb Mosque, which was built in the Fatimid period.

al-Hajjaj ibn Yusif (661–714) was a controversial figure in Islamic history and played an important role in laying the foundation for the Umayyad dynasty. His military career and his subsequent rule over Iraq show tremendous cruelty and tyranny. Despite this he is known as a great rhetorician and a deep believer.

Khamasin is a fierce storm that blows dust, sand, and hot wind from the Sahara to North Africa and the Arabian Peninsula.

Laila Murad (1918–95) was an Egyptian actress and singer of remarkable talent. She usually played the role of a charming young woman in love. She had completely disappeared from the public eye by the late 1950s.

Mar Girgis is a Coptic church in Cairo.

Mohamed Mounir (b. 1954) is one of the most important voices in Arabic music today. He is known for mixing jazz with traditional Nubian notes and classical Arabic music.

Nazik al-Malaika (1922–2007) was an accomplished Iraqi poet and women's rights advocate. She was among the first Arab poets to use free verse.

Sami Yusuf (b. 1980) is a British singer and songwriter. His music combines elements of Islamic *nasheed* (chant) with Middle Eastern and western traditions.

"My mother established a **savings club**. . . ." This used to be a common practice among women in Egypt. Each member in the club would contribute a certain amount of money per month, but only one would receive the sum of all contributions each month. For example, a club of ten women, each contributing LE100 per month, would allow each member to receive LE1,000 over the period of ten months.

Sheikh Imam (1918–95) was an Egyptian musician and composer. He was sentenced to a lifetime in jail in 1967 when he criticized the Egyptian role in the June war. He was released in the 1980s and had successful performances in several Arab and European countries. Toward the end of his life, he went into seclusion.

Suliman Khater opened fire on Israeli tourists in Sinai in 1985, killing seven. Students demonstrated on his behalf to protest his closed military trial, which was unconstitutional. His death in 1986 was ruled as suicide but some believed it was staged by the Egyptian government.

Tahia Carioca (1915–99) and **Samia Gamal** (1924–94) were iconic Egyptian belly dancers and actresses. They energized, innovated, and stylized Egyptian belly dance. In addition, they were movie stars of international fame.

Modern Arabic Literature
from the American University in Cairo Press

Bahaa Abdelmegid *Saint Theresa* and *Sleeping with Strangers*
Ibrahim Abdel Meguid *Birds of Amber* • *Distant Train*
No One Sleeps in Alexandria • *The Other Place*
Yahya Taher Abdullah *The Collar and the Bracelet*
The Mountain of Green Tea
Leila Abouzeid *The Last Chapter*
Hamdi Abu Golayyel *A Dog with No Tail* • *Thieves in Retirement*
Yusuf Abu Rayya *Wedding Night*
Ahmed Alaidy *Being Abbas el Abd*
Idris Ali *Dongola* • *Poor*
Radwa Ashour *Granada* • *Specters*
Ibrahim Aslan *The Heron* • *Nile Sparrows*
Alaa Al Aswany *Chicago* • *Friendly Fire* • *The Yacoubian Building*
Fadhil al-Azzawi *Cell Block Five* • *The Last of the Angels*
Ali Bader *Papa Sartre*
Liana Badr *The Eye of the Mirror*
Hala El Badry *A Certain Woman* • *Muntaha*
Salwa Bakr *The Golden Chariot* • *The Man from Bashmour*
The Wiles of Men
Halim Barakat *The Crane*
Hoda Barakat *Disciples of Passion* • *The Tiller of Waters*
Mourid Barghouti *I Saw Ramallah*
Mohamed Berrada *Like a Summer Never to Be Repeated*
Mohamed El-Bisatie *Clamor of the Lake* • *Drumbeat*
Houses Behind the Trees • *Hunger* • *Over the Bridge*
Mahmoud Darwish *The Butterfly's Burden*
Tarek Eltayeb *Cities without Palms*
Mansoura Ez Eldin *Maryam's Maze*
Ibrahim Farghali *The Smiles of the Saints*
Hamdy el-Gazzar *Black Magic*
Randa Ghazy *Dreaming of Palestine*
Gamal al-Ghitani *Pyramid Texts* • *The Zafarani Files* • *Zayni Barakat*
Tawfiq al-Hakim *The Essential Tawfiq al-Hakim*
Yahya Hakki *The Lamp of Umm Hashim*
Abdelilah Hamdouchi *The Final Bet*
Bensalem Himmich *The Polymath* • *The Theocrat*
Taha Hussein *The Days*
Sonallah Ibrahim *Cairo: From Edge to Edge* • *The Committee* • *Zaat*
Yusuf Idris *City of Love and Ashes* • *The Essential Yusuf Idris*
Denys Johnson-Davies *The AUC Press Book of Modern Arabic Literature*
In a Fertile Desert • *Under the Naked Sky*
Said al-Kafrawi *The Hill of Gypsies*
Sahar Khalifeh *The End of Spring*
The Image, the Icon, and the Covenant • *The Inheritance*

Edwar al-Kharrat *Rama and the Dragon* • *Stones of Bobello*
Betool Khedairi *Absent*
Mohammed Khudayyir *Basrayatha*
Ibrahim al-Koni *Anubis* • *Gold Dust* • *The Puppet* • *The Seven Veils of Seth*
Naguib Mahfouz *Adrift on the Nile* • *Akhenaten: Dweller in Truth*
Arabian Nights and Days • *Autumn Quail* • *Before the Throne* • *The Beggar*
The Beginning and the End • *Cairo Modern*
The Cairo Trilogy: Palace Walk, Palace of Desire, Sugar Street
Children of the Alley • *The Coffeehouse* • *The Day the Leader Was Killed*
The Dreams • *Dreams of Departure* • *Echoes of an Autobiography*
The Essential Naguib Mahfouz • *The Final Hour* • *The Harafish*
In the Time of Love • *The Journey of Ibn Fattouma* • *Karnak Café*
Khan al-Khalili • *Khufu's Wisdom* • *Life's Wisdom* • *Midaq Alley*
The Mirage • *Miramar* • *Mirrors* • *Morning and Evening Talk*
Naguib Mahfouz at Sidi Gaber • *Respected Sir* • *Rhadopis of Nubia*
The Search • *The Seventh Heaven* • *Thebes at War*
The Thief and the Dogs • *The Time and the Place*
Voices from the Other World • *Wedding Song*
Mohamed Makhzangi *Memories of a Meltdown*
Alia Mamdouh *The Loved Ones* • *Naphtalene*
Selim Matar *The Woman of the Flask*
Ibrahim al-Mazini *Ten Again*
Yousef Al-Mohaimeed *Munira's Bottle* • *Wolves of the Crescent Moon*
Ahlam Mosteghanemi *Chaos of the Senses* • *Memory in the Flesh*
Shakir Mustafa *Contemporary Iraqi Fiction: An Anthology*
Mohamed Mustagab *Tales from Dayrut*
Buthaina Al Nasiri *Final Night*
Ibrahim Nasrallah *Inside the Night*
Haggag Hassan Oddoul *Nights of Musk*
Mohamed Mansi Qandil *Moon over Samarqand*
Abd al-Hakim Qasim *Rites of Assent*
Somaya Ramadan *Leaves of Narcissus*
Mekkawi Said *Cairo Swan Song*
Ghada Samman *The Night of the First Billion*
Mahdi Issa al-Saqr *East Winds, West Winds*
Rafik Schami *The Calligrapher's Secret* • *Damascus Nights*
The Dark Side of Love
Habib Selmi *The Scents of Marie-Claire*
Khairy Shalaby *The Lodging House*
The Time-Travels of the Man Who Sold Pickles and Sweets
Miral al-Tahawy *Blue Aubergine* • *Gazelle Tracks* • *The Tent*
Bahaa Taher *As Doha Said* • *Love in Exile*
Fuad al-Takarli *The Long Way Back*
Zakaria Tamer *The Hedgehog*
M.M. Tawfik *Murder in the Tower of Happiness*
Mahmoud Al-Wardani *Heads Ripe for Plucking*
Amina Zaydan *Red Wine*
Latifa al-Zayyat *The Open Door*